MCKINNON'S ROYAL MISSION

Amelia Autin

HARLEQUIN® ROMANTIC SUSPENSE

Recycling programs
for this product may
not exist in your area.

ISBN-13: 978-0-373-27916-6

McKinnon's Royal Mission

Copyright © 2015 by Amelia Autin Lam

Printed in U.S.A.

www.Harlequin.com

Trace stared down into Mara's face. Her smile faded and her green eyes widened. And Trace could have sworn the delicate, expensive perfume she wore increased its potency as her pulse points heated up.

Something tugged at him again, something he hadn't felt in years. Not just desire. Not just passion.

He wanted to run the tips of his fingers along the curve of her cheek and banish the loneliness from her eyes. He wanted to pull the clip from her golden-brown hair and have it spill over his hands in a heavy wave, then wind it about his throat, binding them together.

And he wanted to draw her into the shelter of his arms and tell her...

Tell her what?

His face hardened in rejection of his unprofessional reaction to her, and he backed away, muttering a soft imprecation under his breath. Then he turned and abruptly strode out.

But not before he saw an expression in her eyes that stabbed through him.

***

Dear Reader,

When I wrote *Reilly's Return* years ago, the character of Trace McKinnon intrigued me, and I knew I'd have to tell his story someday. Problem was, first I had to tell Cody Walker's story, which I did in *Cody Walker's Woman*. But I managed to work Trace in, as the heroine's movie-star-handsome partner. Now Trace is back and on his own with a scarred past and emotional baggage, and he's guarding an honest-to-God princess—the *last* thing Trace thinks he needs in his life right now.

Dr. Mara Marianescu is a conundrum, out of place in today's world yet trying desperately to live a normal life free of the stultifying protocol surrounding her as Princess Mara Theodora of Zakhar. She arrives incognito in the US wanting nothing more than to live a quiet, simple life of purpose as a math professor at the University of Colorado.

But the world won't let Mara and Trace forget who they are and where they come from—the past is never dead, not for either of them. They both must overcome the sins of the fathers to find love and redemption in each other's arms through their own efforts... And we meet Mara's brother, who will be the hero of my next book.

I love hearing from my readers. Please email me at AmeliaAutin@aol.com and let me know what you think.

Amelia Autin

Amelia Autin is a voracious reader who can't bear to put a good book down...or part with it. Her bookshelves are crammed with books her husband periodically threatens to donate to a good cause, but he always relents...eventually.

Amelia returned to her first love, romance writing, after a long hiatus, during which she wrote numerous technical manuals and how-to guides, as well as designed and taught classes on a variety of subjects, including technical writing. She is a long-time member of Romance Writers of America (RWA), and served three years as its treasurer.

Amelia currently resides with her PhD engineer husband in quiet Vail, Arizona, where they can see the stars at night and have a "million-dollar view" of the Rincon Mountains from their backyard.

Books by Amelia Autin

HARLEQUIN ROMANTIC SUSPENSE

Cody Walker's Woman
McKinnon's Royal Mission

SILHOUETTE INTIMATE MOMENTS

Gideon's Bride
Reilly's Return

Visit the Author Profile page at Harlequin.com for more titles.

For good brothers everywhere, just like mine—
thanks Al and John!—flawed, everyday heroes
who do the best they can day in and day out
and who deserve wonderful women to love them.
And for Vincent...always.

Prologue

"**W**hy me? Why the hell does it have to be me?" Trace McKinnon stared at his boss with a touch of belligerence.

"Because they specifically asked for you," Cody Walker said reasonably with a faint smile. "And in the spirit of interagency cooperation…"

Trace scowled. "That's BS and you know it."

"Yeah." Walker's smile turned sympathetic. "You know it and I know it. But we have to at least pretend to play nice with the State Department and the Bureau of Diplomatic Security." His voice took on a conciliatory tone. "This is the first time another federal agency has asked for our help since we teamed with the FBI to take down the New World Militia and Michael Vishenko," he said, referring to a case that in some respects was still ongoing, at least with regard to testifying at trials. "And look how well that turned out. Weren't you the one who reminded me two years ago we're all on the same side?"

Damned by my own words, Trace thought, frustrated. His boss was right, and on some level he knew it. It was just that he'd recently started on a case that really interested him for the first time in those same two years, and he hated like hell the idea of turning that case over to someone else while he babysat a foreign princess.

"Why does it have to be me?" he reiterated.

Persuasively, Walker said, "Considering she's going to be at the University of Colorado Boulder, at least you don't have to go far from home. And with your background in the US Marshals Service, who better could they get?"

"I would have thought female bodyguards would be better, under the circumstances."

Walker looked uncomfortable. "Yes…well…you see…the thing is…" He cleared his throat. "The Zakharians are somewhat behind the times. They specifically requested men for this job."

Trace snorted. "Don't let Keira hear you say that. It would drive your wife crazy."

"I know. But we can hardly go against their wishes on this, can we?" He glanced at the folder in front of him, sent over from the Diplomatic Security Service—the other name for the Bureau of Diplomatic Security—in an attachment to an email. "Zakhar is a small country, but it's critically important to the US's strategic plan for NATO and Europe. We don't want to piss the Zakharians off on something as simple as this. Especially since they'll be picking up the entire tab for the cost involved. Yeah," he said when Trace raised his eyebrows. "She's a foreign dignitary, but she's not a diplomat, and technically she doesn't qualify for DSS protection, not long term like this. Zakhar's king just wants our expertise guarding his precious sister, and he's willing to pay for it. State agreed for the reasons I just mentioned, and it won't cost the US taxpayers a single dime."

"Okay, I'll buy that. But why does it have to be me?" Trace asked for the third time. "Isn't this something the Diplomatic Security Service would normally handle?"

"The State Department explained that. You were an Embassy marine for six months in Zakhar, so you've been exposed to their culture, and—"

"Damn! I knew it. This is because I speak the language, right?"

Amusement touched the corners of Walker's mouth. "Right."

"I should never have listed that on my agency résumé."

"Too late now."

Frustrated, Trace took a turn around the room. "I can't guard her 24/7. Who else is being assigned?"

"We'll let the DSS figure it out. But I do have some ideas…"

Trace groaned at the thought.

"It won't be that bad," Walker insisted. "It's only for a year, and—"

"A year! You didn't tell me I was going to be stuck with this BS assignment for a year!"

"She's going to be teaching at the University of Colorado for the next year. Some kind of exchange program. And she'll have her own retinue with her, including Zakharian security forces." He hesitated. "But you're not just being asked to be her bodyguard."

Trace froze. "Then what?"

"The king doesn't know it, but the State Department wants you to take note of anything she or her entourage might say…in the Zakharian language."

"I get it now." Trace shot his boss a knowing look. "That's why they want someone who speaks the language. State wants me to spy on her for them."

"I told you Zakhar is critically important. State wants to know in advance if anything is going to change with that alliance, and it's possible you might overhear something." Walker looked at the cover page of the file, on which he'd jotted a few notes. His mouth curved in an expression of distaste. "I'm afraid there's a little more to it."

Trace felt his forehead tighten in a question.

"Oh, hell," Walker said. "There's no delicate way to put it." His eyes met Trace's. "They picked you for a variety of reasons, one of which doesn't have a damn thing to do with anything other than the fact women find you attractive."

Trace uttered a pithy Anglo-Saxon curse. Then he gritted his jaw and pinned his boss with an uncompromising stare, his voice soft but deadly. "I can't believe you have the stones to say that to me. If State wants some sort of honey trap they'll have to look elsewhere."

"I told them you'd say that," Walker said with the glimmer of a smile.

"I've done a lot of things for my country," Trace said fiercely. "Some of those things keep me awake at night. But I've never done *anything* I was ashamed of, and I never will."

Walker held up a hand, palm outward. "Calm down, okay?" he said.

"Damn it, Walker—" Trace growled. His handsome face was a sensitive subject, especially within an agency whose agents prided themselves on fading into the woodwork. And Trace was a damned good agent in every other way. It was just harder for him to avoid standing out in a crowd.

"Forget it," Walker said quickly. "I'll give State your answer, and if they don't like it I'll tell them the agency will pass on their request entirely."

Trace took a deep breath and expelled it slowly, forcing down his anger at the same time. "Sorry," he told his boss roughly. "I should have known you'd back me on this."

"What about the rest of the request? Will you accept the assignment?"

Trace hesitated, then nodded. "You've convinced me. If State still wants me under the circumstances, I'm on board. When do I start?"

"The princess will be here in about a month." Walker stood up and held out his hand. "Thanks, McKinnon. I knew I could count on you." Trace shook the outstretched hand, and Walker continued in a completely different vein. "So Keira wants to know, are you going to make it to your goddaughter's first birthday party this Saturday?"

Trace's first real smile since he'd walked into this office spread over his face. "Wouldn't miss it for the world. I've already bought her birthday present—she'll love it."

"You spoil her."

Trace laughed. "Like you don't?" He headed for the door, his mood lightened by the thought of his goddaughter, Alyssa Tracy Walker. He'd been blown away when his former partner asked him to be her daughter's godfather. He hadn't had to think twice about accepting. And Alyssa was a darling, just like her mother. She already had all the men in her life wrapped around her baby finger.

"McKinnon!" Walker's voice stopped him just as he was going through the door. "You'd better take this." *This* was the folder that had been sitting on Walker's desk, the one he'd referred to from time to time as he'd convinced Trace to accept the new assignment. Trace's thoughts were dragged away from his goddaughter, reminding him of what he didn't want to think about... not until he had to. He sighed and took the folder, tucking it under his arm.

A princess, he thought as he walked out. *Great. Just what I need.*

Chapter 1

"The princess's plane is arriving!" the US State Department's representative said unnecessarily as she bustled over to where Trace stood on the tarmac in the sweltering summer sun with the two Diplomatic Security Service special agents Walker had arranged to work with him—Keira's brothers Alec and Liam Jones. While they'd been waiting for the princess's plane to taxi in from the runway, Trace's gaze had been constantly on the move, making sure the security measures the State Department had put in place to keep the curious—and potentially dangerous—at bay were doing the job. So far so good.

When Trace realized the self-important woman in front of him was expecting some sort of acknowledgment of her statement, he said, "Yes, ma'am. We know.

That's why we're out here already." As if it wasn't obvious.

Then he zoned the woman out, and his thoughts returned to the reason he was here—Her Serene Highness, Princess Mara Theodora. Thinking of the princess brought his favorite picture of her to mind, a picture that had been included in the detailed dossier he'd received, one that had not been formally posed. The princess was dressed in traditional riding kit, standing beside a magnificent black thoroughbred. Her riding helmet was hanging by its strap from one hand, and the other was tangled in the horse's black mane. Her long, wavy hair was casually tossed over one shoulder, as if it had tumbled down when she removed her riding helmet and she hadn't bothered to tie it up. And she was smiling in the general direction of the camera.

It wasn't a knowing smile. It wasn't an I-know-you're-there-and-I'm-posing smile. It was as if she'd been smiling at something else—the horse, probably—and had just happened to turn right when the shutter clicked. Her eyes, which the unknown cameraman had focused on, were green. Not hazel, true green. And Trace had always been a sucker for green eyes ever since he was four and a half years old and had fallen in love with an older woman—the five-year-old girl next door.

That was also the first time he'd been fascinated by female intelligence, but certainly not the last. Maybe that's why he and Keira had hit it off as partners. She had definitely excelled in the brains department, and together they'd solved cases no one else could solve. But

Keira wasn't just a pretty face and a quicksilver mind. She had courage and determination, and a deadly aim with a gun. All of which made her nearly impossible to replace as a partner in the two years since she'd married Walker.

Trace had trusted Keira as he had never trusted anyone else in his life, even his ex-wife. But he hadn't been in love with her. Maybe it was because of Keira's strong reserve, her insistence on being taken as seriously in her job as any male agent. Maybe it was because he hadn't wanted to screw up a great partnership with the uncertainty of a romantic relationship. Or maybe it was just that she didn't have green eyes.

A plane with the markings of the royal Zakharian air force pulled up to a stop in front of them. Two ground support personnel rushed forward to place chocks in front and behind the wheels, while two other men pushed a mobile staircase toward the plane's door. It took a few minutes, but eventually everything was secured and the door opened.

The first to descend the stairway were four young men with a military air about them, even though they were dressed in ordinary suits and ties. But Trace wasn't fooled by their casual stances at the foot of the stairway.

"Her Zakharian bodyguards," he murmured to the Jones brothers, who both nodded in agreement—and approval. Trace knew the bodyguards were armed beneath their jackets, same as he was. Same as the Jones brothers were. There was just something about the way they held themselves—their bodies alert, their eyes sharply watchful of their surroundings—that reminded him of…himself. Especially the way he'd been while guarding a witness during his stint in the US Marshals Service. A man never forgot that mental toughness, not really. For just a moment he let a tiny smile escape. *You can always spot a bodyguard.*

The next person down was a short middle-aged woman—definitely *not* the princess. She carried a square case in her hands as if it contained the crown jewels. *Hell,* Trace thought with sudden amusement, *maybe they* are *the crown jewels.* When the woman reached the bottom he saw a movement above her head, and the princess appeared in the doorway.

He recognized her instantly. Even if he hadn't seen her pictures, he would have known who she was— there was just something in the way she carried herself. Regal. Not superior. Not conceited. Just…regal. And composed, as if she knew the eyes of the world were always upon her. She was wearing a kelly green skirted suit that shrieked *money.* Her long, honey-brown hair was pulled back into a soft chignon at her nape, and there was a small green hat with a curled brim perched atop her wavy locks. She looked complete to a shade and exactly what she was—the kind of woman the paparazzi buzzed around for a very good reason.

There weren't any paparazzi here—this area of the airport had been cordoned off, ensuring the princess's safe and inconspicuous arrival—but Trace made one last check of their surroundings to be sure. The king of Zakhar had made that condition quite plain, despite being couched in diplomatic terms, and the State Department had been quick to agree. Trace wasted a few seconds hoping the princess maintained her anonymity—it would make the job of guarding her so much easier if the general public and the press had no idea who she was. Not to mention anyone who out-and-out wished her harm.

Then the princess clutched the handrail for a moment to steady herself, and Trace took a step forward, wondering if she was just about to tumble down the stairs. The faint smile remained plastered on her face, but she was deathly white beneath her delicate, understated makeup. He was a second away from making a dash up the stairway to catch her if she fell when she pulled herself together with iron determination, pressed her lips together in a firm line and descended the stairway with her chin tilted up, her hand only lightly touching the rail. One of her bodyguards moved forward to take her arm on the second to last step, but she said something to him in Zakharan. Her voice was clear and light, but cold, and it carried.

"Do not touch me—I do not need your help," Trace translated easily. The bodyguard stiffened and stepped back, freeing her arm. She turned abruptly from him toward the US State Department's representative, who had moved forward to greet her.

Bitch.

The word popped into Trace's head, and he couldn't erase it. Something about the cold detachment in her voice was all too familiar—it reminded him of the way his grandparents had always spoken to him, the morally outraged grandparents who'd raised their unwanted bastard grandson from a sense of duty, not a sense of love. The grandparents he hadn't seen since the day he joined the US Marine Corps when he turned eighteen. The grandparents who'd been eager to see Trace walking out their door, never to shame their doorstep again.

Now his heart went out to the young man who had only been trying to help, but who had been cut off at the knees by a touch-me-not princess. *A whole year,* he thought grimly. *I have to spend a whole year guarding this green-eyed bitch?*

The princess was smiling graciously now, speaking with the State Department representative in English that held only the barest hint of an accent. Trace remembered from her dossier she spoke five languages fluently—one fewer than he did—and had a PhD in mathematics, but he was no longer impressed by her intelligence. *Brains, but no heart. I'll take heart over brains every time.*

"Your Serene Highness, may I introduce Alec Jones and Liam Jones," the State Department representative said, turning to present to the princess the men who would be guarding her during her stay in Colorado. "And Trace McKinnon. He's the head of the team, and will be your primary bodyguard."

"I am pleased to make your acquaintance," the princess said with a lovely smile. She shook each man's hand. The Jones brothers, trained as they were in diplomacy, said all the right things. But when she offered her hand to Trace he looked down at her, remembering how she had withered one of her Zakharian bodyguards with a few carefully chosen words. *She won't wither me.*

He smiled and shook her hand, but his smile didn't reach his eyes. "Princess," he said softly. The insulting inflection was so subtle the State Department representative didn't catch it, but the Jones brothers did, and they both shot sharp glances at Trace. He didn't care about that. All he cared about in that instant was whether or not the princess got the message. She did. She had been pale before, but Trace could have sworn she went a shade whiter. Her lovely smile faded and her eyes took on a guarded expression.

"Mr. McKinnon," she said in a voice that never wavered, that never betrayed what he knew she must be thinking. "I have been told you once spent six months guarding the US Embassy in my country. I would enjoy talking with you about that experience sometime."

How the hell does she know that? he wondered in shock. He glanced at the State Department representative who shook her head slightly, indicating that information hadn't come from them. He recovered quickly. "Special Agent McKinnon," he corrected her. "And I think you'll find Colorado reminds you a lot of Zakhar," he said smoothly. "Especially the mountains."

She nodded and turned toward the Rockies, looming smoke blue and haze purple in the distance. When her gaze returned to Trace's face, her smile returned, too. "That is one reason I chose to teach at the University of Colorado. I hope to soon feel at home here."

More people had deplaned during the introductions, including two more men Trace tagged as part of the princess's security detail, and now there was a sizeable retinue gathered around the princess, including the four men he'd originally pigeonholed as bodyguards. *Six al-*

together, Trace noted approvingly. *More than enough. But better too many than too few.*

"This way, Your Serene Highness," the State Department representative said, indicating several limousines that had discreetly pulled up behind them.

The princess began walking toward the first limousine in the line, her low heels clicking faintly on the concrete tarmac, but Trace steered her firmly to the second one. "No, Princess," he said. "It will be safer for you this way. One of my team will ride in the car in front, and the other will ride in the car behind. You'll ride in here, with me."

She turned startled eyes on him, and Trace found himself falling into those deep, green depths. "I did not realize," she said, for his ears only. "Am I really in such danger here?"

Trace shook his head. "After today there will only be one bodyguard at a time. Other than your Zakharian bodyguards, that is. But until we get you settled in and establish a routine, I'd feel better if we play it safe."

She wrinkled her brow. "Play it safe?" she asked. "I am sorry, but I…"

"Don't take any unnecessary risks," he explained. "Take extra precautions."

"Oh." A self-deprecating smile flitted across her face. "Thank you for explaining. My English is—"

"Your English is probably better than mine," he replied. "Unless you're native born, though, a language's idioms can be difficult to master."

"True," she said, with a smile that invited understanding.

But Trace wasn't feeling particularly understanding at the moment. He held the door open for her. "If you please, Princess."

Her eyes sought his, and he could see the question she wouldn't voice engendered by the subtle insult embodied in that one word. *What have I done to you?*

He couldn't tell her he'd heard her cruel words earlier, not without giving away he understood Zakharan. And that would defeat half his purpose in guarding her. *I'd better tone it down,* he told himself. *No matter what I think of her personally, I've got a job to do.*

When she was seated inside, he turned to the bodyguard who had tried to help her earlier. "If you want to sit in the front with the driver, go ahead. I'm going to ride shotgun." And he slid into the seat beside the princess.

The cavalcade had already begun before the princess asked him, "Ride shotgun?"

Trace chuckled at the innocently curious note in her voice. He couldn't help himself. "It actually means sitting beside the driver of a vehicle, providing armed protection. Like me, now. You're not driving, but I'm still sitting beside you, armed and ready to do whatever's necessary to protect you."

She said something under her breath he had to strain to hear. "Even though you do not like me."

"Yeah," he said, "even though." Her head snapped up, as if she was surprised he'd heard her. Or surprised he openly acknowledged his dislike.

She stared at him for a moment, her green eyes widening. Then she drew a deep breath and said, "I think we have somehow started incorrectly." There was honest contrition in her face. "If I have offended you in some way, I apologize."

Trace couldn't hide his surprise. An apology? From her? That didn't jibe with her insulting words earlier to her Zakharian bodyguard. But he couldn't have misunderstood. It was a knack he had with regard to languages. Just as he had been able to soak up the Afghani language during his tour of duty there, not to mention the various tribal dialects that confused the hell out of most of his fellow soldiers, it hadn't taken him more than three months to master the rudiments of the Zakharian language. And by the time he'd left Zakhar three months later he was speaking the language like a native.

No, he couldn't have misunderstood her. But maybe, just maybe, there was an explanation. *It's not like me to jump to conclusions,* he thought. *Why did I?* He had a suspicion, but he didn't want to admit it. Especially not with the effect those green eyes were having on him. *Safer to dislike her.* But it was a tenuous safety at best.

The cavalcade drove through the iron gates of the palatial estate the king of Zakhar had purchased in the Boulder foothills and furnished for his sister's year-long stay. Even though Trace had been here weeks earlier checking out the security measures and having new ones installed, he still couldn't help mentally whistling through his teeth at the size and grandeur. But now that he'd seen the number of people accompanying the princess he realized the estate wasn't too big—not if it had to accommodate a small army.

Trace had previously gone through every room in the house in minute detail, especially the bedrooms, and in his mind he'd already assigned rooms to the princess and the key personnel he knew were accompanying her. But the princess had other ideas, and wasn't shy in the least about expressing her opinions.

"No," she said immediately when he showed her to the large, sumptuous bedroom he'd picked out for her.

"Why not?" Trace dug in his heels. Not only was this the largest bedroom, it was the most easily defensible, situated as it was on the east side of the house with a vast expanse of open lawn in front of the long windows, no cover for anyone who might make it past the iron gates.

"I did not come to Boulder to look at grass," she said firmly. "No matter how well kept. I wish to see the mountains from my bedroom window."

She wandered through the house, oblivious not only to the beehive of activity around her, but also to Trace following behind her like a tall, grumpy shadow. She peered into room after room, commenting favorably or unfavorably on each of them in her native language, and once or twice Trace was hard put not to respond. But he knew she was talking to herself, not to him. And besides, she wasn't to know he understood.

"This one," she said finally in English, surprising him yet again. The bedroom was neither the largest nor the most opulent, although it had its own attached sitting room and luxurious bath. But when he joined her at the window from which she'd drawn back the drapes he realized why she'd picked it.

The Rockies soared in majestic wonder—layer upon snow-capped layer of blue and purple mountains filling the horizon. All at once Trace remembered Zakhar's capital city, Drago, nestled deep in a mountain valley surrounded by towering, jagged peaks, and the princess's words at the airport, *I hope to soon feel at home here.*

She turned abruptly, not realizing how close he was behind her, and bumped into him. "Excuse me," she said, looking up at him with a faint smile. But Trace didn't back away. The expression on her face in the seconds before she ran into him held him mesmerized. He knew that expression. Knew the emotions it sprang from. He just never expected to see it on the face of a princess.

Loneliness.

Why the hell should she feel lonely? It's not as if she has no one here with her from home—she brought a bevy of people with her. Every one of them here exclusively to see to her comfort and protection. Just like me.

He stared into her face. Her smile faded and her green eyes widened. And Trace could have sworn the delicate, expensive perfume she wore increased its potency as her pulse points heated up. Something tugged at him again, something he hadn't felt in years. Not just desire. Not just passion.

He wanted to run the tips of his fingers along the curve of her cheek and banish the loneliness from her eyes. He wanted to pull the clip from her golden brown hair and have it spill over his hands in a heavy wave, then wind it about his throat, binding them together. And he wanted to draw her into the shelter of his arms and tell her…

Tell her what?

His face hardened in rejection of his unprofessional reaction to her and he backed away, muttering a soft imprecation under his breath. Then he turned and abruptly strode out. But not before he saw an expression in her eyes that stabbed through him. An expression he knew would keep him awake that night—and many nights to come—trying to figure it out. An expression so markedly different from the avid one he'd seen in the eyes of countless women over the years that he would never be able to erase it…or her…from his mind.

She was attracted to him. And it surprised the hell out of her. But that wasn't what tore at his heart. That wasn't what would haunt his nights. It was her quiet expectation—and acceptance—of his rejection that told Trace more than words just how little she expected from the men in her life. Princess or no princess, no one as young and lovely as she was, no one with her impressive string of accomplishments and with her whole life ahead of her should feel that way. Ever.

Chapter 2

Mara watched Special Agent McKinnon go, watched him walk away from her as she had expected. *Why should he be any different?* she thought. But she was still surprised deep down…and *that* surprised her. He had seemed so unique, so different from all the men she knew, men who either treated her with kid gloves and a stultifying protocol, or the ones she had always studiously avoided—men who looked at her with conquest in their eyes, wondering what it would be like to bed a princess.

Trace McKinnon had done neither. He had reminded her of her brother, Andre. *No, that is not correct,* she told herself with a little shake of her head, wondering why her first instinct was to liken Special Agent McKinnon to her beloved brother when they were nothing alike. Not in physical appearance, and not in their attitudes toward her.

Andre had always called her *dernya* as far back as she could remember, which meant "little treasure" in Zakharan. That had been his pet name for her ever since childhood, because, he said, she was the most precious gift he'd ever received. She'd always tried in word and deed to live up to Andre's estimation of her, even though it had sometimes meant sacrifices few people would have understood. Andre had never insulted her the way Special Agent McKinnon had, slicing through her defenses with that one word, *Princess.* But the protective air, the way he'd taken charge, yes, that was Andre. And she knew that despite how Special Agent McKinnon felt about her she was safe with him.

But there was something more. Just a flicker—perhaps she had imagined it—but for a few seconds she thought his eyes had softened as they gazed at her. Softened, and warmed. Not the way some men looked at her with avarice or sexual conquest in their minds, as if she were a prize to be won. No, his eyes had seemed to plumb the depths of her lonely soul. As if he understood loneliness. As if they shared some special bond. Then he had cursed under his breath and walked away, and the spell had been broken.

Who are you, Trace McKinnon? she wondered. *What have you seen in life that makes you the man you are?*

She remembered the dossier on him that her country's secret intelligence service had prepared when they'd been told who would be guarding her during her stay in the United States. There had been dossiers on all three men, but Trace McKinnon's had been the one that intrigued her right from the start.

Was it just his incredibly handsome face and honed physique that had caught her attention? She didn't think so—she wasn't that susceptible to a handsome face, no matter what kind of body went with it. She'd encountered her share of physically attractive men before, and they'd all left her cold. The other two US agents assigned to guard her were attractive men, too, with tall, reassuringly muscular builds and watchful eyes that told her they took their jobs as seriously as Special Agent McKinnon did.

No, it wasn't just the way he looked. And anyway, his pictures didn't do him justice. The pictures hadn't prepared her for the sledgehammer impact to her senses when his large, masculine hand had engulfed hers, and those bluer-than-blue eyes had stared down at her from a tanned face that could have been carved by Michelangelo. And his slightly shaggy dark hair hadn't detracted from that perfection. It merely added just the right touch of dangerous masculinity, which kept him from being *too* perfect.

She was tall for a woman, but next to him she didn't feel tall, she felt just right somehow. As if she would fit into the protective curve of his shoulder without the slightest need for adjustment. As if she belonged there, in his arms.

And for the first time in her life she knew what it meant to be a woman, understood why nature had designed men to be hard where women were soft. For the first time she had met a man who made her realize something vital was missing from her life. Even though she'd still been recovering from the motion sickness that always overwhelmed her whenever she flew despite the numerous medications doctors had prescribed—none of which really worked for her except by knocking her out, and that she refused to allow—even though she'd still been a little shaky, something deep inside her had responded to his blatant masculinity and those gorgeous blue eyes. Her breath had caught in her throat and her heartbeat had stuttered.

But then he'd said that one word, *Princess.* The deliberate insult had been unmistakable. And her daydreams had been banished as swiftly as if they'd never been.

Her father had been like that. Sometimes he had called her Mara, and when he did she knew he'd forgotten to hate her. But the other times, when he'd called her by her full name—Mara Theodora—then she'd trembled at the implacable hatred in his eyes, the bitterness in his voice. She knew why her father had felt that way. She just didn't understand why a man she had never met before today would feel such contempt for her.

She turned back to the bedroom window, gazing out at the mountains. *He was right,* she thought. *The Rockies remind me of the mountains in Zakhar.* She stood there a long time, letting the peace of the mountains settle over her. "'I will lift up mine eyes unto the hills,'" she whispered to herself in Zakharan, quoting from a favorite psalm, a litany that never failed to soothe her.

Calmer now, her thoughts returned to the man who had stood beside her earlier—Trace McKinnon— wondering again what forces had molded him. She knew the facts of his life, but not the man. He was thirty-six and handsome in a way that would only improve with age. That was obvious. He had served in his country's military with honor and distinction for four years, and had worked for one branch of his government before switching to another.

He had been married at one time, but no longer, and she wondered about that now. What had caused the breakup of his marriage? Had he been unfaithful? With his movie star looks and his dangerous air of masculine strength, most women would melt at his feet. Married or not, he would be a challenge most women would be unable to resist, and they would fall all over themselves trying to attract his attention. Perhaps he hadn't been able to resist temptation himself and his wife divorced him—divorce was common here in the States, but not so much in Zakhar.

Zakhar. Special Agent McKinnon had spent six months in Zakhar as a young military man. Had he loved it the way she did? Had he been sorry to leave it, as she was now? A familiar wave of homesickness swept through her, but she fought against it. Her brother had wanted her safely out of Zakhar for a time, and so she was here. She would have done anything to make Andre's life easier, and if that meant suffering the pangs of homesickness—as she'd done all those years she'd studied at Oxford—that was the way it had to be. For the next year she would be teaching mathematics at the University of Colorado.

Other than Andre, her few close female friends, and her horses—especially her favorite, Suleiman—

mathematics was her only love. There was something comforting about the preciseness of mathematics; something reassuring about its unchanging nature: a squared plus b squared *always* equaled c squared. You always knew where you stood.

Even as a small child she had known this. She had devoured her math textbooks, demanding more and tougher problems to solve from her tutors and her teachers, racing ahead of them, and then soon outstripping their abilities. She had delved into mathematical intricacies instead of playing with dolls; had challenged herself to achieve scholastically instead of dating the highborn men her father found for her; had attended Oxford in pursuit of her PhD instead of marrying the man her father had tried to force upon her. The only equation she hadn't been able to solve was the one dealing with human hearts. No matter what she did, no matter how she excelled, she could not win her father's love. And now she never would.

Trace rendezvoused with the Jones brothers Alec and Liam in the privacy of the sun room. A year apart in age, they looked like two peas in a pod—tall, rangy; honed to muscle, sinew and bone, just as he was. Both had that competent air instilled in them by their years in the US Marine Corps and the Diplomatic Security Service. And both had auburn hair, which they kept close cropped. Not for them their sister's red-gold tangle of curls, although neither had the milky complexion and freckles that usually accompanied hair that color.

Alec at thirty-four was a year older and a shade taller

than his brother, whereas Liam was a tad broader in the shoulders. But both inspired confidence on sight, something Trace had been relieved to see. They were Keira's brothers and former marines, so they *had* to be damned good, but still…

"So the plan is," Trace explained, "to guard the princess whenever she's out and about. We'll get regular threat assessments from the State Department and your own agency, the DSS. *My* agency is also in the loop, and I've been assured we'll get all the cooperation we need along those lines—or anything else for that matter. All we have to do is ask. And State has requested the NSA keep them and us posted on any chatter it comes across on terrorist channels. You know what I'm talking about, so I don't have say anything more on that topic."

"Anything pop up on the radar yet?" Alec asked.

"Not so far. Let's hope it stays that way," Trace replied. "You'll know the minute I know anything." He glanced toward the sunroom's closed door, reassuring himself they still had privacy. "The princess has her own Zakharian security team to guard her here on the estate, as I'm sure you've already noted. State cleared them for concealed carry, so I'm not worried too much about an assault on this house. But she doesn't step outside the door without one of us in attendance. Is that clear?"

"Crystal clear," Liam said, answering for both of them. "But does she know?"

"She should, but if she doesn't, she soon will," Trace said. "And her limo driver knows he doesn't drive her anywhere unless one of us is in the limo with her. This isn't coming from the State Department—this is coming from her brother, Zakhar's King Andre Alexei the Fourth. I don't know how much you know about Zakhar, but—"

Alec smiled and cut him off. "We've been briefed. We've learned enough to know that Zakhar isn't a constitutional monarchy, the way Great Britain is. The king *is* Zakhar, and vice versa, so a command from him carries considerable weight."

"Exactly." Trace was glad he wasn't going to have to paint them a picture. "I know neither of you speaks Zakharan, but—"

"Lubyentok marsai cherentziune todai," Liam said.

"I'll be damned." Trace stared at him.

Alec tossed in, *"Makopescht lycobeschy petzeque."* He grinned. "We had a three week crash course. Can't say we really *know* the language, but we've got the basics down pat. Enough to get by."

Trace's admiration for the DSS shot up dramatically, not to mention his admiration for the Jones brothers. "You've even got the accent and inflection nailed," he said.

He asked each of them several questions in Zakharan, and their answers proved they understood what he was saying. Their responses were more simplistic than his questions, but he'd expected that. Mastering an unknown language starts with understanding what you're hearing. Speaking the language takes longer and fluency even longer than that. And *thinking* in the new language, which was the talent he had, is something few people ever really achieve when the language is learned as an adult.

Still, understanding what they heard would be a definite plus when it came to the second part of their assignment—noting anything important the princess or her entourage might say in Zakharan and reporting it to the State Department. He figured they'd already received instructions on this from the DSS, but he went ahead and outlined things anyway.

"I'm not expecting a blow-by-blow translation of everything anyone says in Zakharan. But anything meaningful needs to be reported. And I want to see the reports before they go in. Understood?"

"Yes, sir." Liam and Alec answered in unison.

"Oh, crap," Trace said. "We're not in the Marine Corps anymore and I'm not your commanding officer. I'm not even a DSS special agent. I'm the head of this team, that's all. So cut out the 'sir,' okay?"

"Yes, sir." Liam and Alec both grinned unrepentantly at him.

Trace's eyes narrowed and he uttered an earthy curse. In Zakharan. Alec glanced at Liam, who shook his head. "Me, neither," Alec said.

Trace gave them a superior look, then relented and grinned. "You won't hear it used in diplomatic circles. Ask me when this is all over, and I'll tell you what it means," he said. "But whatever you do, don't repeat it in front of the princess. She'd probably faint from the shock to her delicate ears."

"Speaking of the princess," Liam said, "how did you want to work the schedule?"

"I've got her teaching schedule here, along with a few other things," Trace said, reaching into his inner jacket pocket, and handing copies to each man. "Classes don't begin until the end of August, but she'll be starting work at the university on Monday. The limousine will take her to the campus every weekday, Monday through Friday, leaving at seven sharp, and will pick her up on campus at five, returning her here."

He grimaced. "Weekends are going to be a nightmare unless I can nail her down to a set schedule. The same goes for weekday evenings if she wants to go out. Word from Zakhar through diplomatic channels is that she doesn't intend to act in any way that will draw attention to herself. Apparently the princess is sincere in wanting to do nothing more than teach. But time will tell."

He looked at the Jones brothers. "I thought it would be best for us to take it in rotation—two days on and four off, then on again. That means three long working days out of every seven for the three of us. But it gives us full coverage of the princess when she's out of the house, and we all get plenty of time off. How does that sound?"

Liam glanced at Alec, who nodded. "Works for us," Liam said.

"I'll take the first rotation, starting tomorrow," Trace said. "Decide between the two of you who'll take the second rotation—just let me know what you decide, and I'll post a schedule. If something comes up and you need to switch off, I'm okay with it as long as I know in advance. There might be occasions when I'll have to switch off with one of you myself—I could be called to testify in a couple of trials that are still pending on an old case, but I'll know well in advance and we'll work something out."

He looked at Liam and Alec and saw no objections, so he continued. "You both have rooms here on the estate, as do I. I've already been over the entire house, as well as the estate's outbuildings and the grounds, and I'll show you around in a minute. You can stay here every night, or make your own arrangements for the days you're off duty—it's up to you. Again, this has all been prearranged with the king, so I don't expect any opposition from the princess. And in order to carry out State's request we're going to need to be around her as much as possible, even in the house."

"Understood," Alec said promptly. "What kind of security does the estate have?"

"Active and passive. Some of the systems were already here, some were just installed two weeks ago. I've got a list of the specs, and when I brief the princess and her staff later on, I'll give both of you copies. This really shouldn't be anything new for them—I'm told the palace in Drago has a similar setup. But there might be some little quirks, and I don't want anyone to set off an alarm accidentally. Just in case someone does, you'll both have all the keys and codes necessary. Anything else you need to know?"

"That'll do it for now, I think," Liam said with a quick look at his brother.

"Oh," Trace said. "One more thing. I plan to spend much of my time here, even when I'm not on duty. I live in Denver, but I'm subletting my condo for the duration, so I'll be around a lot. I've also got a cabin outside Keystone, so if I'm not here or visiting your sister and my goddaughter, that's most likely where I'll be. I'll give you the address later." He fixed them both with a sharp look. "You've already got my cell phone number. If anything happens, the second thing you do is contact me."

"And the first?" Alec asked.

"Protect the princess."

Night had fallen and Trace was exhausted as he made the rounds of the estate. The day had been even more hectic than he'd expected, mostly due to the fact that the princess wasn't what he'd expected. In addition to the dispute over the bedrooms, she'd taken immediate exception to Trace's insistence that she be guarded every time she stepped out of the house.

He'd caught her walking out that very afternoon, cool as you please, dressed for riding and heading for the stables—her horses had been shipped by sea and rail and had arrived the week before—and Trace had taken her to task. That had started a battle royal, which he'd won only by invoking the name of the princess's brother. "You may ride," he'd told her in no uncertain terms, "but not alone. Period. End of discussion."

That hadn't been the end of the discussion, not by a long shot. But when Trace had finally told her the orders weren't his, they were the king's, she had stopped arguing instantly. *I'll have to remember that for the future,* he told himself now with a wry smile. He wasn't sure whether it was the king or the brother she was deferring to, but either way he'd discovered the magic word.

"In the future, Princess, let me know when you want to ride," he'd told her, "and I'll make sure one of us is prepared to ride with you."

Unfortunately, when he'd raised the issue with Alec and Liam, he had a rude awakening. "Sorry, McKinnon," Alec had said with regret. "We don't ride."

That just left him to accompany the princess, and he foresaw a curtailment of his free time if she insisted on riding on the days he wasn't officially working. He didn't think she would be amenable to riding only three days a week, and not even the same three days each week at that.

Then there had been the issue of meals. He, Alec and Liam all had rooms in the estate's guest house, which came complete with an adequate kitchen and a well-stocked pantry. Trace had planned to fend for himself at mealtimes, and had assumed Alec and Liam would do the same. But the princess had other ideas.

"That is silly," she'd told him. "There is a perfectly good meal already prepared, and will be every night. My chefs are Le Cordon Bleu trained—*artistes*—and they would be insulted to think you prefer to eat your own cooking instead of theirs."

When Trace had tried to explain that the hired help didn't expect to share her table, her green eyes had flashed. "I do not eat in solitary splendor," she'd told him firmly. "There are many in my household who eat with me." He'd given in with as good grace as he could muster, not wanting another battle, but then he'd realized she'd actually done them a favor. Their presence at her table would be the perfect opportunity to listen to the conversations between the princess and the rest of her household, whether spoken in English or Zakharan.

Then, when they were all at the dinner table, he'd noticed she wasn't eating. Not much, anyway. She'd passed on several dishes that were offered to her, settling for a plain piece of bread without butter and a dish of custard. She hadn't made a big deal out of it, and no one else in her household had seemed to think it worthy of comment, but he'd noticed. And wondered. It wasn't until he was wandering through the kitchen after dinner and overheard her cooks—*chefs*—he'd reminded himself, talking to each other in voluble French about that very same custard that he learned why.

Motion sickness.

Why hadn't it occurred to him before? He'd been concerned when she first appeared in the plane's doorway, had suspected something was wrong, but then had let himself be distracted by her peremptory demand that her Zakharian bodyguard let her go. Maybe that even explained her curt response to the man's offer of help. Maybe she hadn't meant to be so cold, but was just feeling out of sorts the way anyone might when they were sick.

The princess was full of contradictions. Maybe that's why he felt so tired—he never knew what to expect. Guarding her had become an impossible mission already, and it was only the first day—things could easily get worse. Trace murmured to himself, "'Your mission, Jim, should you choose to accept it,'" using a phrase *Mission Impossible* had made famous, making the impossible seem possible. Then he laughed ruefully. If they could accomplish impossible missions, so could he—he'd done it before, hadn't he? All he needed was a *little* cooperation from the princess.

A shadow moved out of the corner of his eye, and he turned sharply, his right hand automatically reaching for his SIG SAUER. Then he cursed softly under his breath when he saw who it was. So much for cooperation. "Princess!" he called.

Startled, she turned toward him. "Oh," she said. "Special Agent McKinnon. I did not see you in the shadows."

"What are you doing outside the house…alone?"

Her brow wrinkled. "I do not understand. I am not riding alone. That is what you told me my brother said, yes? I am not to ride alone?"

He sighed. "Look, Princess, your brother's orders were quite explicit. You're not to step outside the house alone."

"But—"

"No, no, and no. Do I agree with him? No. Do I think you're in danger here within the grounds? No. But am I going to let you go against his express orders? No."

She stared at him, her green eyes betraying her contrition…and uncertainty. "I would not…that is not what I…" She stopped then started again. "So I am a prisoner here?"

Now it was Trace's turn to look puzzled. "What do you mean, a prisoner? You're not a prisoner. You're free to go wherever you want, so long as one of us is with you."

Her face contracted. "I thought…here…where I am not known…I would not be in such danger."

"I don't know what kind of danger you were in at home. But even in this country there are dangers for people like you."

Her voice was very small when she asked, "People like me?"

"Rich. Well known. Well connected. Putting aside any threats against you because you're a political target, there are crazies out there who kill for no other reason than to become famous by killing someone who is already famous."

She glanced away, staring toward the Rockies in the distance, hulking dark shadows against the night sky. "I was guarded at Oxford. Every minute of the day. And in Zakhar, of course. But I did not realize here, too…" She closed her eyes for a minute and sighed noticeably before her eyes opened again. "I was hoping my life would not be so restricted here in Boulder."

Trace felt a flicker of pity for her. "Don't worry, Princess. That's why you've got me. To make sure nothing happens to you. But I'm not your jailor. With just a little cooperation on your part, you can be nearly as free as you'd like to be."

"But I can't just be Dr. Marianescu, can I?"

"Who's that?" The question slipped out before Trace made the connection.

A peal of laughter escaped her, and it startled him. It was such a normal thing…but not for her. The sound of her laughter slid inside his defenses, just as her eyes did. "*I* am Dr. Marianescu," she explained, still laughing. "That is my family name. Mara Theodora Marianescu. When I received my doctorate from Oxford two years ago, I became Dr. Marianescu."

Her laughter faded away, and a wistful expression came over her face. "Andre was there. He was so proud of me—earning my doctorate so quickly. If not for him I doubt I would have accomplished it. At least, not when I did." At Trace's questioning look she added swiftly, "I cannot explain…there are reasons…it is not something I want the world to know." She shook her head as if shaking off an unpleasant memory. "But I achieved my PhD despite everything. And if not for Andre I would have had no one with whom to rejoice."

"What about your father? Wasn't he alive then?"

She went still all over, emotion erased from her face as if a curtain had fallen over it. "Yes," she said, her voice flat and unmusical. "He was still alive. He did not die until two months later." She stood there for a moment without saying anything else. Then she turned and walked back to the house, leaving Trace standing there staring after her, a hundred questions running through his head. But no answers.

Chapter 3

The estate's active alarm system went off in the dead of night three days later. Alec was on duty, but both brothers responded immediately, guns drawn. By the time they made their way from the guest house to the main house, the princess's household had been roused from sleep by the blaring alarm. Her staff was milling around, but surprisingly no one had tried to turn off the alarm. Her entire contingent of Zakharian bodyguards—only two of whom had actually been awake and on duty when the alarm went off—were already stationed in and around the princess's sitting room, armed and dangerous. Two of them whirled and drew down on Liam and Alec before they recognized the two DSS agents.

"Don't apologize," Liam told them when the two

bodyguards stiffly began to do so as he and Alec entered the princess's sitting room. "You did the right thing," he said, pitching his voice to carry over the noise. "What's the situation? Has anyone seen anything?"

Alec left the room for a minute, then the raucous alarm was mercifully turned off. When he returned he said, "The passive alarms didn't go off. I noticed that right off the bat. So whoever or whatever set off the active alarm didn't come from outside the estate."

Both Alec and Liam focused on the princess, who'd been drawn from her bed by her bodyguards and spirited into her sitting room, and was perched in an armchair in the corner of the room farthest from the window, surrounded by three of her bodyguards. She was still in her nightdress, but someone had handed her a silk dressing gown in a deep shade of peach, which she had quickly wrapped around her person. And her long hair had been bundled up, tidily out of the way. Alec glanced around and asked abruptly, "Does anyone know what set off the alarm?"

No one answered at first. The Zakharians in the room turned to the princess, and she shook her head, taking charge in a calm and composed manner. "I do not know," she replied in a steady voice. "I do not think it was one of us."

Liam already had his cell phone out and was pressing a speed dial button. Everyone was startled when a cell phone rang nearby, and all eyes were drawn to the doorway from the bedroom into the sitting room, to the tall man who suddenly stood there as if he'd materialized out of the darkness.

"I set it off," Trace said in his deep voice, as he casually silenced his cell phone and leaned against the doorjamb, his gun safely in its shoulder holster. But there was nothing casual in the way he took in the status of the room, and he nodded approvingly to himself. Everyone had reacted exactly as they should. The princess's bodyguards had quickly moved her from her bedroom to the safest, most defensible place in the sitting room, and were shielding her with their bodies. Alec, who had the duty today, had responded promptly. His brother, Liam, who Trace had known was sleeping in the guest house even though he wasn't on duty, had also responded exactly as Trace had hoped—guarding the princess wasn't the kind of job where a man was ever really "off the clock," not if he was anywhere around her.

And the princess? She obviously wasn't hysterical. She wasn't even frightened by the alarm, not that he could see anyway, just alert and wary. And that surprised him. Somehow he'd thought she'd be the weak link, terrified at the potential threat, and he grudgingly gave her points for remaining cool under duress. He wondered if this was the first time she'd ever faced this kind of situation, or if there had been attempts on her life before. There hadn't been anything about that in her dossier, but then he'd already realized the State Department's dossier on her was woefully incomplete.

Both Alec and Liam had holstered their weapons at Trace's initial statement, and now Alec said with a touch of humor in his voice, "Fire drill?"

"Yeah." Trace straightened and walked farther into the room, heading right for the princess. "I'm sorry," he told her gently, "but it was necessary. I had to be sure everyone knew what to do in an emergency. Your men *and* mine."

She stood up, and her bodyguards deferentially moved to one side. She tightened her belt around her waist with a decided snap, then she looked up into Trace's eyes. "It was a test?" she asked levelly.

"Yes."

Her next question was unexpected. "Did we pass?"

"With flying colors." When her brows drew together, questioning what he meant by that proverbial phrase, he explained, "Honorably successful."

"Ahhh." She nodded as comprehension dawned. "Good." She tore her gaze away from his and glanced around the room at everyone there. "Does this mean we can all go back to sleep now?"

Trace couldn't help it, a smile tugged at his mouth as she asked the question in a practical, no-nonsense tone. "Yes, ma'am," he told her, for once not using the word *princess.* "Everyone can stand down." Before she could ask, he added, "That means suspend and relax from an alert state of readiness. Return to normal. And since it's—" he glanced at his watch "—two-fifteen in the morning, yes, everyone can go back to sleep."

Everyone but me, he thought, but didn't say. He had a report to write. And since the report would no doubt end up in the hands of the king of Zakhar, passed along by the State Department, it needed to be thorough… and reassuring.

* * *

From a short distance away, the three armed men treading in the shadows of the estate's perimeter had heard the alarm go off. They circled back to their prearranged meeting point, shot questioning glances at each other, then shrugged their shoulders without speaking a word. They were as certain as they could be that no one had breached the estate's walls—if anyone had attempted that they would have known—and none of them had set off the alarm.

There was little or no movement around the estate that they could see from their vantage point, even with the advanced technology that night-vision goggles provided. And though the men were prepared to disappear if necessary—considering the amount of illegal equipment they carried—no police responded to the alarm. That was a telling point. All three men noted the time, the exact responses…and the lack thereof. These details would be included in their report, which would be forwarded up the chain of command.

Their orders were clear, although none of the men knew the exact reason behind them. But they didn't need to know. As were all the men who worked in their organization, they were intensely, militarily devoted to the man at the top. They *believed*. Arrest and incarceration was a definite possibility, but it wasn't one that concerned them unduly.

Shortly thereafter the alarm was silenced. When the estate had finally settled down and the normal night sounds returned, the men resumed their catlike stalking from a distance, notating each potential weakness in the estate's defenses for future use.

On the first day of the semester Mara woke early, with a sense of excitement barely contained. Today she would begin teaching again, but this time things would be different. For the past two years she had taught at the University of Zakhar in the capital city of Drago. She was a good teacher—she knew it—but she had never been able to fit in. Everyone at the University of Zakhar had known who she was. The faculty hadn't been able to separate the princess from the professor, not to mention her students. Everyone there had kept her at a distance, just as she'd been isolated at Oxford. That wasn't going to happen this time. Not if she could help it.

Ever since she could remember her secret dream had been to be an ordinary woman. Not a princess. Not an icon. And certainly not someone whose face and life story were used to sell magazines. And such stories! She made an expression of distaste at the memories of the fictional stories—all supposedly true—that had been written about her over the years. Andre had told her not to read them because they upset her so much, but she'd never been able to resist. It was almost a morbid fascination. Then she would throw the magazine against the wall, or rip the pages into tiny fragments, muttering dire threats she wished she could carry out. If only the world knew the truth! No one would want to read about her real life, so the tabloids were forced to make things up.

But that was all behind her now, and Mara hummed

to herself as she dressed. She had taken note of what the women professors at the university here wore, and had gone shopping with a vengeance. No one at school except the president of the university and the dean of her college knew that Her Serene Highness Princess Mara Theodora and Dr. Mara Marianescu were one and the same person. Mara was determined to keep it that way, even though it meant camouflaging herself by wearing clothes bought off the rack and donning eyeglasses with plain glass lenses instead of prescription ones she didn't need. All her adult life she had downplayed her looks; preferring to remain in the background rather than stand out. Now she was glad of it. Most people saw only what they expected to see. And even though her photograph had been plastered across the pages of magazines for years, no one would expect to see her here in Boulder, a simple math professor in a university that ranked in the top hundred in the US, but not in the top ten or even the top fifty.

Mara smiled to herself, remembering the battle she'd fought with Special Agent McKinnon over her insistence on being just like everyone else. That meant the limousine and chauffeur had to go. It had required a phone call to her brother, but in the end Andre had relented. She would be allowed to drive herself to and from school without her Zakharian bodyguards in tow—just one of the special agents assigned to her "riding shotgun." Mara laughed with delight as she thought of it. English was such a colorful language, full of imagery and idioms.

Then her laughter faded. Special Agent McKinnon

would be guarding her today. She was already on excellent terms with the other two special agents, the ones from the Diplomatic Security Service, Alec and Liam. She called them by their first names now, and although they had both refused to call her Mara, and she had refused to allow them to call her Princess Mara, they had laughingly agreed to call her Dr. Marianescu.

And while Alec and Liam zealously guarded her, they treated her like a normal person, which was what she so desperately wanted. She knew all about their large family—mother, older brothers, younger sister and her daughter, their one-year-old niece. They had shared with her a little of their dreams and aspirations, and knew something of hers, too, and how much she wanted to belong.

But Special Agent McKinnon was different. When she was with him she always felt on edge, and it wasn't just because his face and physique set her senses jangling. It was as if he were judging her and finding her wanting, and that hurt more than she'd ever thought possible. He never told her anything about himself, either. After more than a month she knew no more about him than she had that first day—the facts in his dossier and the effect he had upon her senses.

Because of him she had drastically restricted her rides on Suleiman, a real sacrifice. Neither Alec nor Liam rode, so if she rode she was forced to do it with Special Agent McKinnon at her side. That meant riding only on the days he was on duty, instead of every day as was her habit. The first time he had appeared on horseback on one of his days off Mara had been startled. He hadn't said anything about it, and it was so difficult to talk to him about anything. So she'd asked Liam, who was officially on duty that day. After that she had requested a copy of the duty roster every week, and planned her rides accordingly.

But Special Agent McKinnon didn't seem to appreciate her sacrifice. Didn't seem to appreciate *her*. Sometimes in bed at night she thought about him before falling asleep. Wondered what kind of woman would appeal to him. Wondered why he didn't like her. And she wanted him to like her. So much so that she wondered what it would take to change his mind. Wondered what it would take to make him stop calling her *Princess* in that subtly mocking way she hated.

She watched him when he wasn't looking, especially on horseback. She rode English and he rode Western style, but that didn't mean she didn't admire the way he rode. Man and horse seemed as one, and she imagined he had been born in the saddle. He was such a superb horseman she would even have trusted him with Suleiman—and she had never let anyone but Andre ride her precious Suleiman.

But it wasn't just the way he rode. He did everything well, from training her household on security measures—including the two additional alerts in the past few weeks and his no-nonsense dissecting of everyone's actions, including hers—to picking a veterinarian for her horses, to dealing with the hundred and one problems that cropped up as her staff adjusted to life in a new country. Competent. Self-assured. Liked and respected by everyone, from her housekeeper to her chefs to her chargé d'affaires. Everyone in her household turned to him as the final arbiter. Alec and Liam didn't say much about him, but she could tell they, too, thought highly of Special Agent McKinnon.

You do, too, she told herself sadly. It wasn't his handsome face she was drawn to, although looking at it filled her with the challenge of making him smile at her. A real smile. A private smile, just for her. And it wasn't that incredibly fit body of his, either, although her thoughts had followed a forbidden path more than once as she imagined what it would be like in his arms. No, it wasn't either of those things, but something entirely different. Even though he made her nervous and edgy, she trusted him implicitly where her safety was concerned. She *knew* nothing could happen to her when he was there, the same way she felt with Andre. Safe. Secure. Sheltered.

And something more. She wasn't sure what that was. Not exactly. But she wanted to find out. If only he didn't dislike her…

The order to stand down two days before had come as a surprise to the men who had covertly surveilled the estate for weeks. They had quietly discussed the order among themselves, but there was no question of disobeying. The reason behind their original posting and their withdrawal order was beyond their need to know. They had filed one last report, then disappeared as if they had never been there, leaving no trace of their passing. What, if anything, had been learned from their observations would be used—or not—at the discretion of the man whose word was law to his men. Their operation was over…for now.

Trace woke late, with barely enough time to shower, shave, brush his teeth and grab some breakfast in the guest house's kitchen. He was *not* in a good mood. He'd had big plans for the weekend—his first full weekend off in a month—but nothing had gone according to plan.

First, Keira had called him early Saturday to say his goddaughter was running a fever, and it would probably be best to postpone his visit to another day. He'd really been looking forward to spending time with Alyssa. Not to mention he'd wanted the opportunity to favor Alyssa's father with a few choice words about the current assignment he'd been suckered into taking on.

Then his date Saturday night with the tall hot blonde who was subletting his condo had turned into a complete washout. Not that she'd given him the cold shoulder. On the contrary. He wasn't cocky or conceited about it—at least he tried not to be. But he knew when a woman was giving him the green light. And the green light had been flashing all evening. The problem was… him.

Don't lie to yourself, a little voice in the back of his head mocked. *It's not that you didn't find her attractive. It's just that she didn't have green eyes.*

Green eyes fringed with long, delicately tinted lashes that owed nothing to artifice. Hair the color of wild honey. Lips that wore just a touch of lip gloss; that curved into an open, natural smile more often than not. And a voice like water trickling through a mountain stream bed, cool and clear, with just the faintest hint of an accent.

Sunday he'd gone to his cabin near Keystone, but that hadn't been a success, either. He'd done the long-overdue yard work and prepped the cabin for winter until his body was aching and dripping with sweat. But his thoughts continually strayed to the princess, wondering what she was doing on her last day before the semester started. Wondering what she'd think of his rustic cabin in the mountains if he ever dared take her there. Wondering what it would be like to kiss her until her lips were naked of anything but the color of passion.

When he'd caught himself thinking along those lines he'd severely chastised himself, but it hadn't done any good. It had only been a month, but she was slowly driving him crazy with wanting her. How was he going to make it through the rest of the year?

Trace had reminded himself he had no intention of falling into the trap that falling for the princess would eventually become. Hadn't he made it quite clear to his boss and to the State Department that he would not, under any circumstances, use his looks to attract her the way the State Department had wanted him to do? That he would not compromise the princess that way? But who would believe him if he said now that he was drawn to her for reasons totally unrelated to his job? Even he'd have a hard time believing it of himself, though he knew it was the God's honest truth.

He'd returned to the estate last night in a foul mood. Then he'd lain awake until the wee hours of the morning, unable to banish the princess from his mind. Think-

ing about the way she watched him when she thought he
wouldn't notice, and what that meant. Thinking about
the way she looked on Suleiman, how she handled the
high-spirited thoroughbred with ease and rode as if
she and the horse communicated on a higher plane.
Watching as she groomed Suleiman with firm and sure
strokes—she never left that manual chore for her groom
to do, earning Trace's respect for her as a true horse-
woman. Hearing in his head her gentle voice as she
talked to her horse in Zakharan when she thought no
one could hear, all soft and sweet and loving, nothing
held back.

Would she be like that with a man? With him?

He'd finally fallen asleep, for all the good it did him.
She haunted his dreams, memories of the times he'd
spent in her company interwoven with fantasies. Vivid
fantasies. Erotic fantasies.

Now Trace tried to shake off the remnants of his
dreams as he dressed in the jeans and casual shirt she
insisted her bodyguards wear on campus so as not to
stand out. Then he strapped on his SIG SAUER, automatically checking the action and the clip before shrug-
ging on a blazer to cover the gun and its holster and
heading out.

He wasn't looking forward to today. Guarding the
princess meant he'd have to sit in on her classes. And
since she didn't want anyone to know she was being
guarded, he was going to have to pretend he was a student. *A little long in the tooth for a student,* he thought,
smiling wryly. But that meant he couldn't read the news-

paper, couldn't do the crossword puzzle, couldn't do anything but sit there, listen and pretend to take notes.

Why did she have to be a math teacher? Well, maybe he'd learn something. He couldn't imagine how it might apply to his job, but you never knew. He'd just have to make the best of it.

He started out the door, but was called back by the ping of the secure fax machine indicating an incoming fax was pending. He quickly keyed in the code to release the fax, then waited impatiently for the two sheets of paper to print. His brows drew into a frown as he perused the latest intelligence report from the State Department. It was disquieting, to say the least, to think that the estate might have been under observation by a person or persons unknown. The good news—if you could call it that—was that *if* there had been surveillance, which the State Department was by no means sure of, that surveillance had since been withdrawn.

Trace considered things for a moment, correlating known facts with this latest intel. No one had been following the princess, he was sure of that. And no one had attempted to penetrate the estate's perimeter. So the reason for the surveillance—if there *had* been any, he reminded himself—was unknown at this point.

He didn't like it. He didn't like unknowns, but there wasn't much he could do about it, except kick up their state of readiness, just in case. He made a mental note to discuss the situation with Alec and Liam. Before he mentioned anything to the princess and her Zakharian bodyguards, he wanted to get the Jones brothers' take on it. He had to be careful about how much he revealed regarding his government's secret intelligence reports—especially if they showed his government in a poor light the way this one did. He considered how he might word a warning to the Zakharians as he folded the pages and tucked them securely in an inner pocket of his jacket before he walked outside.

The princess's chauffeur had parked the brand-new midnight blue Lexus SUV in front of the main house in preparation for her, leaving the keys in the ignition, and Trace took a minute to look the vehicle over. On the one hand it wasn't a vehicle many college professors could afford to drive. But on the other hand it wasn't completely out of the realm of possibility, either. If she wanted to fit in, as both Alec and Liam had made a point of telling him, at least the SUV would be less noticeable than the limo and driver.

The princess had already driven the two DSS agents to and from the university, getting a feel for the SUV and learning her way about town. They'd both assured him she was a good and careful driver, if a little nervous at times. *Only to be expected,* he thought. *Zakhar doesn't have the kind of traffic we take for granted, and she probably didn't have much opportunity to drive herself there anyway. The same goes for the time she spent in England.*

The front door opened and the princess walked out alone. She was dressed as casually as he was in jeans topped with a pale green blouse open at the throat, exposing a creamy expanse of skin. A brown leather purse was slung over one shoulder, she carried a leather briefcase in her other hand and brown leather flats were on her feet. A delicate gold necklace, a discreet gold watch and tiny gold studs in her ears were all the jewelry she wore. Her hair was pulled back into the chignon she customarily wore in public, a style that begged for a man's hands to undo to let her wavy tresses flow free.

Her makeup was understated, as always, as if she didn't want to draw attention to herself. And the disguising horn-rimmed fake eyeglasses were firmly in place—they really did make a noticeable difference in her appearance, although they didn't really hide her lovely green eyes. Not from him, anyway.

"Good morning," she said, smiling hesitantly.

His heartbeat quickened when her eyes met his, and he had to steel himself to be brusque. "Good morning, Princess."

Her smile faded, and she took a deep breath. "Please do not call me that. Not today. Today I am Dr. Marianescu. Only that."

She's right, he thought. *She's gone to a lot of trouble to fit in, and it would defeat the purpose if anyone overhears me calling her Princess.*

He knew why he called her Princess. It was his only defense against her, against the way she tugged at his emotions, the way his body responded to her. It was the only way he could remind himself of who and what she was. Not to mention who and what *he* was. She was a royal princess, sister to a reigning monarch. He was a man who didn't even know his father's name. And while Trace was as egalitarian as they come, there was still a vast gulf between them. Too vast to cross.

"Dr. Marianescu it is," he told her. Her smile returned, and it was like the sun rising over the horizon. He almost smiled back, but then stopped himself and added, "At least while we're at school."

An odd expression flitted over her face and her eyes darkened behind the clear lenses, but she kept the smile in place with an effort. Something about that forced smile made him feel as if he'd kicked a defenseless kitten—not a good feeling at all. Trace wished he hadn't said it, but it was too late for that. "We'd better get going," he said curtly. And despite telling himself not to, he couldn't keep the mocking inflection out of his voice when he added, "You don't want to be late on your first day, Princess."

Chapter 4

That day set the pattern for Mara for the days that followed. She was teaching four classes this semester. One, a calculus course, was what her fellow professors at the university called "general education," or "gen ed" for short. This class contained upwards of a hundred students, and was taught in a large lecture hall five days a week.

Her other three classes—advanced undergraduate courses in ordinary differential equations and partial differential equations, and a graduate course in partial differential equations—were taught on Mondays, Wednesdays and Fridays, and were all small, where she could really interact with her students. Those classes were where she was really pinning her hopes as a teacher.

Differential equations were her specialty…and her passion. No one knew it yet except the dean of the College of Arts and Sciences and the head of the mathematics department, but she was secretly working on a differential equations textbook. She hadn't even told Andre—she wanted to surprise him.

Other than her early morning calculus class, she didn't teach on Tuesdays and Thursdays, but she had office hours. Her door was always open to her students, who soon learned that Dr. Marianescu was one of the more approachable professors in the mathematics department, and were quick to take advantage of her willingness to spend time with them one-on-one. By the time Friday of her first week teaching rolled around, Mara had established herself in a satisfying if exhausting routine.

Tomorrow was Saturday, and she'd promised herself she would devote the entire day to researching her textbook. She hadn't had a chance to work on it since last weekend—starting a new semester was always a challenge, mentally and physically, and she'd been too tired when she'd arrived home from work every night this week to even think about her book. She was determined to make progress, though, so that by the end of the school year the book would be finished. Then she'd tell Andre—he'd be so proud of her.

But Sunday? That was a different story entirely. Mara had overheard two of the professors who had offices near hers discussing the upcoming closure of the top of Mount Evans. When she'd asked what they were talking about, they'd assured her Mount Evans was definitely something she didn't want to miss during her stay here.

"It's only sixty miles west of Denver, and it's the highest paved road in North America," one professor explained. "You can actually drive all the way to the top of the mountain—over fourteen thousand feet. But they close the road past Summit Lake the day after Labor Day, and they don't reopen that five mile section until Memorial Day."

"When is that?" Mara had asked.

"Memorial Day's the last Monday in May, so it won't be open again until next year. This weekend's your last chance to go up there this year. After Monday it'll be closed."

When Mara diffidently approached Special Agent McKinnon after breakfast Sunday morning about visiting Mount Evans, he gave her a long, considering look. Then he said, "Okay, if you want to go, that's fine. But you can't drive—you can only go if your chauffeur drives us."

"Why can I not drive myself the way I drive to the university?" Mara insisted. "It is not that far—only sixty miles."

"Look, Princess," he explained patiently. "I've driven up Mount Evans…and I've driven with you behind the wheel. You're not a bad driver, but you'll need a lot more experience before I'll let you attempt those switchbacks."

"What is that?"

"Sharp turns, steep inclines. Just going as far as Echo Lake can be difficult because there are some hairpin turns even an experienced driver would need to be care-

ful on, and that's just the first fourteen miles. Between
that and Summit Lake it's even more tricky. And after
Summit Lake, forget it. There's no guard rail, and very
little shoulder. Go over the edge of the road even a little
bit, and it's a long way down with nothing to prevent it."

"Oh." Mara considered this for a moment. "You
could drive," she offered.

"Not and do my job at the same time," he said flatly.
"So either your chauffeur drives us—and frankly I don't
see why that's a problem; he hasn't had anything to do
this past week except wash your SUV and keep it filled
with gas—or we don't go."

When Special Agent McKinnon spoke that way Mara
knew she didn't have a choice. It was his way or no way.
"If you insist," she said finally. "But not in the limousine. It is too noticeable, and I…" She willed him to understand how she didn't want to stand out in a crowd the
way she did in Zakhar. Even in England the paparazzi
had followed her around, and she desperately wanted to
avoid that here. The public—not to mention the press—
didn't know she was here in the US, and she wanted
to keep it that way as long as she could. "He can drive
my SUV, yes?"

He chuckled. "You don't have to worry about that. I
had no intention of going in the limo. Not on that road."

The trip soon turned enjoyable for Mara despite the
unpromising start. She'd left her fake eyeglasses at home
for a change—even after more than a week she still
wasn't used to wearing them, and the unaccustomed
weight, slight though it was, gave her a headache when

she wore them too long. She thought—hoped, actually—
no one would recognize her today in her casual jeans
and sweater even without the disguising glasses. And besides, even though she was dressed casually she wanted
to look her best…for some strange reason.

Silly, she scoffed at herself, not wanting to delve too
deeply into her motivations. Nevertheless, she left the
glasses at home.

Even with her chauffeur in the front seat able to overhear everything they said, she felt as if she were a normal woman on a normal outing with a man. A very
special man. A man who made her react in ways she
never had before. A man who made her realize that
being a woman wasn't such a bad thing after all, no
matter what her father had said.

Special Agent McKinnon knew a lot about the Mount
Evans Scenic Byway—not surprising for someone
who'd lived in the area for years—and it had only taken
a few adroit questions from Mara for him to open up
and act as a tour guide.

They turned off I-70 at Idaho Springs, stopping at
the National Forest information center to check on the
road conditions and for Mara to view the exhibits. Then
they headed for Echo Lake, the road climbing in elevation with every mile. Mara pressed the button that
rolled down the window so as not to miss any of the
scenic vistas, letting the cool wind blow on her face.
It reminded her so much of home she turned a smiling
face to Special Agent McKinnon.

"Does it not remind you of the mountains around
Drago?" she asked him just as a strong gust of wind

caused her hair to tumble down from its chignon. "Oh, no!" She grabbed for the large clip that normally held her hair so securely, but which now was dangling precariously behind her. She couldn't reach it.

"Here, I've got it," he said, unhooking the clip and holding it out to her. "And yeah, it does remind me."

Mara deftly twisted her hair into a knot and affixed the clip. "I have wanted to ask you," she said shyly. "I know you spent six months in Drago when you were a young man." She realized he might find that comment a little insulting, so she quickly added, "Not that you are an old man now. Just older."

He laughed. "Not to worry, Princess. I knew what you meant."

Special Agent McKinnon's laughter changed him, made him more approachable somehow, and Mara asked, "Someday, would you tell me what you remember most about the time you were there?"

"Homesick?"

"Just a little." She turned to look out the window again. "But not when I am in the mountains this way— they remind me of home." She smiled at a particularly good memory. "Andre used to take us hiking in the mountains sometimes."

"Us?"

"Juliana and me. She was the daughter of the US ambassador. We were at private school together, and we were best friends until she went away to college here in the States."

"What happened after that?"

Mara's smile faded. "I do not know," she said softly.

"I called her. Wrote to her. But she never wrote back after the first two months. Never returned my calls." She shrugged, pretending to herself the loss of her closest friend hadn't mattered, even though that loss had reduced her small circle of friends to pitiful proportions. "Perhaps she was too busy. The next year I started college myself, and Juliana went to Hollywood and became a famous actress. I suppose she no longer needed my friendship after that. Then her ambassador father retired to Virginia, and she never returned to Zakhar. I never saw her again."

Special Agent McKinnon frowned. "Juliana...famous actress...you're not talking about Juliana Richardson, are you?"

"Yes, that is her name."

He whistled. "Beautiful woman. Terrific actress." He looked at Mara, his curiosity piqued. "So you knew her?"

Despite the remnants of hurt and bewilderment she still felt at the loss of Juliana's friendship all those years ago, Mara allowed herself a tiny smile. "Yes, but when I first met her she was not beautiful as she is today. Except for her eyes. Her eyes were always the same as they are now. Andre always said Juliana's eyes could bring men to their knees."

"He was right."

The shaft of pain that lanced through Mara had nothing to do with losing a friend, and everything to do with envy. For the first time in her life she wished she had violet eyes, a heart-shaped face, ebony hair and stood only as high as a man's heart. Instead she had green eyes set in a pretty but certainly not beautiful face, light brown hair and came up to Special Agent McKinnon's shoulders.

Not that Mara thought she was ugly, but her mirror told her the truth and she had no illusions about her appearance. No one would ever call her dainty. Nor would they ever call her beautiful, especially since she did almost nothing to enhance her appearance as many women did, as her own mother had done in all the portraits Mara had seen of her—Mara had never wanted to stand out.

She had also wanted to downplay her resemblance to her dead mother, especially when her father was around. And even though he was dead now, that habit was engrained in her. Unadorned by anything more than the faintest trace of makeup, her face was reasonably attractive but indistinguishable from the faces of thousands of other women. Her eyes, her best feature, she discounted.

As for her body, in a long-ago era her figure would have been much admired, but not in today's fashion conscious world, with its emphasis on thin bodies. Fashion designers still wanted to design clothes for her to wear, but only because the world took notice of what she wore, not because she was model thin.

She wasn't fooled either by the paparazzi who had followed her everywhere she went before she came to America incognito. They weren't photographing her because she was drop-dead gorgeous as Juliana was now. They just wanted to sell pictures. And pictures of a princess sold well. And if the pictures were embarrassing in any way, that only added to their salability.

Mara sighed to herself and shook those thoughts off. She'd had a lot of practice walling off her emotions, putting them in little boxes where they couldn't hurt her. Or at least, where the hurt could be contained. She had never cared before about her appearance this way. Had never cared about appealing to a specific man. But then, she had never met Special Agent McKinnon before.

She pasted a smile on her face. "Tell me about Mount Evans, please. You have been here many times, yes?"

Mara listened quietly as Special Agent McKinnon talked, loving the sound of his deep voice; watching the animation on his face. He was a complex man, and she wished she knew more about him. Wished she knew if there was a special woman in his life. Wished she had what it would take as a woman to make him lose that iron self-control.

When they reached Echo Lake Special Agent McKinnon directed the chauffeur to pull into the parking lot, and told her, "We've got to stop here. I've been all over the world, but I've never seen anything like Echo Lake."

Mara saw the pathway leading from the parking lot. "Can we walk all the way around the lake?"

He shook his head. "No, but we can walk as far as that cove over there," he said, pointing. "See the piece of land that sticks out into the lake?" When she nodded he added, "The walkway stops right before that. It's fairly flat so it's not a difficult walk, but it's a bit of a distance. Are you up to it?"

Mara shot him a look of incredulity. "I told you I have hiked the mountains surrounding Drago. This is nothing compared to that."

He laughed. "I stand corrected." She started to get out but he stopped her. "Take your jacket," he warned. "We're above ten thousand feet elevation. It might seem warm now, but it can get chilly if the wind picks up."

They walked together in companionable silence for several minutes. Special Agent McKinnon automatically shifted positions a couple of times to put his body between hers and those of strangers they passed, but he let her set the pace. She knew she'd surprised him when they quickly outdistanced most of the crowd of people milling around Echo Lake Lodge.

The lake was beautiful, the water crystal clear, like glass, reflecting the blue of the sky above them. The scent of pine trees was overpowering, and the trees were mirrored in the still waters. "You are right," Mara told him softly after a while. "I have not been all over the world, like you, but I have been to many places, and it is like no other lake I have seen."

They stopped for a minute at a point where the walkway came right up to the rocks at the water's edge. "Tell me about some of the places you have seen," she invited. "Not Zakhar—we will talk of Zakhar another day. But where else have you been that you cannot forget?"

Special Agent McKinnon propped one foot on a boulder in front of him, leaned an arm on his knee, and contemplated the view across the lake for the space of several heartbeats. Mara watched him, scarcely realizing she was holding her breath as varied emotions crossed his face. Finally he said, "I've seen a lot of beautiful places that will stay with me forever—places I want to remember. But there's only one place I can't forget—and wish I could."

"Where is that?" she asked in a voice barely above a whisper.

"Afghanistan."

She let out the breath she'd been holding. His expression was troubled, and she knew he wasn't seeing Echo Lake, he was seeing a mountainous, largely arid, war-torn country, a battleground for millennia. "You fought there," she guessed. She started to tell him her brother had fought there, too, but changed her mind, not wanting to distract Trace from anything he might share with her about his own experiences.

"Yeah." He looked at her, and she could see the scars on his soul reflected in the shadows in his eyes. "There's no real winning in Afghanistan. Alexander the Great fought there. So did Genghis Khan, the Soviets, and the US under the United Nations banner. But even if we all left tomorrow, war would continue, innocent civilians would still suffer and children would still die. The tribal leaders fight among themselves, and nothing will ever change that." He breathed deeply. "There are some breathtakingly beautiful places in Afghanistan, but few people will ever know about them. All they know is war and devastation and death."

"How long were you there?"

"Two years. The Corps wanted me to re-up—that means reenlist," he explained in an aside, "because I was able to sp—" He stopped abruptly, and Mara wondered what he had been going to say. "But I'd had enough. I'd already served four years by that time, two of them in Afghanistan. Two years in hell."

He was silent for another minute, and Mara didn't say anything. Couldn't think of anything to say to take away the pain his memories invoked. But she wanted to. More than anything she wanted to erase that desolate expression from his eyes.

Finally he gave himself a shake. "How did we get on that subject?"

"I asked," she said in a small voice. "I am sorry—I did not wish to make you sad."

"It's okay, Princess," he said, but she could tell his lighthearted tone was forced. "It was a long time ago. A lifetime ago." He smiled briefly. "Shall we go on? Or did you want to turn back?"

"I want to go to the end," she answered. "I do not like half measures."

He laughed softly. "No, you wouldn't," he said, and Mara could tell something had distracted him from his sadness. "Let's do it, then."

They walked to the end in silence, passing several other couples along the way. Just as before, Special Agent McKinnon unconsciously interposed his body between those other people and Mara. He didn't make a big deal out of it, but his protective air was as unmistakable as it was unshakeable.

Mara glanced at the people they passed, realizing the marked difference between those people and Special Agent McKinnon and her. *They are lovers,* she told herself, watching the way the other couples walked arm in arm or hand in hand. Echo Lake *was* romantic and quietly beautiful, the ideal place for lovers.

Her throat ached as she cast covert looks at the tall man beside her, wishing he would hold her hand. Or put his arm around her. Or look at her with tenderness. But that was wishing for the moon. *You should just be glad he does not look at you with dislike,* she reminded herself, realizing with a little start of acknowledgment that not once today had he done so. She hugged that knowledge to herself with a tiny smile. Even when she had made him remember a place he wanted to forget, he had forgotten to dislike her.

Chapter 5

When they finally made it back to the SUV Special Agent McKinnon checked his watch and told her, "We should probably just go up to the top now—not stop at Summit Lake. We can stop there on the way down if you want."

"Why?"

"Because it's a good idea to visit the top of the mountain in the morning, and be gone by noon. Thunderstorms are common in the afternoon, so unless you want to take a chance on missing the view…"

"But the view is what the other professors told me I should not miss."

He smiled. "Exactly."

They drove straight to the top, with Mara exclaiming the entire way. There were several places she was tempted to cry out "Stop!" so she could take in some particularly scenic view, but she didn't say anything, trusting Special Agent McKinnon's advice to visit the top first, then stop on the way down.

The road twisted and turned sharply, almost bending back on itself in places, and the incline was steep, so the going was slow. And as he'd told her that morning, there was no guard rail and very little margin for error. Mara wasn't afraid—not exactly—but at one point she admitted, "I am glad you would not let me drive."

One corner of his mouth quirked up in a smile, but he didn't say anything. Then they turned one last corner and pulled into the almost full parking lot at the top of Mount Evans. Mara's chauffeur found a spot to park and carefully backed into it. When the SUV stopped Mara drew a deep breath and exhaled slowly, then thanked her chauffeur in Zakharan. "I am glad you were driving," she told him with her best smile. "I felt safe with you at the wheel."

"Thank you, your highness," he replied, touching his cap. "It was my pleasure."

"I know you stayed with the car at Echo Lake," she said. "But please…please go see everything for yourself here. I am told it is an experience not to be missed. Do not wait for me." She'd already broken him of the habit of holding her door for her, not wanting to draw undue attention to herself.

"I will do that now," he told her, opening his door and getting out.

When he was gone Mara turned to Special Agent

McKinnon. "I am ready," she told him. "What should I see first?"

He reached into the pocket of his jacket. "Before you do anything else," he said. "Put some of this on." He handed her a tube of sunscreen. "We're over fourteen thousand feet up," he explained. "That means you have fifty percent less protection from the sun, and I wouldn't want you to get sunburned."

Mara squeezed some sunscreen into one hand, rubbed both hands together, and tried to apply it to her face. But it was difficult without a mirror. Then she rubbed the remainder on her forearms and the backs of her hands.

"Uh, you have a little too much here," Special Agent McKinnon said, raising a hand to her face and gently wiping away excess cream.

Mara's startled gaze met his. His fingers were strong, firm, warm. And the masculine touch she wasn't used to sent shivers through her so that she trembled. Noticeably. "Thank you," she said when he finally removed his fingers and she was able to speak in something approaching a normal voice. "What of you?" she asked.

"I never burn," he assured her.

"But that is silly." She took the tube, squeezed a small amount onto her fingertips, and dabbed it on his cheekbones and the bridge of his nose before he could stop her. Then she rubbed the cream into his skin, feeling his muscles tensing under her touch. Their eyes met again, and even though he wasn't touching her, she was touching him, Mara shivered, and trembled again. "There," she said at last. But she didn't draw her hand away.

There was something wrong with her breathing. A tightness in her chest made every breath she drew ragged. As if in a trance her fingers slid slowly down his cheek, feeling the slight beard stubble of a man who had shaved very early that morning. Without volition, her thumb brushed itself against his lips. Strong, firm, unyielding. Like him.

He caught her hand and dragged it away. "Not a good idea, Princess."

Suddenly Mara realized what she had done, and she felt her cheeks flame with embarrassment. "I am sorry," she whispered, turning away and fumbling for the door handle. She scrambled out of the car, appalled at herself. She wanted to run away and hide, but wherever she went he would go, too—there was no escaping him. Except one place. She bolted for the ladies' room in a small building beside the ruins of the Crest House.

Five minutes later, composed but still ashamed, she walked out of the ladies' room and found Special Agent McKinnon waiting for her, leaning one shoulder against the stone wall. There was an expression on his face that defied her ability to read it, but at least he wasn't looking at her with the mocking expression that would have shriveled her.

"I am sorry," she said again, humiliated, but determined to salvage her trip to Mount Evans if she possibly could. The day had been wonderful so far, right up till the moment when she'd practically thrown herself at him.

"It happens," he said dismissively, as if women routinely made unwanted advances toward him that he had to fend off.

Not surprising, the way he looks, she thought. But she didn't want him to think she was like all the other women he knew, only interested in his handsome face. She knew in her heart she would have been drawn to him no matter what, but would he believe her?

"It does not happen with me," she told him, her eyes crinkling in an expression she hoped didn't betray how vulnerable she felt at that moment. "Truly."

A muscle twitched in his cheek, but all he said was, "Don't worry about it." He smiled faintly. "Now that that's out of the way, did you want to walk to the real top of the mountain. The summit?" He pointed at the outcropping on the other side of the parking lot. "The climb is only a hundred twenty feet, but at this altitude it's not easy—the air is thin and you could tire easily. It's up to you."

Mara was grateful for the way he was trying to act naturally. "What is at the top?"

He grinned. "Nothing much. Just a USGS marker."

"What is that?"

"That stands for US Geological Survey. Fourteen thousand two hundred fifty-eight feet. And the highest view you'll probably ever see. Are you game to try it?" His voice was a definite challenge.

Her eyes narrowed, taking the dare. "I do not like half measures."

"Then let's do it."

Mara stood at the top of the summit, gasping for breath. Special Agent McKinnon hadn't lied—the lack of oxygen combined with physical exertion had made climbing the hundred twenty feet seem as if she'd climbed the entire mountain from its base. Without him ahead of her, encouraging her, Mara wasn't quite sure she would have made it. At one point he'd even taken her hand to help her over a rough patch, but then he'd let go, so she could struggle up the last few feet on her own.

The view was worth it, once she finally caught her breath. She could see in all directions, and when she turned westward Special Agent McKinnon pointed out Mount Bierstadt, Grays Peak and Torreys Peak. "Those are three of what are called Colorado's fourteeners—mountain peaks that exceed fourteen thousand feet, like Mount Evans," he told her. "And from up here you can see a good portion of the entire state."

"What are those mountains to the south?" she asked.

"Those are the Sangre de Cristo Mountains."

"Blood of Christ," she translated automatically. "Why?"

"Supposedly because of their red color at sunrise and sunset."

"What about those mountains to the north? What are they called?"

Special Agent McKinnon laughed. "Would you believe that's the Never Summer Mountain Range?"

Mara laughed, too, delighted. "Never Summer. How appropriate for mountains." She rotated slowly, gazing at everything, imprinting the picturesque vistas in her mind. "Thank you," she said simply. "I will always remember this."

He looked at her, a quizzical expression on his face.

"I just realized you don't have a camera with you. If you'd told me I could have brought mine."

Her smile faded. "I do not like cameras," she said, feeling suddenly so cold she shivered. "Photographs..."

"I don't get it."

At first she thought she couldn't tell him, but there was something about his expression that told her he wasn't just asking out of idle curiosity—he really wanted to understand. She drew a deep breath. "Ever since I was a little girl, the paparazzi were everywhere I went in public. Even in Zakhar. No privacy. No way to escape. I was their prisoner, and it was as if they felt they owned me. *Thousands* of photographs have been taken of me against my will."

She struggled to find the words. "I learned early never to show emotion in public. Never to let them see what I was thinking. Never to display a single vulnerability they could exploit—I was always on display. I would turn around, and there they would be—the paparazzi. *Click. Click. Click.* I used to have nightmares when I was young, and for a while I was even afraid to take a bath, that is how paranoid I was."

Her eyes burned with unshed tears as she remembered another princess, hounded by the paparazzi to her death in a Paris tunnel, and she whispered, "I honestly believe if I were being raped or murdered and the paparazzi were there, instead of trying to help me they would just photograph it. That is why I hate cameras."

She covered her face with her hands, suddenly shaking. Then gentle arms enfolded her, wrapping her protectively in warmth. "Shhh," a deep voice said over her head. "It's okay, Princess. I'm sorry I asked. I'm sorry I made you remember."

Mara knew she should withdraw from his embrace, knew it was dangerous to let herself seek shelter and comfort in his arms. But he was so warm. So strong. So understanding. So much the man she'd dreamed of in her lonely bed. In this instant it was as if she could be herself with him. Just Mara. Not a princess of Zakhar. Not even Dr. Marianescu. Just Mara, no more, no less. A woman with a man.

They were past the worst of the switchbacks on the way down when storm clouds moved in, shrouding the top of Mount Evans from view. And by the time they reached Summit Lake, an alpine lake nestled in the cirque formed by Mount Evans and Mount Spalding, it had started to snow. Dainty flurries, wind born, that didn't even require the use of windshield wipers.

"Better not stop," Special Agent McKinnon said, viewing the Summit Lake parking lot, which was rapidly emptying.

"But this might be my only chance," Mara protested. "They close the road the day after tomorrow."

"We're still close to thirteen thousand feet elevation here," he explained to her. "We need to get at least as far as Echo Lake before it really starts snowing."

"Half an hour," she pleaded.

He gave her a considering look. "Fifteen minutes. But if the snow thickens, we start back immediately."

They pulled into the parking lot, and although the chauffeur had his pick of spots, he kept driving until he got as close to the lake as he could. Before Special Agent McKinnon could say anything, the chauffeur told him in his thickly accented English, "I will wait with the car." Mara saw the two men exchanging meaningful glances, and realized they were both worried about the weather.

She jumped out of the SUV and walked as quickly as she could toward the lake, zipping up her jacket and fumbling for her gloves, which she soon realized she'd forgotten. It had gotten colder ever since the storm clouds had blotted out the sun, so she thrust her hands into her pockets to keep them warm. Snow flurries were swirling, but the lake was still easily visible, the cliffs and ridges surrounding it mirrored in the water's surface.

She heard Special Agent McKinnon behind her, but she didn't waste any of her precious seconds turning around. She breathed deeply, pulling the crisp, clean air into her lungs as she drank in the view, wanting to preserve this memory. Someday, when she was old and gray, she would bring it out of her mental photo album and remind herself of this special day—the lakes, the mountains, the meadows, the man. Especially the man, but she didn't need to see him again to remember him. He was already imprinted in her mind…and her heart.

The wind picked up suddenly, sending ripples across the surface of the lake, carrying heavier snowflakes with it. The few small groups of people still wandering around the lake's edge turned and headed for the parking lot. The last couple was just passing them when Special Agent McKinnon said, "We should go, too, Princess." Perhaps he raised his voice to be heard over the wind, or perhaps the wind itself carried his voice farther than he intended. Because that's when it happened.

"Wally! Wally! Look!" the woman of the couple said excitedly, tugging at the arm of the man at her side. "It's her. That's Princess Mara! I'm sure of it. I saw her on a TV special last summer!"

The man named Wally turned, camera in hand, and before Mara could shield her face he had snapped a picture of her.

"No!" Mara couldn't prevent her cry of dismay. But even before the word left her mouth the man named Wally was staring down the business end of a SIG SAUER held in the steady hand of Special Agent McKinnon.

"Camera," he demanded, his voice as cold as the icy wind blowing across the lake.

"What?" said the man named Wally, as he and the woman with him stared in sudden shock and horror at how quickly the incident had escalated into something neither of them had expected.

"Give me the camera," Special Agent McKinnon said, holding out his left hand while his right hand never wavered. Mutely, the man named Wally held out the camera, which was snatched from his hand. "You've got three choices," Special Agent McKinnon said, his voice as implacable as his face. "One, I can toss the camera in the lake. You're out an expensive camera, as well as any pictures you've taken today. Two, I can take the memory card. Then you've only lost whatever pictures are stored on it. Or three, I can erase one picture. But to do that I need two hands. It's your call."

The man named Wally seemed too terrified to speak, but the woman with him said, in a high-pitched voice, "Just erase the picture," and she huddled behind the man she was with.

That quickly the gun was holstered and Special Agent McKinnon stepped back a few paces. He reviewed the camera, his gaze flicking from the camera to the couple in front of him, and back to the camera. Then he pressed one button, and another. Finished, he told Wally, "Catch," and tossed the camera to him. The man juggled the camera, but caught it. And when he looked up the gun had been drawn again.

"Put the camera in your pocket, turn around, and walk to your car. Don't stop for any reason. If you stop, I'm going to assume you're a threat." He paused. "And if you *ever* take anyone's picture again without permission, especially hers," he said, indicating Mara with a tilt of his head, "you're a dead man. You got that? And if you talk about this, just remember that means I'll know where to find you."

Both the man and the woman nodded. The camera was quickly stowed in a jacket pocket. The couple backed away, then turned, and practically ran toward their car in the parking lot. The car engine roared to life, the car backed out, then gravel spurted as the car shot out of the parking lot and onto Mt. Evans Road.

Mara watched in silence as Special Agent McKinnon holstered his weapon. He looked up and saw the expression on her face. "We should go, Princess," he told her gently. "The snow's really coming down now."

He held out his hand, the hand that had drawn the gun so quickly. Mara looked at it for a moment, then up at his face, her thoughts, her emotions, swirling like the snowflakes falling around her. She had been as shocked as the couple who'd just left at how quickly Special Agent McKinnon had reacted. It was as if his body had responded before he'd even had time to assimilate what had happened, but she knew that wasn't the case. Thought had preceded action, but only by a split second.

She'd known he had to be good at his job, or else the US State Department wouldn't have assigned him to head up the team guarding her. She just hadn't realized how good. Nor had she realized how far he'd go to defend her. Not just physically, but emotionally, too. He'd learned only a short time ago how much it upset her to have her photograph taken, yet he'd already incorporated it into his protective shield around her. And while she knew he would never have killed anyone over a photograph, he hadn't hesitated to use whatever leverage he had to protect her.

Just like Andre.

Her shock faded with that thought. She glanced at his outstretched hand, smiled tremulously, and took it. Then she raised her eyes to his.

Chapter 6

Her second week of teaching behind her, Mara said goodbye to her teaching assistant Friday afternoon, then smiled a little tiredly at Liam as she packed up her briefcase. "Are you doing anything special for the weekend?" she asked him.

"Not really. Our family has a cabin southwest of here in the Rockies, near Dillon Reservoir. You don't know that area, do you?" She shook her head. "Our cabin's between Silverthorne and Keystone, maybe an hour and a half from here. Alec and I were thinking of going there together since we're both off."

"That sounds nice," she said with a touch of wistfulness. "What do you do there?"

"The usual stuff. Hike. Fish. Laze around. Sleep late and neglect to shave." He grinned at her. "Hike and fish some more. What are you doing this weekend?"

Her smile faded. "Whatever Special Agent McKinnon lets me do, since he is on duty. Grade papers, I suppose." She started to walk out of her office, but Liam stopped her.

"That's not fair to him," he told her. "McKinnon's not like that. Didn't he take you to Mount Evans last weekend? If there's something you want to do, just tell him, the same way you tell Alec and me."

It is different with him, she thought, *especially now,* but she couldn't say that to Liam. Instead she said, "That is the problem. Other than riding, there is nothing I can think of to do. I do not know many people here, not yet. And I do not know of any place to go. If I were at home in Drago there would be many choices. But I am still a stranger here."

"Why don't you just ask McKinnon to show you around? He lives in Denver. I'm sure he knows the area like the back of his hand." He hesitated. "McKinnon's got a cabin, too. Near Keystone, he told us. I bet he'd take you there if you asked him. The mountains are especially beautiful this time of year."

Mara forced herself to smile at Liam, knowing she would never ask Special Agent McKinnon—and not because of what had happened on Mount Evans. Because of what had happened the next day. *I could ask you or Alec,* she thought. *But not him. Never him. Not now.*

That night after dinner Trace heard a knock on his door. "It's open," he called, putting down his third newspaper of the day, the one he hadn't gotten around to finishing that morning. He read three newspapers daily cover to cover: *The Denver Post*, *The New York Times*, and *The Washington Post*. He preferred actual, physical newspapers he could hold in his hand, as opposed to reading his news on the internet. Keira used to tease him about it when they'd been partners, but he'd been reading newsprint since he'd been a twelve-year-old boy reading the newspapers he delivered, and he wasn't going to change, not after twenty-four years.

Liam walked in. "Hey, just wanted to let you know the princess is in her bedroom for the night, so I'm done. Alec and I are heading out early tomorrow morning, and I wanted to tell you something before I leave." He recounted what the princess had told him that afternoon, about wishing she had something to do this weekend. "I had an idea, so I called Keira. She said she and Alyssa would be home tomorrow morning if you want to stop by around ten."

At McKinnon's sudden frown he added softly, "All the princess wants is what most of us take for granted—a normal life. She's not a social butterfly—the bright lights and the fast-paced lifestyle don't appeal to her, and—"

"How the hell do you know that?"

"Come on, McKinnon. Alec and I have been guarding her for almost six weeks now, same as you. Don't you think we'd have noticed? She comes home from work and she stays home. She grades papers and plans her classes, and works on her book. She calls Zakhar and talks to her brother or one of her friends, and she rides that horse she loves whenever she can. Except for an occasional outing like Mount Evans, that's it. Speaking of which, in case you hadn't noticed, she only rides on the days you're officially on duty."

"I noticed," Trace growled. "So what?"

"So she's not the kind of woman where it's all about her. She's thoughtful, considerate, and from what Alec and I can gather sitting in on her classes, she's a decent teacher—she really cares about her students. So why don't you cut her some slack? You're pretty hard on her—Alec and I were talking about it the other night."

Trace threw him a forbidding expression, but Liam just smiled. "Yeah, we're not blind, either. We've seen the way she looks at you, and it's not the way she looks at us. If she were any other woman and she looked at *me* that way, I—"

The forbidding expression turned into a scowl, and Trace gritted his teeth. "Get the hell out of here, Jones."

"Yes, *sir*!" Liam threw him a mocking salute. "See you Sunday night."

Liam sauntered out and Trace cursed under his breath. He picked up his newspaper and tried to finish the article where he'd left off, but his thoughts strayed to what Liam had said. And what he hadn't. *Damn it,* Trace thought, throwing his newspaper aside. *Why did he have to bring that subject up? Now I'll never be able to sleep tonight.*

It wasn't as if he hadn't noticed almost from the start the princess wasn't the kind of woman he'd first thought her. And it wasn't as if he hadn't noticed she'd strictly curtailed her own pleasure in riding to accommodate his working schedule. And it *damned* well wasn't as if he hadn't noticed the way she followed him with her eyes.

At least he didn't mention my eyes follow her, too, whenever they get the chance, Trace told himself, taking small comfort in his ability to hide his emotions. "Cut her some slack," he muttered. "Yeah, right. If I don't keep her at a distance emotionally, there's not a snowball's chance I'll be able to keep her at a distance physically, job or no job."

He wanted her. But it was just one of those things he had to live with. He knew there was no future in it, and he wasn't going down that road. Not if he could help it.

Last Sunday had been a near thing, and he'd spent Labor Day Monday distancing himself from her. She'd toppled his defenses on Sunday…and she hadn't done it on purpose. She just had to breathe, to smile, to take his hand, to laugh the way she had at the summit, and his protective instincts kicked into overdrive. He wanted to protect her from everyone and everything…except him. But he was the one she most needed protection from.

He hadn't meant to tell her anything about himself. And he sure as hell hadn't planned to tell her about Afghanistan. But somehow the words had poured out of him like water through a sieve. Then she'd looked at him with compassion in those green eyes, and he'd felt as if he could tell her anything and she'd understand. He'd almost blurted out the reason the Corps had wanted him to re-up, because of his facility with languages. He'd remembered just in the nick of time why he was there with her, and had held his tongue.

Afterward, he couldn't help but notice the way she'd darted wistful looks at him every time they'd passed another couple as they finished up their walk alongside Echo Lake. He'd managed to shunt that to the back of his mind—until she'd touched him in the SUV atop Mount

Evans. *I never burn,* he'd told her, but she'd rubbed sunscreen on him—*sunscreen,* for God's sake!—and the softness of her fingertips had burned right through him, hotter than the hottest sun. Then she'd touched his lips and he'd almost pulled her into his arms.

His reaction to her on every level baffled him. Like when they'd been talking about her one-time friend, the achingly beautiful Juliana Richardson. He'd seen the actress in his mind's eye as they were discussing her, but somehow her perfection had paled in comparison to the warm, animated face of the princess sitting next to him. He couldn't prove it, but he knew in his heart that if he were given his choice between the two women he would choose the princess. Hands down.

Not that you'll ever have either woman, he told himself. The princess was as remote from him as the actress was. But that didn't stop him from wanting her. And it didn't stop him from wanting to shield her from anything that might cause her pain.

His hand had already been reaching for his SIG SAUER when the man called Wally had turned around suddenly at Summit Lake, even before he'd taken the princess's picture. If it had been a gun in his hand instead of a camera, Wally would have been dead before he got off a shot. But Trace's brain had registered *camera,* not *gun,* and he hadn't fired. Then he'd heard the princess's soft cry of dismay, and he'd known in a flash he had to protect her from that, too. Her whole day would have been destroyed if he hadn't destroyed that picture.

Yeah, but you didn't have to threaten the guy after you erased it, did you? Weren't you just grandstand-

ing for the princess's benefit? he asked himself. But the answer he got back was, *not really.*

Part of his threat had been aimed at making sure no more pictures were taken of her, especially once the guy was out of gun range. But another part of the threat was reaction to something he'd never understood before until the princess had expressed it—the *violation* someone might feel at having their picture taken against their will, especially when it was repeated…endlessly. He couldn't enforce his threat, but maybe the guy would think twice before he took someone else's picture unawares.

When the princess had taken his hand afterward, when she'd looked up at him with unalloyed trust in her eyes, he'd had the slow-motion feeling of falling. He hadn't expected the trust. Not so quickly after he'd seen the shock on her face at the sudden threat of violence she'd witnessed. But her hand had nestled trustingly in his all the way back to the SUV. She hadn't said much on the long drive back to Boulder. But her eyes had spoken for her, and they had scared the hell out of him.

He'd spent most of Monday rebuilding his defenses, but to do that he'd had to resort to treating her as he had before the trip to Mount Evans, with that slightly mocking attitude. He'd watched the smile fade from her eyes, replaced by a flicker of hurt, then blankness—that lack of emotion in her expression she'd told him she'd learned early to keep the paparazzi from knowing what she was thinking. As if that weren't bad enough, the blankness was followed by the acceptance of his rejection he'd seen in her eyes that first day, an acceptance that contrarily made him so angry he'd wanted to shake her.

Fortunately for him he'd been off for the next four days, and he hadn't had to see her...except in his mind. He hadn't had to think of her...except every other waking moment. And he hadn't had to dream about her and her lovely green eyes...except he had. The dreams weren't erotic—not at first. He'd dreamed of her standing on the Mount Evans summit, her green eyes vivid in the smiling face she turned to him. He'd dreamed of her at Summit Lake, snowflakes swirling, her green eyes not smiling at him this time, but filled with trust. And he'd dreamed of the way her green eyes had hurt for him as he talked about the futility of Afghanistan.

Then the dreams had turned erotic. Each memory had ended with a twist that was fantasy, not reality. Each dream had ended with the throbbing release he was fast coming to fear he could only find with her. Then he'd woken each time, hard and aching from the release he *hadn't* found.

Cut her some slack, Liam had said. *Right.*

Then he remembered the other part of what Liam had said, about taking the princess to visit Keira and Alyssa. Maybe he should. At least with other people around—people he felt at home with, unlike her household staff—he'd be distracted from thinking about her all the time. And maybe she'd enjoy the novelty of seeing how ordinary folks lived—Liam was right about that. *I'll ask her at breakfast tomorrow,* he thought. *If she turns me down, no harm done.*

Part of him hoped she would turn him down. He didn't want to see her the way he'd seen her last Sunday, as a normal woman with normal wants, needs, desires—

too dangerous for his peace of mind, especially after what had nearly happened on Mount Evans. He didn't want to think of her as anyone but the princess she was.

But another part of him was hoping she would accept his invitation, the part of him that had led him into his often dangerous line of work. The part of him willing to take risks. The part of him willing to step into the line of fire.

And that's *exactly* what he'd be doing if he let himself get too close emotionally to the princess—deliberately stepping into the line of fire.

With Special Agent McKinnon directing her, Mara drove to Keira and Cody Walker's house in the small city of Golden, Colorado, west of Denver. When he'd casually invited her at breakfast, she'd jumped at the chance to meet someone close to him, despite the way he'd been treating her ever since their trip to Mount Evans. She already knew from Alec and Liam that Keira had been Special Agent McKinnon's partner for three years, and the two DSS agents had been full of praise for their younger sister. Mara wanted to see how he acted around other women—was it the same with every woman he came into contact with, or was it just her?

"Turn here," Special Agent McKinnon told her. "This is it." Mara pulled into the driveway, drove through the open gate and up the lane, then parked. She stared for a moment, admiring the way the house seemed to blend into its surroundings. Not for the Walkers the cookie cutter look of some of the newer subdivisions they'd driven through. Theirs was an older-looking house, but distinctive and meticulously maintained, set on a fenced acre of land.

"It is nice," Mara said before getting out of the car. "It has character."

"Yeah. Their house is special—and a lot like them. It's also highly defensible."

"Defensible?" Mara was surprised by the word. Special Agent McKinnon looked as if he wished he hadn't mentioned that, so Mara hurried on. "They are your friends, yes? Alec and Liam said—" She stopped short, realizing that Special Agent McKinnon might not appreciate being the topic of conversation between her two other bodyguards and her.

But all he said was, "Yeah. It's a little complicated because Walker is also my boss. But they're good friends. And their daughter is my goddaughter." He smiled to himself, and for the first time Mara realized he was a man who could be emotionally vulnerable. "They even named her after me. Can you believe it? Alyssa Tracy Walker." There it was again—that curious combination of pride and humility. But Mara didn't have time to consider what it might mean because Special Agent McKinnon said, "Come on, Keira's expecting us."

They rang the doorbell, which was almost immediately answered by a lovely woman with red-gold curls, warm brown eyes and a dusting of freckles. "Trace!" she said with a welcoming smile. She looked toward Mara and started to speak, but Special Agent McKinnon interrupted her.

"Keira, I'd like you to meet Her Serene Highness,

Princess Mara Theodora of Zakhar. Princess, this is Keira Walker, my former partner."

Keira held her hand out to Mara. "Very pleased to meet you finally," she said with a warm smile. "Alec and Liam have told me a lot about you." She shot a look at her former partner that Mara didn't understand before she added, "And it's Dr. Marianescu, right? I was so impressed when my brothers told me. There aren't enough women going into math, science and technology careers, even after all this time. And it had to be especially difficult for you, under the circumstances. What I mean is—"

"Can you continue this after we get inside?" Special Agent McKinnon asked drily.

Keira laughed, stepped back, and pushed the door wide. "Sorry about that," she apologized. "Trace knows that once I get started on this subject I can go on for hours."

As they walked in an angry wail came from upstairs. "Oh, dear," Keira said ruefully. "Alyssa's awake already. I was hoping she'd sleep a little longer. Excuse me for a minute, but please make yourselves at home." She started for the stairway, but before she'd taken four steps a tall, rangy man with blond hair and blue eyes walked down the stairs and into the living room, cuddling a one-year-old baby girl in the crook of his arm.

"I've got her," he told his wife unnecessarily, smiling at the baby in his arms. He raised that smile to Mara and held out his hand. "You must be the princess."

"Yes," Keira said, "but that's just an inherited title. She's also Dr. Marianescu, and *that* title she earned."

Mara beamed at Keira, whose words indicated she understood. "Yes, but will you not call me Mara?" she asked both Keira and her husband as she shook his hand. "Alec and Liam call me Dr. Marianescu, but that is because they are pretending to be my students when they guard me at school."

"Of course," Keira answered promptly. "Mara, this is my husband, Cody. And that bundle of inexhaustible energy is our daughter, Alyssa."

Mara looked at the little girl, whose copper-colored curls and angelic face seemed to combine the best of her mother and father. She wasn't crying anymore, and when she saw the tall dark-haired man at Mara's side she gurgled excitedly and clapped her hands together. "Dace!" she babbled, holding out her arms to him. "Dace!"

Mara saw Special Agent McKinnon throw a startled glance at Keira, who told him with an understanding grin, "Oh yes, she's talking now. Her vocabulary consists of about ten words, including Mama, Dada, Gamma—that's my mother," she explained to Mara. "Dace—that's you, Trace," she told Special Agent McKinnon. "And bat—that's bath, which is her very favorite thing in the world."

Special Agent McKinnon walked over and took Alyssa from her father's arms. "Come to Trace, baby," he told her, and she went to him willingly, then smiled contentedly and snuggled against his shoulder.

Mara went very still, feeling as if the world was somehow out of kilter. She glanced from one man to the other, their open love for the little girl reflected

on the faces of both men. Special Agent McKinnon—
no, she thought. *I cannot think of him as anyone but
Trace. Not here. Not holding Alyssa. Here he is a man.
Just a warm, loving man, like Andre.* Trace was talking
to Alyssa in a soft voice, teasing her and tickling her
tummy as she gurgled with laughter again and again.

"He spoils her rotten," Keira told Mara in an aside,
but her voice held amused indulgence. "She turned one
a couple of months ago, and you should have seen what
he gave her for a birthday present."

Mara didn't say anything, but a variety of emotions
churned through her. Wistfulness and honest bewilderment ended up on top. "She is a beautiful child," she told
Keira. "But your husband—did he not wish for a son?"

Keira glanced at her sharply, a frown starting to
form. But then she seemed to see beneath the surface
of the question into Mara's wounded heart. "No," she
said gently. "In fact, before Alyssa was born Cody refused to let them tell us if we were having a boy or a
girl. He said, 'Not knowing now will make it all the
sweeter…later.'"

She smiled at Mara, woman to woman. "And when I
gave birth to Alyssa, Cody was right there in the delivery room—she was born into her father's eager, waiting
hands. That's the only time I've ever seen him cry, but
they were tears of joy, not disappointment."

"Oh." Mara couldn't think of anything else to say.
She needed time alone to consider this. To analyze it
in detail the way she would a complex equation. Because if what Keira was saying was the truth, if it was

right and natural for fathers to cherish their daughters the way they cherished their sons, then...

Trace watched Keira and the princess take Alyssa upstairs to change her diaper. Keira had demurred at first, but Mara had insisted. "Please," she had asked in her pretty, faintly accented voice. And when she'd added, "I have never been around babies, but I would like to learn," Keira had smiled and accepted the offer of help.

After they left, Cody pulled Trace into the kitchen. "Spill it," he demanded, almost before the swinging door closed behind them.

Trace hesitated. "Not sure what you mean."

"C'mon, McKinnon," Cody said. "Something happened."

"It's all in my report."

"Don't give me that. I know you. Maybe the State Department bought that report about what happened on Mount Evans, but I don't. And don't give me that poker-faced look, either," Cody added drily. "Keira's been giving me the high sign practically since the minute you and the princess walked in. So is there a problem? Something I need to know about the princess...and you?"

Trace's jaw tightened. "Not a thing," he told his boss, trying to convince himself at the same time. "There's not a single, solitary thing you need to know."

Cody's expression hardened as he became more the boss than the friend. "You'd tell me if there was, right?"

"Right." Trace almost believed it. Almost.

* * *

That night as Mara lay in her bed she relived her visit with the Walkers and their daughter, Alyssa. And Trace. He was Trace to her now. She would never think of him as Special Agent McKinnon again. Because when he was with his friends, when he held his goddaughter in his arms, he was so much like her brother, Andre, her heart ached.

She tucked a hand beneath her cheek. *But it is not as a brother you see him,* a little voice inside her head tormented her. *He is a man who makes you understand what it is to be a woman.*

Mara remembered the way Trace had held Alyssa, remembered the expression on his face as he gazed at the little girl. Remembered also the look on Alyssa's face as she smiled up at him and cuddled in his arms. She adored her "Dace" as she called him, and he could not have loved the little girl more if he had been her fath—

Father. But fathers didn't love their daughters. Did they? Or was her own father the aberration? She had known for years that her father wasn't just indifferent to her, he actually hated her, and she'd known why. And except for her brother, it was reinforced by the attitude of the majority of men—particularly those in power—all around her. But why had she accepted her father's hatred? Why had she accepted his assessment that she had no value, that she was a worthless addition to his family?

Andre had never felt that way about her. She was special in her brother's eyes. He had protected her, fought for her, loved her. And she had made him proud of her when she obtained her PhD, something she might never have achieved without his assistance.

She smiled softly to herself. She would never forget the mingled love and pride on Andre's face as she'd accepted her Oxford diploma and the trappings of her new status in a ceremony that dated back centuries. Then her smile faded. Why had that not been enough for her? Why had she looked in vain for her father beside her brother? Why had there been a gaping hole in her heart as she realized that even in this, her supreme moment, she had failed to win her father's love? *The fault was not in me,* she realized with a sense of shock. *The fault lay in my father. Andre was right all along. It was not anything I did or did not do.*

Her thoughts returned to today. *Keira said her husband cried tears of joy when Alyssa was born. That is how a father should feel. That is what my father should have felt at my birth. He did not. I could have brought him great joy, just as Alyssa has brought to her father. But he chose to turn away from me, chose to hate me instead. That was his loss. Not mine. All these years wasted seeking his approval. Seeking his love.*

It hurt terribly to realize now just how much of her life had been wasted pursuing something that could never be. It hurt even more to realize she'd allowed her father to control her emotionally, had allowed him to make her fear rejection so much she'd come to expect it and steel herself against it, afraid to risk her heart with any man other than Andre. Even though her father had been dead for more than two years he was still controlling her through that fear. But no longer.

Chapter 7

You have been a coward long enough, Mara told herself with sudden conviction. Not a physical coward—she'd never balked at taking a fence when she was riding, and had been thrown more than once. She'd always picked herself up, dusted herself off and climbed back into the saddle, determined not to let fear control her. But that same dauntless courage had failed her time and again when dealing with her father.

Not anymore, she vowed. *He is dead, and he will not control me anymore.*

Mara felt like a butterfly emerging from a chrysalis, struggling to free herself from the confining cocoon that had bound her for years to a false conclusion—that her father hadn't loved her because somehow she was unworthy of love. Yes, Andre loved her, but her brother had always been a perfect, God-like being in her eyes, so far above mere mortals that she had discounted his love for her as the exception. Andre's love was like God's love—immutable. It was her father's lack of love she'd always struggled to overcome. Her father's assessment of her as worthless she'd always fought to disprove.

If that wasn't true…if her father had been wrong…if she could be loved for who she was…not as a princess, but as a woman, loved by a man…

A picture of a man rose in her mind—a tall, handsome man with dark hair and bluer-than-blue eyes, with a smile that made her heart ache and her body tingle. A man who handled a gun and a baby with the same easy competence. A man who made her keenly aware of herself as a woman, with a woman's body, a woman's heart, a woman's emotional needs. A man who looked and was dangerous, but who also paradoxically made her feel safe.

Trace.

Mara turned over restlessly, the silk sheets rustling. *Trace.* He already filled her thoughts, day and night. He even filled her dreams. But until now she had accepted his dislike for her as just something that *was*, the way she'd accepted her father's hatred.

If she could pick one man to love her, she would pick Trace. Not because he was drop-dead gorgeous, although he was. Not because he had a body that rivaled Michelangelo's David, although he did. Not even because he made her feel safe, although that was true, too. She would pick him to love her because there was a deep well of love within him he kept hidden from most of the world, love such as the overwhelming love he showed Alyssa, a child not his own. If Trace loved a woman, there would be nothing held back. Nothing he would not do for her. Nothing he would not share.

Could she win his love? Was it possible? She'd never been able to win her father's love, but now she knew it was because he had no love to give—his love had died with her mother. But Trace wasn't like that. There was love in him to be won…by the right woman. And if she was worthy of being loved, why not try?

Determination grew in Mara, the same determination she'd once dedicated only to riding and mathematics. *Yes,* she told herself with a new confidence. Keira had understood—Mara had *earned* the title of Dr. Marianescu by dedication and hard, grueling work. She could *earn* Trace's love the same way.

Starting tomorrow she would map out a plan of campaign. Starting tomorrow she would put that campaign into action. But now…just for tonight…she would let herself dream of him. She would let herself imagine what it would be like to be loved by him in every way a man could love a woman.

She needed to visualize the goal in order to achieve it, just as she'd done when she'd learned to ride. Just as she'd done when she achieved her PhD. And she desperately wanted to achieve this new goal of earning Trace's love…because she was fast falling for him.

The next morning Mara woke early. She propped herself up against the pillows and set her mind to work planning her campaign. She briefly considered getting a complete makeover—turning herself into the glamorous woman her mother had been. She could probably do it. She knew she resembled her mother closely enough that it was possible to achieve that polished, beautiful veneer, but she discarded the idea almost immediately. If she changed herself in obvious ways, not only would she be uncomfortable with herself, she might draw unwelcome attention from others, especially the paparazzi. And besides, Trace would see it for the ploy it was. A man with a face and body like his probably had all kinds of women angling for his attention.

No, it had to be something subtle, something that would make him look at her in a new light, but in a way that wouldn't push him behind that impenetrable barrier. *Surprise is the essence of attack.* Where had she heard that before? She needed to take Trace by surprise, to make him see her as something other than the princess he was guarding.

Mara ran a finger along her bottom lip. What was that English expression? Come up on his blind side? That was all well and good so long as she didn't do it literally—she'd seen how fast he was at drawing his gun, and she didn't want him to shoot her.

She chuckled, wishing she could share the joke with someone. Wishing she could share the joke with *Trace*. But that was out of the question. Then an idea occurred to her. *Perfect*, she thought. Andre had taught her the basics years ago, but no one—no one meaning Trace—knew it. Trace would be the ideal teacher. And he wouldn't be able to say no. Not under the circumstances.

* * *

Trace stared at the princess in disbelief. "You want me to teach you how to what?"

"Shoot," she said composedly. "I wish to learn how to protect myself."

"That's not necessary," he told her bluntly. "You've got three federal bodyguards dancing attendance on you, not to mention the security team you brought from Zakhar."

"Yes, but I wish to be like Keira," she told him.

"You're planning on walking into a bullet?"

The princess was distracted for a minute. "Is that what she did?"

"Yeah," Trace growled. "Two years ago. No," he corrected himself, "more than that now. Took her almost a year before she recovered full use of her right arm."

She looked at Trace with curiosity. "But you were her partner. How is that possible?"

Trace felt himself flushing under his tan. He'd asked himself that same question at the time. And numerous times ever since. Never mind that Keira, Walker, Ryan Callahan and he had been operating as a team, and Callahan had been closest to her at the moment it had all gone down. Never mind that Keira had deliberately stepped in front of Callahan to take a bullet meant for him. She'd still been Trace's partner then, and he'd blamed himself for not keeping a closer eye on her.

But he couldn't tell any of that to the princess. That operation was still a closely guarded secret—and there were still trials pending. Not to mention the princess was a foreign national who did *not* have a need to know. "Long story" was all he said.

She considered him for a minute, and he was afraid she was going to ask more questions, but all she said was, "I do not wish to 'walk into a bullet' as you say, but I would still like to learn. If you do not think you can teach me…" she added so artlessly that Trace shot her a sharp, narrow-eyed look, suspecting she had something up her sleeve. But she met his look with one of such innocent inquiry he figured he had to be mistaken…until he got her on the shooting range.

Trace swore under his breath. This was *not* going as planned. He'd brought the princess to his favorite shooting range and made her sit through three hours of gun safety class before he ever let her step outside with a gun in her hand. Sweetly appealing in her jeans and rose-pink sweater that hugged her curves, with her hair piled with seeming carelessness atop her head in a way that let a few curls dance tantalizingly every time she moved her head, she'd listened intently to every word he said. She'd even asked questions that proved she was following what he was saying. He'd shown her different kinds of pistols, talked to her about ammunition, about rimfire versus center-fire and various calibers of bullets. He'd had her load and unload bullets into a clip, and had demonstrated how to load a clip into a pistol and chamber a round. He'd explained what a safety was, and the importance of utilizing it.

But the minute she stepped onto the range with a Smith & Wesson 22-caliber pistol it was as if he'd wasted his breath. *No one can be that incompetent with a gun,* he told himself. Either she hadn't really been paying attention, or he was a lousy teacher.

"No, Princess, you're holding it all wrong," he said with a touch of exasperation. "And *never* point a gun at a man unless you intend to shoot him," he added when she swung around in his direction. "Even if the safety's on." He grabbed her gun hand and forced it downrange.

She removed her headphones, letting them hang around her neck, and stared at him. "Would you have shot him?"

Trace removed his own headphones. "Shot who?"

"The man at the lake. The one who took my photograph," she explained. "You just said I should never point a gun at a man unless I intend to shoot him." Her face was solemn. "So would you have shot him?"

He thought about it for a moment, wondering exactly what she was asking. And why. "If that had been a gun in his hand and not a camera—yes. He would have been dead before he got off a shot. Dead before he hit the ground."

"But it *was* a camera," she said stubbornly. "So would you have shot him?"

He shook his head. "But I had to make him think I would. I had to scare the hell out of him so he'd give me the camera."

"Why?"

"Because I—" He stopped, not wanting to tell her the truth, but not wanting to lie to her either. He remembered her soft cry of dismay when the shutter had clicked, and his protective instincts had kicked in. *Noth-*

ing was going to be allowed to hurt her in any way when he was around to prevent it. No matter what he had to do.

She was still looking up at him, a question in her eyes. "Because it's my job to protect you," Trace said finally. And while it was the truth, it was a far cry from the whole truth.

She didn't say anything, just nodded, as if his answer matched her expectations. She turned back to the gun range and slipped her headphones back on. "Can you not help me?" she asked again in a sweetly helpless way.

Trace sighed and positioned himself behind her for the third time, fitting his right hand around hers. "It's not that difficult, Princess," he told her with as much patience as he could muster. He brought her arm up with his and aimed at the target. "You just find your point of aim and shoot."

This close to her the smell of her delicate perfume was mesmerizing, not to mention what the feel of the back of her body cuddled up against the front of him was doing to his breathing. He quickly disengaged and stepped backwards, slipping his headphones back on. "Now you try it," he told her with a voice that wasn't quite steady. "No, take the safety off first."

She complied. This time she faced the target, aimed, and for the first time, fired. She didn't hit the target, but she didn't flinch—and that's when the suspicion hit him. Despite the noise-canceling headphones she wore, she should have flinched at the sound and kick of the pistol she'd just fired for the first time—most newbies did. Which meant she probably wasn't a newbie with a gun. So why was she pretending she was? Why had she dragged him out here? Why had she patiently sat through gun safety class? And why had she asked him to demonstrate by positioning her arm time and again?

Then he figured it out, and he wasn't sure if he should swear or feel complimented. While he was still trying to decide, another question came to him. Should he tell her he knew the truth, or should he let her go on pretending, wasting both their time? She turned to him just then, looking for direction. "Again," he told her automatically. "Keep trying until you empty the clip."

Slowly she fired one shot after another, and by the time the clip was empty Trace realized he couldn't tell her he knew. That expression he'd seen the first day he'd met her came back to him, the same expression he'd seen on Labor Day after he tried to set her at a distance. The patient expectation and acceptance of rejection he'd been shocked and then angry to see told him there was something going on with her he needed to handle with kid gloves.

Friday night Liam had told him he was pretty hard on the princess, and he'd been right. Maybe she was just trying to overcome what she saw as his dislike of her by getting him to see her in a different light. Or maybe she just wanted to practice her feminine wiles on someone she saw as safe. Whatever the reason, if he told her he'd seen through her little charade she'd be embarrassed. And worse, humiliated, just as she'd been on Mount Evans. *She doesn't deserve that,* he thought protectively.

She turned to him again, her brows raised in a question. "I emptied the clip."

Silently he reached into his pocket, pulled out the spare clip, and handed it to her. "See if you can change the clip," he said. "Then try again. Keep trying until you hit the target at least once."

The next evening Trace was watching *Monday Night Football* in the guest house living room with half his attention and doing the crossword puzzle with the rest when the phone rang. He muted the sound of the football game and reached for it. "McKinnon."

"It's Alec. I'm out here in the stables with the princess, and—"

"What the hell is she doing riding without me?"

"She's not," Alec assured him. "She just came out to visit her horses like she does most evenings after dinner, but there's something wrong with Suleiman and I don't—"

"Where's her groom?" Trace asked sharply, then answered his own question. "It's Monday so he's off, damn it. Call the vet and get him out here," Trace told him. "The number's posted beside the phone. Do you see it?"

"Yeah."

"Keep the princess calm, if you can. I'll be right there." Trace headed for the stables in a hurry. *She loves that horse,* he thought, perturbed. *If anything happens to him...*

When Trace arrived Alec was just hanging up the phone. "Vet's on his way," he said.

Trace heard him on one level and nodded, but he only had eyes for the princess. She was in Suleiman's stall, trying to get him up. Suleiman was thrashing around on the ground, in obvious pain, and she was tugging on his mane, calling to him urgently in Zakharan, but Suleiman either wouldn't—or couldn't—rise.

When Trace entered the stall she turned a face of desperate pleading toward him. Two tears had trickled down her cheeks, leaving trails that glistened, but she ignored them. She said one word in Zakharan, then shook her head as if angry at herself, and switched to English. "Colic."

Trace had understood her the first time. "Let me get in there, Princess." But his hands were already on her arms, moving her firmly out of the way. To Alec he said, "Got to get him up—colic can be a killer if the horse rolls around on the ground and gets his intestines all twisted up." He grabbed a halter from where it hung near the stall and quickly strapped it to the horse's head despite the way Suleiman tossed his head in an attempt to resist, forcing the bit between the horse's teeth and into place. Then he tugged hard, bracing himself against one wall for extra leverage, his muscles distended.

"Call to him, Princess," he ordered.

"Suleiman! Up, boy, up, up!" she repeated, in a mixture of English and Zakharan.

With a shrill neighing sound, the horse staggered to his feet. Trace stroked the horse's neck soothingly. "Good boy," he praised in a calm tone, although he was feeling anything but calm. Just because Suleiman was standing didn't mean he was out of danger. "Get back, Princess," he told her curtly when she started forward. "Let's make sure he doesn't become violent."

"Not with me," she assured him, careless of her

safety, her eyes anxious for her horse. "Suleiman would never—"

"Not normally, no. But with colic you can't be sure. If the pain gets too bad he could lash out, and I don't want you too close to him." He started leading the horse out of the stables. "I'll walk him until the vet arrives."

It was nearly midnight before Trace finally fell into bed. It hadn't taken long for the veterinarian to confirm the princess's and Trace's diagnosis when he arrived, and apply the proper treatment. Trace had been tremendously relieved it hadn't been anything worse than impaction colic that didn't require surgery. But it had been bad enough...and messy. Not just for the vet. He'd been surprised at the princess's active participation, but then realized he shouldn't have been—nothing was too much for her where the horse she loved was concerned.

Afterward, Trace had told Alec to take her back to the house so she could clean herself up, and he'd returned to the guest house himself for a shower and change of clothes. But he'd been quick about it because he'd had a hunch the princess would be back, and he'd been right. The princess had stayed with the vet while he gave Suleiman intravenous fluids merely as a precaution, then stayed, even after the vet left.

Trace stayed with her, Alec hovering in the background until Trace told him he might as well turn in. "No sense both of us hanging around," he told the other man. "And you're on duty tomorrow, so you'd better get some sleep."

Trace glanced at the princess from time to time after

Alec left, but didn't say anything. He wanted to tell her there wasn't anything more for her to do, so she might as well go to bed, too. But he knew that wouldn't happen, not until she dropped from fatigue. At one point when he looked at her she caught his gaze and held it. There was gratitude in her lovely eyes, and something more. Admiration. The kind of expression that made a man feel ten feet tall and invincible.

"Thank you," she said softly.

"No big deal," he replied. "You already knew what the problem was, and the vet got here fast. We were lucky it wasn't anything more serious."

Yes," she agreed. "But I could not get Suleiman up. It could have been so much worse if you had not—" She caught her breath and her eyes darkened.

He shrugged. "I just happened to know what to do, that's all."

Her eyes betrayed her curiosity. "Yes, but how did you know? You are not a veterinarian. Were you raised with horses? I have wondered…"

Although Trace laughed, he felt a touch of bitterness. "No, Princess," he said. "I was raised by my grandparents, and they couldn't have cared less about horses… or me." He caught himself up quickly, realizing he'd revealed something he would rather not have revealed.

She didn't say anything at first, just turned to watch Suleiman for a minute. Without looking at Trace she said, "But you are a natural horseman. There is no question of that. So how, if you were not raised with horses…?"

"I was cowboy crazy when I was a kid," he said with

a half-smile of remembrance for the boy he'd been. "I delivered newspapers, mowed lawns in the summer and shoveled snow in the winter to earn money to take riding lessons when I was twelve."

This time when she looked at him her admiration was for the single-minded determination of the boy he'd been, not just the man he was. "I understand that kind of dedication," she said, her green eyes shining, and Trace remembered this woman had obtained her doctorate at the age of twenty-five. Since most math PhDs took five to six years to complete in addition to a four year undergraduate degree, that meant she had to have started very young, putting aside everything else in her drive to achieve her goal.

"When I was fourteen," he continued, "I was 'hired' by the stable where I took lessons, and I worked there for the next four years. At first they just paid me with more lessons and free rides, but when I was older they paid me in cash, too. I cleaned out stalls, groomed horses, fed and watered them, led trail rides, and even gave lessons myself toward the end." He smiled at her. "So yeah, I've seen colicky horses before, not to mention a few other ailments. Haven't lost one yet, though some of it was just plain luck."

"But you are not a cowboy now. Why did you stop working there?"

"I joined the Corps at eighteen. The US Marine Corps," he clarified. "I wanted to see the world." He chuckled. "That used to be the recruitment line for the US Navy—'Join the Navy and see the world.' But I didn't want to be a sailor. I wanted the toughest bunch of SOBs this country had to offer, and I got it." Then he realized who he was talking to. "Sorry," he apologized. "Sometimes my language is a little rough around the edges. Blame it on the cowboy, not the marine."

Her green eyes twinkled mischievously. "It is nothing," she assured him. "I have heard worse." She laughed under her breath and said something in Zakharan, the earthy curse he'd thrown at Alec and Liam the first day.

Trace was hard put not to display his shock, but he managed it. *How the hell does a princess know that?* "Sounds like a curse," he said, wondering if she'd tell him.

She laughed again, this time with delight. "It is, but I dare not translate it for you." Then her eyes turned wistful. "It is Andre's favorite curse. Not in public of course. He is very circumspect in public, very much the king. But I have heard him use it…on occasion." Her face retained its wistful expression, but an amused, remembering smile touched the corners of her lips.

"You miss him a lot, don't you?" The question popped out before he realized he was going to ask it.

"More than anything in the world," she said simply. She blinked several times, then looked at Trace, and there were tears in her eyes. "He is…special. And so precious to me. I cannot explain. He is my king, yes. But he is my brother, first and last. He would give his life for me, and more no man can give. If not for him…" She wiped the tears from her eyes unashamedly. And what she said next took his breath away. "You remind me of him. So very much."

"Me?" he asked ungrammatically, not believing he'd heard correctly.

"Yes. I cannot explain, not with words. It is something in here," she said, raising a hand and pressing it to her heart. "I know I am safe with you. Alec and Liam—they guard me well. Do not think otherwise. But they do not remind me of Andre." She drew a deep breath, sighed and said softly, "I just wish you did not dislike me."

Trace didn't know what to say. He didn't dare tell her the truth, that he liked her far too much for comfort. Far too much for safety. Hers...and his. "I don't—" he began, but she cut him off.

"When I saw you with Alyssa, I saw the man you really are. Gentle. Loving. So very protective. And she is not even your own daughter."

"Any man would feel that way about a child," he said, not quite understanding what she was getting at. "Especially a sweet little girl like Alyssa."

She went very still, as she had once before, and at first her face was like a blank, emotionless slate. This time, however, he saw a struggle in her eyes instead of that passive acceptance, and he knew he was on the verge of some cataclysmic revelation. But then she said no, ducked her head and turned away. "It is late. Thank you again for saving Suleiman."

She walked out of the stables, her head held high. But there was something about the gallant figure she made as she walked away that tore at his heart. Something about the way she'd said that one word, *No*. Something that made him feel like crying.

He wanted to call her back, to ask her what in God's name she meant by it. But he was afraid. Afraid that if he knew the answer, his defenses against her would be irrevocably breached.

Chapter 8

September segued into October. The aspen groves displayed the bright golden color for which they were justly famous, drawing flocks of tourists, and though the sun still shone the average temperature dropped by ten degrees. Snow fell in the mountains west of Boulder, and jackets became the norm.

Trace sat in the guest house living room on the first Sunday night in October, toasting his feet in front of the fire in the fireplace. The one beer he allowed himself when he wasn't on duty was sitting half forgotten on the end table beside him as he reviewed the meticulously prepared case reports from the Jones brothers covering the past week. Nada. Zip. Zilch. There was nothing in their reports worth funneling upward to the State Department. And his own reports weren't any more informative. Still, the reports would be filed as they'd dutifully been filed every week since the assignment began. The State Department's bureaucracy demanded it.

Not for the first time Trace thanked his lucky stars the agency he really worked for was free of that monotonous bureaucracy and paperwork. If there was nothing to report, there was nothing to report, and you didn't have to go into excruciating detail while saying it. That wasn't to say his fellow agents didn't prepare periodic case reports. Sometimes the absence of something was just as important to the overall picture as its presence, so case reports were still required. But the agency trusted its agents to make the judgment call on what and when. The agency had better things to do than drown in needless paperwork.

Trace tossed the last report aside with a little sound of frustration, picked up his beer and drained it in one long swallow. For a minute he longed for his real job with the agency, missing the never-ending challenge, the excitement of pitting his wits against terrorists and criminals. Even without Keira as his partner he missed it. Then he cradled the empty bottle in his hands as he stared into the dancing flames, his thoughts turning inevitably to the princess who was never far from his thoughts, waking or sleeping.

His obsession with her had been bad enough before she'd begun what he called her campaign to deliberately attract him. In any other woman he'd have thought it laughable, but that wasn't the emotion her attempts to gain his attention aroused in him. Far from it. Each attempt merely made him feel more protective of her…and at the same time drawn deeper under her spell. It was becoming increasingly difficult to maintain his distance.

A little niggling voice inside him said he should ask to be taken off the team guarding her. And he'd do it, too, if he felt his objectivity had been compromised. But he was handling it like the professional he was. Wasn't he? And he'd hate like hell having to tell anyone—even Walker—why he wanted off.

No, he'd see the assignment through to the bitter end. He'd never called it quits on an assignment before, and he wasn't about to start now. No matter the cost to himself.

Mara had been teaching for six weeks when she woke to a Monday morning world of swirling white. She stood at her bedroom window, marveling at how the landscape had been transformed overnight. She wanted to bundle up, go outside and frolic in the snow as she had done when she was a little girl. She longed to be young enough to catch snowflakes on her tongue, to be pulled on a sled by a laughing Andre, to make angels in the snow.

A tap at her bedroom door startled her out of reverie. "Come," she answered automatically in Zakharan, refusing to take her eyes from the winter wonderland outside, and the happy memories it invoked.

Mara's personal assistant entered and spoke a few soft words in Zakharan, dragging Mara back into the here and now. Her heart skipped a beat as she retied the belt of her robe and told her assistant, "Bring him." But before she was prepared Trace walked into her bedroom.

Trace stopped short on the threshold, transfixed by the sight of the princess standing by the window from which she'd drawn the drapes, with her hair hanging around her shoulders in glorious sleep-tousled waves. He'd only seen her once in person with her hair down like this, and she'd quickly bundled it back up, but the photo of her with Suleiman and her hair loose was one of his most cherished possessions.

His eyes slid from her hair downward, taking in the soft fleece of the pale green, floor-length robe that hugged her curves like a lover. Like he wanted to do. A wave of heat slammed through him, and it was all he could do to remember why he was there. "Good morning, Princess," he said finally. "We have a slight problem."

"Yes?" Her voice was early morning husky, and sent tendrils of desire streaming everywhere through his body.

Trace ignored the feeling, ignored the unmade bed that gave him forbidden ideas and pointed to the snow swirling outside the window. "How much experience do you have driving in snow?"

"Oh," she said blankly. "I did not think of that." She turned away to stare wistfully out the window. "I was just remembering when I was a little girl."

When she said the words Trace saw a vision of her as she must have been when she was young and carefree, before her world was bounded by protocol and paparazzi, and tenderness was added to his desire. But that tenderness was even more dangerous than the desire he was barely able to control.

"That's why you have me," he said. And when she

threw him a puzzled glance he clarified, "To think of these things. So how much experience do you have?" As soon as the words left his mouth he realized the unintended double entendre, and hoped the princess wouldn't realize what his question could be referring to.

Her startled eyes met his, and he could see by her sudden intake of breath that she hadn't missed a thing. She stared at him across the room, and Trace knew nothing had changed since the day she'd touched his lips on Mount Evans. She was as vibrantly aware of him as a man as he was of her as a woman. Maybe even more so. "None," she admitted finally, her voice low and trembling.

For just a second Trace wondered which question she was answering. "Then…" He cleared his throat. "Then it's probably best if your chauffeur drives us to and from school today." He held up his hand before she could dispute him. "Trust me on this, Princess."

"I was not going to object…I am not stupid," she said with some heat, lifting her chin in the obstinate way she had the first day. "I was merely going to say I do not mind if he drives the SUV." She stared at him for several seconds as varied emotions flitted across her face, then added, "I would not risk my life…or yours. Not until I have more experience." She took a deep breath, as if gathering her courage, and walked slowly toward Trace until she was standing right in front of him. "Will you teach me?"

Desire roared back in full force, and he longed with all his heart to be the one to teach her. Not just how to drive in snow, but how to please a man and be pleased in return. To teach her what her body was capable of, to awaken her desire to the point where she knew what hunger was, the way he hungered for her. He longed to sink his body deep into hers; to carry her with him on rising waves of passion until the whole world disappeared, leaving only the two of them…and their need for each other.

He fought the hunger biting through him, curling his hands into fists to keep from reaching for her. *Driving*, he reminded himself. *She's talking about driving.* But his body didn't want to listen. "Sure, Princess," he told her, letting the slight mocking tone creep into his voice, his only defense against her. "I'll teach you…anything you want to learn." He turned and walked out of the room, but not before he saw the hurt in her eyes.

Two days on, four days off. Trace had had four days to try to build his defenses against the princess on something solid, something with more strength to it than deliberately hurting her, again and again. The subtle mocking inflection to the word *princess* was banished now, never to return. He'd reached the end of the line where that pitiful defense was concerned. Each time he hurt her he hurt himself now, and he couldn't do it anymore. She didn't deserve it…and he couldn't bear it. Something had changed in their relationship—she *mattered* to him. It was a hell of a thing to have to admit, but he couldn't deceive himself anymore.

Maybe it was that day at the shooting range when he'd realized she was deliberately creating excuses to have him touch her, hold her. Or maybe it was the way she'd looked at his goddaughter the day before that—

wistful, bewildered, yearning. He didn't understand the emotions that had flitted across her face, but he'd known she was vulnerable. Damned vulnerable. Maybe it was the way she'd said he reminded her of her beloved brother, Andre, the night Suleiman had colic. That shock had left him reeling. It was almost as much of a shock as hearing that earthy, Zakharan curse on her lips accompanied by a mischievous expression.

Or maybe it was everything. Everything about her. Every day spent in her company. Every minute spent listening to her musical voice, so full of enthusiasm as she taught. Every sidelong glance she cast at him when she thought he wasn't watching. Every naive attempt to draw his attention. Every aching, erotic dream about her. Every time he saw her lovely, green eyes—smiling, solemn, wistful, hurt. Even blank, the way he'd seen her eyes a few times when that curtain had come down over her emotions. Her eyes owned him.

He didn't want to like her...but he did. He didn't want to want her...but he did. He didn't want to need her...but he was afraid it was already too late. *You're in over your head, McKinnon,* he warned himself sternly. *You're drowning.*

But he didn't care. Not anymore, and it was as if a weight had been lifted with that determination. He wasn't going to fight what he felt for her. He wasn't going to act on it, of course—she was as much off limits to him now as she'd always been—but what was the harm in enjoying her company? A little light flirtation, a little friendly conversation. And maybe she'd answer some of those questions about her past that had been slowly driving him crazy.

Tomorrow was Sunday, and he'd be back on duty. He was going to do what she'd asked him to do last Monday morning—teach her how to drive in the snow. As the week had progressed the temperature had warmed somewhat. Most of the snow here in Boulder had melted, and even the side roads were clear. But he'd let her drive up into the mountains a little way, just as far as his cabin outside Keystone. I-70 would be dry as a bone, as would the other highways, but they never plowed the long dirt road that led nowhere except to his cabin, and there should still be snow there.

That road would be ideal for her to practice on since there would be no other traffic; if she skidded, she couldn't hit much of anything. Then they could take a break in his cabin before starting for home. He'd always wondered what she'd think of it, and now he'd find out. The water was turned off, but he could turn it back on for the time they'd be there, then shut it off again without too much trouble.

I can handle this, he assured himself. *Look but don't touch.* It wouldn't be the first time. He'd had lots of experience doing just that in Afghanistan. The same for when he'd been married. His ex-wife had never believed him, but he'd been completely faithful to her in the years they'd been married. Hell yes, he'd looked at other women. He was a man and had a man's appreciation for women in all their interesting variations. And with his looks women had always thrown out lures. But his vows had meant something to him, and he'd never succumbed to the many temptations that had crossed his path. Not once.

Janet just hadn't believed him. And her constant suspicions, her lack of faith in him had eroded whatever love he'd once felt for her, until…at the very end, when she'd demanded he give up his new partner, Keira Jones, accusing him of caring more for his partner than he did for his wife, he'd realized she was right. Not that he was having an affair with Keira. He just no longer cared for Janet, couldn't bear her lack of trust a minute longer. And that had been that.

A sudden memory surfaced—the princess taking his hand at Summit Lake, an expression of utter trust in her lovely green eyes. She should have been terrified, or at the very least she should have been on guard against him after his violent confrontation with the man who'd taken her picture. But she'd trusted him implicitly, had known somehow that the violent side of him would never be turned against her. Had known, too, that he would protect her with his life…and not just because he was her bodyguard.

That memory triggered a new line of thought. *Maybe that's when you first realized she mattered to you,* he told himself with a flash of insight. Trust was such a rare and precious commodity. Other than his former partner, what other woman in his entire life had ever trusted him? Really trusted him?

The princess did. Even though he'd pushed her away emotionally, time and again, even though he'd resorted far too often to that mocking tone of voice to drive her away, she trusted him. And she didn't hide it from him. Her hand had lain trustingly in his all the way back from Summit Lake. And her eyes…her eyes had spoken volumes.

The sun was shining brightly Sunday morning, the temperature hovering in the high thirties, and the air was calm and still when Mara walked out the front door to where Trace was waiting for her with the SUV. She was bundled up against the cold he had warned her they could experience at the higher elevation of Keystone no matter what the temperature was in Boulder, and her face was glowing with the anticipation of a child. When he'd casually mentioned his plans at dinner last night she'd been excited, all the more so since he indicated they wouldn't need her chauffeur to accompany them. A chance to spend time alone with Trace was as exhilarating as it was unexpected.

He was dressed in jeans and a navy blue wool sweater with a Norwegian reindeer pattern across his broad chest. Boots and leather gloves, of course, and an unzipped down vest, also in navy blue, completed his ensemble. He was leaning casually against the SUV, and looked wonderfully masculine to Mara's eyes.

"Good morning," she told him with an uninhibited smile. "Are you sure you do not mind doing this?" One corner of his mouth quirked up in the little smile she was coming to know meant she'd somehow amused him, and she rushed to add, "Yes, I know you would not have offered if you did not mean it, but…"

"I see you took my advice and dressed warmly" was all he said, still with that private grin.

Mara stopped. "Too much?" she asked anxiously.

She looked at her fur-lined boots into which her jeans were tucked, then at her heavy down parka in a shade of green that matched her eyes, and finally at her well-insulated mittens.

He took two steps toward her, and his smile was kind, not mocking. "Let's just say you look more prepared for a hike through snowbound mountains than a drive in a heated SUV. You might want to swap those mittens for gloves that will let you control the steering wheel better. But," he added gently, as if he'd noted the sudden dismay in her eyes, "bring the mittens, too. If we break down and have to walk for help, you'll be ready. And that's a good thing—better safe than sorry, especially in the Rockies."

He turned slightly and hooked a thumb over his shoulder, indicating the back of the SUV. "I've got an emergency kit in there—thermal blankets, flares, water and rations. Not to mention a small snow shovel."

Mara didn't say anything, just nodded and went back into the house. When she returned she'd matched his outfit as nearly as she could—sweater, down vest and leather gloves—but she carried her down parka and mittens. Trace took them from her without a word and stowed them in the back, then held the driver's door open for her. With that same kind voice he said, "Your chariot awaits, Princess."

Mara drove along the clear streets of Boulder and picked up Highway 93, taking that south until she reached I-70 westbound. Trace kept up an innocuous conversation the entire time, conversation that soothed any flutter of nerves that cropped up. Not only that, he didn't make any comments about the fact that she adamantly stayed in the right lane and drove below the posted speeds. Instead he gave her general driving tips and quizzed her about dealing with a variety of road issues.

"You're doing fine, Princess," he assured her when she cast him an anxious look as another car passed them.

"Yes, but there is no snow," she said.

"Not yet" was all he said. "Wait until we get off the interstate."

They reached Silverthorne after nearly two hours of driving, and stopped at a gas station to top off the tank and to use the facilities. Mara knew from things Alec and Liam had told her that it didn't normally take two hours to drive from Boulder to Silverthorne—less than ninety minutes was the norm—but Trace hadn't complained at her cautiousness. The two hours of steady driving had given her an increased confidence in her driving abilities, something she didn't get just driving the few miles to and from the university. And she was actually enjoying her driving lesson.

The elevation had risen with every mile they'd driven west on I-70, and the temperature was definitely colder. The wind was blowing, too, and Mara was glad to get back into the warmth of the SUV.

"Tired?" Trace asked her as she buckled up her seatbelt.

"No," she told him honestly.

"We leave I-70 here and take US-6 toward Keystone,

but we don't actually go all the way—the turnoff to my cabin comes before we get to Keystone Lake. Maybe six miles. Are you sure you're up to it?"

Mara gave him a look of determination. "I do not like half measures," she reminded him.

"So you said before," he acknowledged. "Then let's do it."

An hour and a half later Mara finally admitted to herself she'd had enough. She'd driven to and from Trace's cabin more than a dozen times along a winding, snow encrusted road, stopping, starting, stopping again, deliberately going too fast on a turn to provoke a skid so she could learn how to handle one. She'd learned how antilock brakes actually work *with* a driver's panicked slam-on-the-brakes response to a skid. She'd learned how to steer *into* a skid and not against it.

And she'd learned something else, knowledge she cherished. Trace had infinite patience—when he wanted to. Not once had he lost his temper or raised his voice, not once had he been anything but a patient and kind teacher, even when she'd skidded so far off the road he had to shovel the tires free and rock the SUV back and forth to gain the traction to get them back onto the road.

But though she admitted to herself she was ready to stop, she wasn't ready to admit it to him. So she was surprised when he stopped her from turning around when they reached his cabin once more. "Let's call it a day," he told her. "Don't forget we still have to drive back this afternoon. And I don't know about you, but I'm ready for lunch."

Mara shifted into Park and turned off the engine, grateful for the respite. She hadn't realized just how tense she'd been until she removed her hands from the steering wheel and found she was trembling. "How did I do?"

Trace took the keys from the ignition and pocketed them. "I've never had a better student," he told her with a twinkle in his blue eyes.

Mara gave him a steady look. "How many people have you taught to drive?" she asked, fairly sure she already knew the answer. "And how many people have you taught to drive in the snow?"

A grin slashed across his face. "Well, there you have me. You're my one and only." She chuckled, which allowed much of her tension to bleed out, but then her face turned serious when he added, "Might be a good idea to teach you some defensive driving tactics, too."

"What is that?"

"Ways to shake someone following you. Ways to evade capture, to keep yourself from being boxed in by bad guys out to take you down. Stuff like that."

Mara's heart suddenly jumped. But she wasn't going to let fear control her. "Is that necessary? I did not think…has someone been following me? Nobody said—"

He cut her off. "No. No one's tailing you that we know of. And as far as we know you're not in any more danger now than you were the day you arrived. But it wouldn't hurt to learn what to do, just in case."

She took a deep breath and let it out slowly as the sudden fear drained away. "You are right, of course. It never hurts to be prepared. And you could teach me, I am sure. Look how you taught me to drive in the snow. You are a good teacher," she confided. "Even Andre could not have done better."

An expression she couldn't read crossed his face. "Thanks," he said. "That's praise of the highest order." They stared at each other for several seconds, and Mara wished she knew what he was thinking. Wished she had the courage to ask. When she finally looked away he said, "Come on, you can rest inside for a little while before we start back."

They ate lunch in the cabin's tiny kitchen talking about nothing in particular. Trace had showed her the entire cabin in two minutes, then had left her to go outside and turn the water on. After lunch he made them each a cup of hot chocolate, which they took into the main room. Mara shivered as she sipped the hot brew, letting it warm her insides.

"Cold?" he asked her.

She put her cup down and rubbed her hands on her arms. "A little. But I can put my vest back on."

"I could build a fire…unless you want to head back right away."

"No, I…I would like to stay." She smiled hesitantly at him. "But it is your cabin. I do not want to put you to any trouble."

"No trouble," he assured her.

The wood was already laid in the grate, and once Trace kindled the fire it didn't take long for the blazing logs to begin warming the small room. Mara curled up on the lambskin rug in front of the fireplace, her knees tucked beneath her. She stared into the fire, smiling, enjoying the crackling sounds, the dancing flames, the way the heat came and went in waves. Then a memory surfaced, and her smile faded.

"Penny for them."

Mara came back to herself with a start, realizing she wasn't with her father in the palace in Drago; she was in Trace's cabin in Keystone…with Trace. "Excuse me?" she asked, not sure she'd heard him properly.

"I offered you a penny for your thoughts," Trace said. "It's an expression. It just means I was wondering what you were thinking." He came over to the fireplace, picked up the tongs and shifted a log into a better position, then stood the tongs back up in the holder. He hesitated, as if of two minds about continuing, then explained, "You looked…sad all of a sudden."

Mara turned back to the flames. "I was remembering."

"It didn't look like a happy memory."

"No."

There was a long silence before Trace sat himself cross-legged next to her in front of the fire and said huskily, "You seem to have a lot of those." Mara raised her eyebrows in a silent question, and he added, "Unhappy memories."

There was a little catch in her voice when she asked, "Why do you say that?"

"Little hints you throw out without realizing it," he said simply. "Except for when you talk about your brother, I get the impression you didn't have a very happy childhood."

"You misunderstand," she said quickly.

"I don't think so. I can spot the signs a mile away."

Mara was surprised and perturbed. She hadn't realized she'd betrayed so much of her unhappy past to the man she loved. "It…it is complicated" was all she said. A long silence followed, the only sound the crackling of the fire. Then a log broke with a hissing sound, sending sparks flying, and Mara asked quietly, "Would you tell me something?"

Chapter 9

Trace was instantly on the alert. "If I can," he temporized.

"Why were you raised by your grandparents? What happened to your parents?"

Whatever Trace thought she might ask him, he'd never imagined this, and he laughed humorlessly. "Good question. If I ever run across them, I'll be sure to ask."

"I do not understand."

"Hell, Princess, I didn't know my father," he said roughly. "I don't even know if my mother knew who he was, and she didn't hang around long enough to tell me one way or the other."

"I would give anything not to have known mine." The words were torn from her throat, a harsh sound that ripped through his emotions, shattering what he thought he knew about her. They stared at each other for a minute as the realization of what she'd admitted was reflected in her face, and Trace tried to comprehend the enormity of what she was saying.

"My father was..." She hesitated. "In my country only men can sit on the throne. My father already had an heir—my brother, Andre. My mother's doctor had warned her against a second pregnancy, but my father wanted another son, just in case. What he got instead was me."

She smiled, a tight little smile that didn't reach her eyes. "And my mother, whom my father loved until the day she died, died giving birth to me. He hated me for that, and for not being the son he expected. The son he sacrificed my mother for—needlessly. That is why he named me Mara Theodora." In her voice were all the things she would not say, the devastating pain of growing up knowing herself unwanted. Unloved. A pain Trace understood all too well. "Mara Theodora," she repeated, barely above a whisper. *"Bitter divine gift.* God's joke on my father. My father's revenge on God... and on me."

Trace's throat ached. "I'm sorry, Princess," he said gently as her words sank in. And he saw much more than those few words revealed. "I didn't understand before."

"Do not feel sorry for me," she said swiftly. "I had my brother. He tried to explain to me about my father. He even tried to make it up to me...when he was around. But he was so much older—five years is a large gap in children's ages. Also, my father was grooming him to ascend the throne someday, and Andre was often away for long periods of time. And since there was no way I—or even any of my children—could ever take the throne, I was useless to my father. But I had my studies and my horses, and a few friends. They sufficed."

He needed to ask. "How old were you when you realized..."

Her eyes stared into the distance. "Five, I think," she said softly. "Yes, that was when I knew for sure. But part of me knew long before, I just did not understand." Her eyes squeezed shut for a moment and she shook her head, as if she were shaking off memories too painful to bear. When her lovely green eyes opened again, they were clear and calm, accepting of a past that could not be changed.

"I was five, too," Trace confessed in a low tone, wanting to share with her something of his own bitter past in exchange for her confidences. "That's when I learned I was a shameful burden to the grandparents my mother had dumped me on."

Her hand touched his briefly in comfort. "But you did not have an older brother, did you?"

He shook his head. "I was a lonely only. Just as well, since my grandparents didn't even want to be stuck with me, much less another bastard to care for."

"Do *not* use that word," she said fiercely, eyes flashing, surprising him. "There is no such thing as a bastard child. Only bastard parents. If there is a sin, it is the sin of the parents. Children are innocent. They cannot help being born—they have no choice in the matter."

Trace turned his hand so that it was clasping hers.

Startled, she tried to draw her hand away, but he held tight. Slowly he raised her hand to his lips, and pressed a kiss into the palm. "Thanks, Princess." His voice was husky, the words a caress. Her hand was on the small side for a woman as tall as she was, and delicate. But his lips felt the calluses on her palm, and he knew where the calluses came from—she was no pampered princess, as he'd known in a corner of his heart almost from the beginning. It had just taken him a while to accept it.

Her breath caught when his lips traveled from her palm to her wrist, and he could feel her pulse quicken under his caress. His pulse quickened, too, and an urgent desire swept through him to pull her into his arms, to taste those soft, vulnerable, slightly parted lips. But he didn't. Slowly, reluctantly, he let her hand go.

"I…I have made a life for myself," she said raggedly, and he knew she was as affected by him as he was by her. "It is not the one most people think. But I do not care about that." Her face was solemn and her green eyes darkened. "I learned early to downplay my resemblance to my mother, especially as I grew older. It only made my father resent me all the more—salt in his wounds, I think is what you say here." A haunted expression crept into her eyes, but after a minute she shook it off and continued.

"And Andre looks out for me, truly he does. Things are not so good in my country right now. The monarchy is under attack from certain factions because of the changes Andre is trying to implement. It was Andre's idea I come here for a year, to get away from the danger. He knows I am a target no matter where I go in Zakhar, because there are people within my country who would use me for their own purposes. The military remains loyal to him for the most part, but even there…"

Her lips tightened. "There is always a chance that this man is not loyal, or that man carries a secret agenda. Even within my own household, within my own body-guards, who can say for sure?" Her eyes met his. "There have been two attempts to assassinate Andre since he ascended the throne. The second attempt I was stand-ing right next to my brother when the would-be assas-sin drew a gun and aimed it. He was killed by Andre's bodyguards before he could open fire, but still…"

Trace nodded at the confirmation of what he'd won-dered about the first night he'd deliberately set off the estate's alarm—the princess had faced danger before. And while she wasn't sanguine about it, it didn't para-lyze her with fear either.

"That is why Andre insisted your government pro-vide protection for me while I am here," she continued. "That fear for me is always there. Not for himself—he is a man who will always be stronger than anyone who goes against him, and he would never be afraid for himself. But he is vulnerable where I am concerned."

She drew a sharp breath. "I do not want that for him. He is a good king for Zakhar—he could even be a great king. He is not my father's son in that respect. He cares passionately about what is best for our country, even if it is unpopular with the people. Someday they will see that, but until then…"

"Until then, you're in danger."

"Yes. Both of us. So Andre sent me here. He had the

leverage to bend your government to his will, to ensure my safety, and so…" She shrugged.

"What happens when the year is over? What happens when you go back?"

She refused to look at him, just whispered something under her breath in Zakharan. But his sharp ears caught her words and translated them. *For such is the will of God that by doing right you may silence the ignorance of foolish men.*

It sounded like a Bible quotation and he wanted to ask her to explain the reference and its context, but caught himself just in time. He couldn't let on he understood.

"I will face that challenge when it arrives," she said to him in English, and her sad smile as she turned away tore at his heart. He could no more prevent what he did next than he could willingly stop breathing. His hand shot out, capturing her arm and drawing her inevitably closer. A tremor ran through her, but she didn't resist, didn't fight him, and he knew in his soul that she wanted this from him as much as he did…maybe even more.

She raised her face to his as trustingly as a child, and when his lips claimed hers she responded. Ardently. Like a flower turning toward the sun. He deepened the kiss, his tongue making a foray into her mouth to capture her tongue, and she made a little sound deep in her throat. She strained closer, her body trembling. One hand holding her tight, Trace let his other hand wander downward, stroking, caressing, arousing her as much as she aroused him just by her presence in his arms.

"Sweet," he muttered between kisses. "So sweet."

"Am I?" she breathed when he finally let her breathe, and he could hear the uncertainty in her voice…and the desire to believe. "Oh, Trace, am I truly?"

"Like honey," he said softly, knowing the word didn't even come close to describing the sweetness of her. Not just her taste, not just her incredible softness, but the trust that let him touch her like this. "Like the sweetest gift God ever made."

His lips made a voyage of discovery, traveling from her passionate mouth to the vulnerable spot behind her ear. She shivered and moaned when his teeth tugged at her earlobe, and when his tongue dipped into the delicate shell of her ear she cried his name.

Had a woman ever responded like this to him? He couldn't remember. All he knew was *this* woman, *this* moment, and the shivering, unraveling sounds of her passion bathing him, luring him, telling him without words that she needed him. Wanted him. Trusted him.

One hand slid around and felt for the clip that held her hair, and with a practiced flick of his fingers released it. Then he was drawing those honey-brown waves forward as he'd dreamed of doing, wrapping them around his throat, binding them together. Soft, delicately perfumed, they burned his flesh like a brand, and his erection throbbed, swelled and strained tightly against the confines of his jeans.

He laid her oh-so-gently on the sheepskin rug in front of the fireplace and pressed himself against her, letting her feel the need she'd created. She caught her breath. Her slight withdrawal was nearly imperceptible, but he felt it and started to pull away. Then she softened and her hands hesitantly grasped his hips, anchoring him in place.

She opened her eyes and stared up at him, her breathing as ragged as his, and those lovely, innocent green eyes told him everything he needed to know. Desire for him battled her instinctive fear of the unknown… and won.

"Trace…I…" she whispered. "I want to…but I have never…"

"I know, Princess." And he did know. He hadn't needed the words.

He kissed her again, but this time it was just for her. His lips aroused but soothed at the same time. His right hand slid down, cupping her full breast momentarily through her blouse and bra. Her nipple hardened and she caught her breath, but then his hand slid away, across her flat stomach, to the zipper of her jeans. The zipper yielded on the first try, and he popped the button open with equal ease. Then his hand was slipping into the opening, sliding beneath the silk panties to the silkiness of her skin, seeking and finding his warm, damp target.

Her hips arched and she moaned against his mouth when one finger brushed against the nub he coaxed from hiding, and her hands clutched at his arms. Then his fingers slid lower, seeking the moisture he knew he would find.

"No…." Her protest was faint.

"Yes," he said. "Let me do this for you." And as his finger slid delicately inside, he thrust his tongue between her lips. Then his tongue was mimicking his finger—advance and retreat, advance and retreat—

until she melted all over him and surrendered under the dual sensual onslaught. Her legs trembled but they parted, allowing him complete access.

Part of him wanted to just rip away her jeans, pull her to him and bury his body so deep in hers that she would never lie in another man's arms without remembering him. That same part of him wanted to grind against her, again and again, until she dug her nails into his flesh and cried his name, begging him to bring them both to a climax so shattering neither would ever accept anything less again.

But she trusted him, and he didn't have any way to protect her. Nothing with him to prevent unwanted consequences. Her earlier words came back to haunt him—*there is no such thing as a bastard child...only bastard parents...*

He gritted his teeth and fought for control. He couldn't make love to her the way he desperately wanted—she would remain a virgin despite their mutual desire. But he could give her this gift. And she would never forget the man who had given it to her. Never forget *him.*

His fingers damp with her essence, he slid them upward, cherishing her secrets along with her trust. And she responded. Her hips rose and fell involuntarily as he alternately stroked her and soothed her, and her breathing became erratic. She whispered his name as a question, her hands clinging to him as he drove her higher and higher. "I cannot..." she said, but he knew from her tone that she could. "Oh, please..."

"I will, Princess," he whispered against her perfumed skin. "I *will* please you."

"I cannot…" she repeated, but then her legs stiffened and he knew she was close. So close. "What are you… Oh, I cannot…" He rubbed faster, his fingers dipping into the honey he'd called forth from her body, sliding it over the delicate nub that was now swollen and begging for release. "Oh, please…please…"

Then her fingernails were digging into his arms as her hips surged upward. Her head thrown back, she cried his name again and again, little sobs tearing through her chest. Involuntary tremors shook her, and he could see as well as feel her shattering climax. Gently he slid one finger inside her, needing to experience as much of her orgasm as he could, and her body clamped around his finger, holding him prisoner for endless seconds as she throbbed around him.

A minute later she sighed and relaxed bonelessly against his body. He removed his hand reluctantly, but he couldn't help one last stroke over her swollen flesh, and she trembled against the pleasurable aftershock.

"Trace?" His name was a question again, but this time she was asking something different. "What of you? I want to—"

"It's okay, Princess," he whispered, cherishing her, brushing kisses against her eyelids and forcing her eyes closed. "This was for you."

"But I…"

"No."

She opened her eyes and stared up at him for long seconds, varied emotions flitting across her face. Finally she said, "I do not understand. Do you not want me?" Her voice wavered, and her eyes held such pain and fear of rejection it broke his heart.

He took her hand in his and dragged it down his body, forcing her to cup him, to feel the throbbing intensity of his desire. "Tell me I don't want you," he rasped.

Hesitantly at first, her fingers stroked, squeezed, measured, and Trace groaned. He couldn't get any harder...but then he did, and the ache between his thighs threatened to overwhelm his good intentions.

"You want me," she whispered, the startling revelation reflected in her lovely green eyes, and then she smiled at him, shyness replaced by a womanly resolve. "You *do* want me." She strained toward him and brushed her lips against his.

No man ever had a woman offer herself to him so sweetly. No man ever had to fight so hard not to take what was offered. A shudder tore through him as savage as his desire to possess her completely. "No," he said, tearing himself away from her. He hunched over, pain wracking his body in waves that seemed endless, and all he could hear was his own tortured breathing.

Eons later he glanced back at her, only to find her watching him with confusion written across her face. "I'm sorry, Princess," he said, gently caressing her cheek. "You don't understand. I have no way to protect you. And I won't be like my father, whoever he is. I've never made love to a woman without protecting her." He clenched his jaw fiercely. *"And I never will."*

Her face was solemn as she took in his words. Then she smiled at him as Eve must have smiled at Adam in the Garden of Eden. "I cannot ask you to be less than the man you are," she said softly, sitting up and moving closer to him, so that he could smell the sweet fragrance of her. "But I *can* ask you to let me be a woman for you."

Her hand slipped down to stroke him through his jeans, her green eyes darkening with desire as he swelled against her touch. "Please," she said, that one word sliding through his shattered defenses. "I *want* to do this. For you. Only for you."

Helpless against her, helpless against his own raging desire, he didn't resist as she slowly popped the button and unzipped his jeans. One small hand reached in and caressed him through the opening she'd created, through the cotton fabric of his briefs, but suddenly it wasn't enough. He needed her touch against his naked skin, wanted her to see what she did to him, what she would always do to him merely by her presence. He caught her hand. "Wait," he said. Then he raised his hips and forced his jeans and briefs down together, revealing himself to her. Hard. Achingly hard.

She breathed deeply, but she didn't shy away. She took his erection in her hand, her fingers encircling him, and he groaned. "You like that," she said to herself in Zakharan, a tiny smile of discovery playing over her mouth. She raised her gaze to his as her fingers tightened around him. In English she asked, "You like that, yes?"

"Hell, yes," he said, more harshly than he intended. Part of him wanted to take her hand and show her the rhythm he needed, but another part of him wanted to let her discover it for herself—if he could stand the torture.

She stroked him, petted him, all the while her breathing quickening along with his. She whispered to him in Zakharan, little words of praise he didn't think she even realized she was saying, and which he desperately wanted to respond to…if he could let her know he understood.

Then she bent over him, her golden brown hair falling in soft, cooling waves against his heated skin. She whispered something in Zakharan, words his mind processed automatically but which his brain refused to consider in the heat of the moment. And when she took him into her warm, moist mouth he thought he'd die from the exquisite pleasure. Unable to stop himself, he arched upward, head thrown back, eyes closed. He groaned again. "Princess… Oh God, yes!" Shudders wracked his body when her tongue swirled around him.

His eyes flicked open, and he propped himself on his elbows and watched her, the sensations she was creating with her touch nearly unbearable, but the erotic picture she made as she loved him with her mouth in the glow of the firelight even more unbearable. He'd had more skilled lovers, but never one like her. He never would again. His body trembling as it had never trembled with a woman before, he surrendered to her without a fight.

When it was all over Trace lay there, his body spent, one forearm across his eyes as he wondered what the hell he was going to do. Wondered how he would survive the endless remaining months as her bodyguard without making love to her, without taking what she'd so sweetly offered. Wondering how he was ever going to let her go back to Zakhar when the year was over.

Because the words she'd whispered—words she hadn't wanted him to hear since she'd uttered them in Zakharan and not English—now came back to haunt him. She loved him. Or thought she did. And now he had no defenses against her. Now the losing battle he'd been fighting was lost. Because whether she loved him or not, whether she wanted it or not, now he knew he loved her, too.

He removed his arm, opened his eyes, and sat up. The princess was kneeling beside him, her hand still wrapped around his sex as she watched his face, waiting for him to say something. Her face was soft and defenseless. Her eyes, those lovely green eyes were so full of love and hope as she gazed at him that Trace said the only thing he could think of, repeating the words he'd uttered earlier. But this time they weren't uttered in the heat of passion even though they were meant just as fervently. "You are the sweetest gift God ever made."

She flushed up to the roots of her hair, but she didn't glance away. "Am I, Trace?" she asked shyly.

"Yes." Gently he removed her hand and kissed her palm, then tugged his jeans into place and zipped up. Other words struggled to escape, but he fought them back. He couldn't tell her the truth. He couldn't tell her he loved her, but that there was no future for him in loving her. No future for them.

He should remove himself from this assignment— he knew that as surely as he knew anything. What he'd just allowed to happen had compromised his objectivity, his professionalism. But there was a part of him that refused to accept what his head was telling him. And besides, what reason could he give for wanting out? Not just Walker—he might have been able to tell Walker the truth. But there was no way in hell he was going to tell the State Department what had happened. No way. Not after what they'd originally asked him to do where the princess was concerned. He could just see the smirks, the sniggering, knowing smiles, the *humiliation* the princess would suffer because of him.

No, he had to protect her from that any way necessary, even if it meant staying on this assignment. He just had to pull back. Had to return—if he could—to the way things had been between them before today. Yes, it would be difficult. Especially now that he knew it was more than just desire…on both their parts. Now that he knew he loved her and she thought she loved him, it would require every bit of resolve he could muster to stay with her and not touch her again. But he had to do it. Not just because it was still his job to protect her, but because he couldn't bear for anyone to know her intimate secrets. And because he couldn't bear for her to think herself rejected again, when that was the last thing he wanted to do.

No, he had to somehow carefully pick his way through the quicksand and find a way to let her down gently over the remaining months of her stay without anyone else being any the wiser. All he could give her was the protection she deserved…and the love coursing through his body and his heart. Not the words. But he could set her free of the chains of her past, and when he let her go—when he was *forced* to let her go—she would know exactly who and what she really was: beautiful, desirable and so damned lovable she'd never believe otherwise again.

But when she left, she would take his heart with her. The heart he hadn't known he still had to lose...until it was lost.

Chapter 10

Mara hummed a joyful little Zakharian folk song from the eighteenth century to herself as she gathered up her books. Another school week was over, but that wasn't why she was so happy. She was happy because she had the whole weekend ahead of her…with Trace. Tuesday and Wednesday this week had been Alec's days on duty, and Thursday and Friday had belonged to Liam.

She'd only seen Trace occasionally since Monday— at dinner, walking around the grounds and once in the stables when she went to check on Suleiman. He had scarcely said a word to her, nothing that couldn't have been overheard by anyone in her household. And when others were around his face wore that professional appearance she knew now was a mask hiding his deeper feelings. But the few times they'd been alone his eyes had been alive with emotion. And the emotion she wanted to believe she saw reflected there was…love.

This weekend—Saturday and Sunday—were Trace's days to guard her, and she had plans to spend as much time as she could with him. She knew she probably couldn't convince him to take her back to his cabin, although she would gladly go there if he would. She just wanted to be with him—to listen to his voice, to watch the way he moved with that silent, graceful power, to read what he felt for her in his gorgeous blue eyes. Doing *nothing* with him was better than doing anything with anyone else.

"You're happy," Liam commented casually as Mara slung her computer case over one shoulder, picked up her briefcase with one hand and her purse with the other, and headed for the door of her office. But there was nothing casual about the way Liam's eyes swept the corridor as he walked out of her office a step ahead of her, his jacket unbuttoned for quick access to his gun. "Starting to feel more at home here?"

"Oh, yes," she assured him.

"The other day Alec said it seemed as if you weren't homesick anymore. That true?"

She allowed herself a tiny smile. "Everyone is so nice to me here. My students—most of them try so hard any teacher would be pleased and proud. My fellow professors treat me as if I am truly one of them. You and Alec take such good care of me. And Trace…" Her tiny smile grew.

"Yeah. Alec and I, we noticed."

Mara shot a quick glance at Liam's face, wondering

exactly what he meant by that statement, but all she read in his expression was the same casual interest. *Liam and Alec cannot know,* she reassured herself. *No one knows except Trace, and he would never tell anyone.*

"So how's the book coming?" Liam asked her as they walked to the faculty parking lot.

She sighed a little. "It would be easier if I could write it in Zakharan," she told him with a droll smile. "Equations are the same in any language, but the text...the right words will not always come to my mind to convey the exact meaning of what I wish to say."

She remembered then how she had whispered to Trace in Zakharan last Sunday. She had wanted to tell him everything she was feeling, had wanted to share with him the glory and wonder of knowing he understood all the things she couldn't bring herself to say about her father, about her growing up years...*and he loved her anyway.*

And then she'd told him she loved him. Not in English. In Zakharan. She hadn't been able to hold back—the words had tumbled out despite her best efforts. But at least he hadn't understood her. At least she hadn't put that burden on him. When he was ready he would tell her. She knew he loved her as surely as she knew she loved him. She wanted to shout it to the whole world, but...

Mara knew she was old-fashioned compared to American women, but that was the way she'd been raised. In Zakhar a woman did not tell a man she loved him...not until he spoke first. And she wanted those words from Trace. She wanted him to tell her what his eyes had surely told her on Sunday...and every time they'd been alone since. Then and only then would she tell him—in English—that his love was returned.

But if she couldn't tell Trace yet, there was one person she *could* share this with. *Andre,* she thought, smiling to herself. *I must tell Andre.*

"So are you going to ask him?" Liam said to Alec in an undertone as the two brothers stripped off their boots and mufflers in the guest house mudroom. "Or should I?"

"Ask me what?" Trace said from the doorway. His stance appeared casual as he crossed his arms and leaned a shoulder and one jeans-clad hip against the door frame. As always when he was awake, he was strapped, his SIG SAUER nestled in its shoulder holster. It was such a part of him he would only have noticed if he wasn't wearing it. He knew neither of the Jones brothers would be intimidated by him openly displaying the weapon as other people might be, so he never bothered covering the shoulder holster with a jacket when he was in the guest house.

But something was up, and Trace had a fairly good idea what it was. He knew Alec and Liam were too smart, too aware, not to have noticed the change in the princess this past week. Not to mention they could probably read the change in him, too. If nothing else, the tension in his muscles right now was a dead giveaway, so he tried to relax. He was only partially successful.

Liam glanced up but didn't reply right away, just removed his coat and hung it on the wall rack above his boots before meeting Trace's eyes and saying, "Is there something we should know...about the princess?"

Trace's face hardened. "Like what?"

Alec answered for both of them before Liam could. "Like the way she looks at you."

Trace's eyes narrowed as he quickly decided the best defense was a good offense. His gaze moved from Alec to Liam. "Weren't you the one who said from the get-go that the princess looks at me differently than the way she looks at either of you?" he asked Liam. He shrugged. "Nothing I can do about that."

Liam glanced at Alec, then back at Trace. "Yeah, but..."

"But what?"

"It's different somehow. *She's* different."

Trace cursed mentally, but refused to allow anything he was feeling to be reflected on his face. Instead he shrugged again, feigning disinterest. "You told me to cut her some slack, so I did. That's all."

Liam started to respond, but Alec put a hand on his arm. "Never mind," he said. "It's not important. 'Cause if it was, McKinnon would tell us. Right?"

His brown eyes, so like his sister Keira's, sought Trace's eyes. And something in that steady gaze made Trace say, "Yeah. If there was anything you needed to know to keep the princess safe, you'd know. That's the only thing any of us have to worry about—keeping her safe."

"Okay then," Alec said, as if that ended the conversation. But Liam looked unconvinced, and Trace wondered just what the Jones brothers thought they knew about the princess…and him.

Once again he resolved to keep the secret of their tryst in his cabin to himself. Alec and Liam didn't have a need to know in order to do their jobs—that was something private and precious between the princess and him, and *no* one needed to know about it. And he was doing his job…difficult as it was. He'd managed to regain his objectivity after an intense internal struggle, and he knew he was providing the princess with the same high standard of professional protection Alec and Liam were, if not higher. So he had nothing to be ashamed of. Nothing he'd done or was doing was putting the princess at risk. Nothing.

He had always known that with great power came great responsibility. He had never hesitated to exercise both when called upon, had never shirked the difficult life-or-death decisions most men never faced. Now he bent a hard stare on the two men standing at military attention in front of him. Young. Proud. Warriors both. The crème de la crème of his fighting corps, men he had trained with. Men he trusted with his life. Men who were nearly fanatical in their desire to protect him—from anything. And even more importantly in this situation, men who would willingly kill or die on his command. Knowing he could be sending them to their deaths, but knowing, too, he had no other choice. *"Quis custodiet ipsos custodes?"* he murmured to himself. That reminder was the final deciding factor.

"Make no mistake," he said abruptly. "You have not

volunteered for an easy assignment. This man has killed before. He could kill again if he perceived you as a threat. Even if you are not killed, you could be captured. Imprisoned. Put to death or left to rot for years, with no possibility of escape. No reprieve. No chance for freedom. The prison doors would open only if you were willing to talk. But that must *never* happen. No one must ever know. Are we clear on that? Lukas? Damon?"

Both men replied with military precision and fervor, and he allowed himself a faint smile. "Good," he said approvingly. "You will be met upon your arrival, and your contact will provide you with cash, documents and everything else you need to maintain your cover. Cars have been arranged that will be nearly impossible to trace, but do not let yourself be spotted. Changing vehicles often will help, so rotate at least twice a day."

He flipped open a file, turned it around so it was facing his men, and spread the contents out on the desk in front of them. He pointed to the picture of a handsome, dark-haired, blue-eyed man only a few years older than he was. "This is your target. He is always armed, and I have it on good authority he has lightning-fast reflexes, so be wary."

He paused for questions and got none. "I want daily reports. Your contact will provide you with the cameras, encrypted computer, virtual private network and internet access account you will need to do this." His eyes narrowed. "Stay in the shadows. Watch him carefully from a distance. Photograph him. But do not kill him. Let me repeat, do *not* kill him. Not yet. He dies *only* on my direct command. *I* say if and when. Understood?"

Affirmation came with the same military promptness. "Good," he repeated softly. "Very good. I am depending on you. Do not fail me in this. You are dismissed."

October slid into November. The days grew colder and shorter, and several times it snowed, although the snow melted after a few days. Now when Mara and whichever bodyguard was on duty left for work the sun was barely up, and when they returned the sun had already set. Trace refused to let Mara ride Suleiman in the dark, so she was restricted to riding him only on the weekends. But Trace rode with her every weekend now, whether or not he was on duty.

And although they did nothing else, they talked. Since that afternoon in his cabin when they'd shared their darkest secrets, it was as if a dam had been breached for both of them. Mara confided in Trace as she had once confided only in her brother. And Trace... Trace did the same—hesitantly at first, but as day followed day and week melted into week, he opened up to her in ways she'd never imagined.

The taciturn man she'd first fallen for was replaced by a man who shared his thoughts, and to a lesser extent his emotions. Not what he was feeling where she was concerned, but other, deep-rooted emotions that played across his handsome features as she watched and listened, enthralled.

"...I was on the bomb squad in Afghanistan—disarming them. A futile effort in a futile war. But someone had to do it. If you've ever seen a child maimed or killed by a roadside bomb, you'll understand why I volunteered

for that duty. Why I'm still alive is a mystery—a little bit of skill, I guess, and a hell of a lot of luck. Not everyone was as lucky. But at least the civilians were protected...

"...I'd worked for D'Arcy as a US marshal ever since I got out of the marines. When he was recruited into a new agency and asked me to join him I couldn't tell him no. I respect him more than any man I've ever known. Don't get me wrong, Walker's a great boss—he's brilliant and his instincts are always right on target. But D'Arcy's in a class by himself, and yeah, there are times I miss working for him...

"...No man likes to admit failure. So when my marriage failed, I refused to admit it for the longest time. I kept thinking if I just tried harder, Janet would realize her suspicions were groundless. I'm no saint, Princess, but I never cheated on her. Never. I can't help it if women find me attractive, but I took my marriage vows seriously. The bottom line was she just couldn't bring herself to trust me, and that defeated me...

"...Keira's special. She was my partner for three years, and we closed some tough cases together. She's a whiz at research and analysis. Except for D'Arcy, I've never known anyone better at solving a puzzle no one else can solve. I was glad for her when she and Walker got married—I really was. But I lost the best partner I'd ever had when she gave up being a field agent and took a research-and-analysis job with the agency, answering directly to D'Arcy—and that still hurts. Not even being Alyssa's godfather quite makes up for it...

"...I saw Keira lying in a pool of her own blood, Walker beside her, desperately trying to save her life.

*And I knew in that instant I had never really loved
my wife, not the way a man should love the woman
he marries. Not the way Cody loves Keira. He would
have taken that bullet for her in a heartbeat, the same
way I—"*

Trace never completed that sentence, but Mara knew
what he was thinking. As her bodyguard it was his job
to protect her, even if it meant sacrificing his own life.
But she wasn't just a job to him, not anymore. He loved
her the way Cody loved Keira, and he would take a bullet for her in a heartbeat. It was in his voice when he
called her *Princess* when they were alone—tender and
loving now, not mocking. It was in his eyes when she
turned around suddenly and caught him watching her
with that deep longing and a hunger she was just beginning to understand. He never let anyone else see, but
she knew in her heart no man could look at a woman
that way and not love her.

Mara blossomed, knowing herself loved. Even
though Trace had not touched her since that time at his
cabin, these were halcyon days for her, each one more
special than the day before, and each one leading to the
inevitable conclusion. And though part of her was impatient for the words of love, another part of her was
content to let Trace tell her when he was ready. She just
wished it would be soon. Andre never asked when they
spoke on the phone, never pushed her for details in any
way, but it had been more than five weeks since she'd
told him she was in love, and she knew he was waiting
for her to tell him more. There just wasn't anything to
tell him…yet.

* * *

"Given the acceleration, which is a second-order differential equation," Mara explained, writing with a dark blue erasable marker on the whiteboard in the small classroom where she taught her grad students, "if you integrate you get the velocity." She quickly added several more figures and symbols, the marker squeaking slightly in her writing haste. "If you integrate again, you get the distance traveled."

She glanced back at her students. "See how that works?" Expressions of intense concentration and comprehension met her questioning gaze. "Remember, while pure mathematics has a beauty and meaning of its own, it is *applied* mathematics that drives our world." She smiled at them. "Engineers in the room, take heart. We are heading into your territory now."

Mara glanced regretfully at the clock. "And that, I think, is all for today." She held up one hand to hold the class for a moment. "Do not forget, your term papers are due next Friday. No excuses," she warned, but with the understanding smile that reminded her students she was available if any of them were struggling with the concepts and needed assistance. She placed the marker in the little trough beneath the whiteboard as the room exploded with sudden chatter and the noise of a dozen students slinging textbooks and notebooks into backpacks or briefcases and surging toward the door.

Trace rose from his seat near the front of the room as they did so, moving quickly yet with an apparent lack of haste toward Mara's side, his own backpack slung over his left shoulder and his right hand casually tucked inside his jacket. Two students whom Mara knew were engineering grad students and study partners stayed back and approached her with questions, which she answered after giving each question careful thought. A third student, a young man of obvious Arabic descent hovered by the door, waiting, and when Mara was free he darted forward to pose his question. After a long and detailed discussion that involved use of the whiteboard again to demonstrate what she meant, the student eventually left.

Through it all, Trace's eyes had never left the face of the young man talking with her. Now he followed the student to the classroom door, closed it behind him and locked it while Mara wiped the eraser over the whiteboard until it was clean. She drew a deep breath and exhaled slowly with a little sound of satisfaction, allowing herself to relax finally as another strenuous week came to an end. She loved teaching, but her students kept her on her toes, especially her grad students. Their questions sometimes stretched her brain to its limit, but tough questions were a good sign. It proved she was reaching them. It proved she was making them *think*, and that was even more important than the concepts she was trying to impart.

Now that they were alone, she turned to Trace and allowed herself to smile at him in a more intimate fashion than she did when others were around. Sometimes he smiled back, but today wasn't one of those days, and Mara hid a sigh. "What is it?" she asked.

"We have new intel on that man," he said curtly, indicating the student who'd just left with a tilt of his head.

Mara's brow wrinkled. "Intel? What is that?"

"Intelligence." When she still looked at him with confusion, he added, "Military speak for information gathering."

Comprehension dawned. "My students?" she asked in disbelief. "You are spying on my students?"

"Not me personally, but yes, the State Department has a dossier on every one of your students. What did you expect?"

Mara sank onto the edge of the desk and removed her eyeglasses, staring at him dumbfounded. "I...I had no idea." She gazed up at Trace. "Why?"

"To keep you safe, of course."

"But...they are *students*." Mara knew her dismay was obvious. "They would not harm me."

Trace shook his head. "You can't know that for sure." He hesitated for a moment. "That young man who was just here, for example. Good student, right? Head of the class. Applies himself diligently. But what do you really know about him? Did you know, for instance, that he has a second cousin in Lebanon with suspected ties to Hezbollah?"

Mara's thoughts flew to the young man in question. So earnest. So polite. So eager to learn whatever she could teach him. She could not envision him as a terrorist, or even as someone with terrorist leanings. "What does that have to do with Zakhar? With me?"

"Maybe nothing. But we can't take chances with your safety. By knowing everything we can about those around you we can plan accordingly, so we've read the dossiers the State Department compiled. And we continue to get updates."

A sudden realization startled her. "Alec and Liam, too? They have read these secret reports on my students?"

"Of course. And not just your students. The faculty and staff here, too. Not to mention the people you brought with you from Zakhar."

Mara covered her face with her palm and made a sound of distress. "I did not know," she whispered. There was silence between them for a minute, then she glanced up sharply. "Does Andre know of this?"

Trace's mouth twitched into a rueful smile. "It was his suggestion. Command, really, but couched in diplomatic terms. Even if he hadn't raised the issue, though, I would have."

"But *why*? I cannot believe…this is worse than the paparazzi. To spy on people. To pry into their private lives. To hold the sins of others against them." Mara knew she was getting worked up, but this was something she had never imagined the only two men she loved in the whole world would have in common. Concern for her safety, yes, even a fierce desire to protect her. That she understood. But to go this far? To suspect everyone?

"Whose life can stand up to such intense scrutiny?" she demanded hotly.

"How did you know when we first met that I once spent six months in Zakhar?" Trace asked reasonably.

"That was—" Mara stopped short. She'd been about to say that was different, but she suddenly realized it really wasn't. She remembered that even before she'd left Zakhar she'd read dossiers, complete with pictures, on all three men who would be guarding her, bare bones dossiers submitted by the US State Department but expanded by Zakhar's secret intelligence service. She hadn't thought about it at the time, hadn't even considered that this was exactly what she was protesting against now.

But no one's life is free of things they would rather keep private, she thought. *Mine certainly is not.* A wave of warm color surged into her cheeks as she remembered the intimate details of everything she and Trace had done at his cabin weeks ago. *There is nothing to be ashamed of,* she reminded herself sternly. *We did nothing wrong.* And yet, she knew she would not want anyone else to know about it. What they had done was personal. Private. A memory she cherished, but not one she wanted broadcast to the world. She didn't even want it contained in some secret report that someone might read.

A thought came to her unbidden, and she blurted it out. "You did not...no," she said, shaking her head as if she could make the thought go away by her denial.

"Didn't what?"

"You would not," Mara reassured herself and him. "You would not betray to anyone what we did in your cabin." Trace stiffened but he didn't respond, just looked at her from under his dark eyebrows, a forbidding expression on his face. She added quickly, "I am sorry. It is a despicable thing to accuse you of, and I know in my heart you would not."

Trace still didn't speak, and a little calmer now, Mara

asked, "Is it even legal for your government to spy on its citizens this way? Zakhar, yes. This I understand. The citizens of Zakhar do have rights, but not the same rights as people in this country, and Andre would do whatever he needed to do to protect me. But that is Zakhar. So I must ask again. Is it legal to do this here?"

"No laws were broken." He moved a step closer and slid his backpack from his shoulder onto the desk beside her. "Before 9/11 maybe, but not now. The world changed after 9/11, and our laws changed, too."

Mara gazed up at him, regret in her eyes. "That was a terrible tragedy. But is not the loss of freedom, the loss of privacy, just as tragic?"

Trace laughed abruptly. "You want to debate US political policy, Princess? Discuss the nature and meaning of privacy and freedom as defined by the US Constitution?"

She shook her head. "No. I am Zakharian, and I have no right to criticize. It is just…" She searched for the words. "Some things should remain private. I do not like to think of people's privacy being invaded." She had suffered too much herself at the hands of the paparazzi and the tabloids over the years, had suffered too much over the loss of her own privacy to easily accept this invasion of privacy being perpetrated in her name.

"This was all put into motion months ago," Trace said gently, holding her gaze with his. "Before you even arrived in this country. It wasn't your decision, and it still isn't. You're not responsible." His hand came up to cup her cheek briefly before he drew it away sharply as if he'd been burned. "But, Princess, you should know by now that just like your brother I *will* keep you safe, no matter what I have to do." He started to say something more, but stopped himself with a shake of his head. Then his face hardened and he repeated, "No matter what I have to do."

And though Trace didn't say the words Mara longed to hear, she knew he wasn't just talking about doing his job. Somehow that thought managed to allay her dismay over what she'd just learned. She still didn't like it. But she understood. Just as she understood why Andre would go to any lengths to protect her, she understood why Trace would, too.

Chapter 11

Mara and Trace were riding together the last Saturday in November when she broached the question she'd been longing to ask. The air was crisp and cold now, and they were both bundled up warmly as they cantered across the snowy landscape. They pulled up when they reached a small rise that gave them an unhindered view of the Rockies; both horses snorted and stamped their hooves, their breath making white clouds in the frosty air.

"I love this view," Mara said, smiling dreamily at Trace. "Every time I come here I think of home."

"Still miss Zakhar?" His eyes were turned outward as he asked the question, scanning the horizon for any sign of a threat, but the landscape was deserted and there was no one to be seen for miles around.

"Not as much as I used to," she answered honestly.

He focused his attention on her finally and asked, "And your brother?"

Mara's smile faded, and she knew her heart was in her eyes. "Not when I am with you." They stared at each other for several seconds, until Trace turned away with a muttered oath. "Andre is sending the plane for me after finals are over, so I will be able to return to Zakhar for Christmas break," she said, apropos of nothing. She took a deep breath. "Will you go with me?"

"Princess..." She hated the regretful way he said that word, knowing a refusal was forthcoming.

"If you cannot, you cannot," she said lightly, and only she knew what effort that lightness cost her—rejection from Trace was still something she found difficult to deal with. "I will only be gone two weeks after all. I would have liked to show you the place where I grew up, introduce you to Andre. But I understand."

Trace guided his horse over so they were facing each other, knee to knee. He held the reins in an iron grip with his left hand, while his right reached out to cup her cheek. His thumb brushed gently over her lips, and regret cast a shadow over his beautiful blue eyes. "No," he said softly, his voice husky with emotion. "You don't understand. You can't possibly understand. I would if I could, but..." He looked as if he were going to add something to that statement, but he tightened his lips to hold the words back.

"Then..." Mara took her courage in her hands once more. "If you will not go with me to Zakhar, will you take me to your cabin tomorrow?"

He couldn't disguise the sudden flare of desire that

slashed across his face. His right arm slid around her waist, pulling her into an embrace so fierce, so ardent, Mara caught her breath as passion exploded between them. His lips demanded a response, and she yielded gladly, hungry for his kisses…and anything else he would give her. It wasn't until her slack hand on the reins allowed Suleiman his head and the horses drifted nervously apart that Trace let her go.

Her lips were swollen; her heart skittered wildly in her chest. She brought Suleiman under control and turned his head so she could reach Trace again. "Please," she said, pride taking a back seat to love. "You cannot know how I have longed for this."

"I do know," he said, as he bent to take her lips again, and his kiss was rough, urgent. "Whatever you're feeling, it's only a fraction of what I feel," he muttered. His tongue dove inside, luring hers, and he tasted of love and danger. "I could take you here, now, and I wouldn't give a damn about snow or anything else," he said between kisses that melted her insides and made her tremble. Then his kiss gentled. "But you deserve better than that, Princess. You deserve the best I can give you." He lifted his head and stared down at her, pain she didn't understand darkening his eyes. Then he seemed to reach a decision. "Yes, I'll take you to the cabin tomorrow."

Trace let her go and turned his horse sharply away, putting a little distance between them before stopping dead in his tracks, his head bowed. And Mara knew something was wrong. Very wrong. She wanted to ask him, but she didn't want to pressure him into telling her what it was. *Maybe when we are alone at the cabin,* she thought as she touched her heels to Suleiman's sides and headed slowly back toward the house. *Maybe he will tell me then.*

Hoofbeats in the snow, the creak of leather and the snorts of the horses were the only sounds that accompanied their return ride, and Mara searched for an explanation for Trace's sudden capitulation…and his withdrawal. She had hoped going to the cabin would give him the opportunity to tell her he loved her. But until they resolved whatever the problem was, she knew he wasn't going to say what she wanted to hear.

Until yesterday Trace hadn't touched Mara in almost seven weeks. Hadn't kissed her the way he yearned to do. The way *she* yearned for him to do. He hadn't drawn her against his body, letting her feel the desperate need that clawed through him, knowing in his heart of hearts she felt the same way. He'd refrained from touching her, knowing that was the only way to maintain a professional distance. He hadn't laid her down and worshipped her body with his, taking both of them to a higher plane where the only thing that mattered was the two of them and the love they shared. Where the only thing that mattered was their two hearts beating as one.

No, he hadn't done any of those things…except in his mind. And he knew—he *knew*—he wasn't the only one dreaming those hopeless dreams. The princess wanted him, too, and she no longer even tried to hide it. The scene yesterday was burned into his mind as he remembered her complete surrender. *She wouldn't have cared about the snow either,* he brooded, watching silently as she drove confidently along the highway toward Keystone, the speedometer holding steady a few miles above the speed limit.

The defensive driving lessons he'd given her these past weeks had paid off, and she was no longer a nervous driver. No longer hesitant. Not about driving, or anything else. There was a radiance about her now. She'd been lovely before in an understated way, but now she walked in an incandescent glow whenever he was around. Happiness and confidence in herself as a woman had wrought that change. Whenever he looked at her his mouth went dry with desire and his body hardened in a painful rush. But it wasn't just lust. He could have dealt with that. It wasn't lust that made his heart skip a beat when she took a dangerous jump on Suleiman. It wasn't lust that filled him with helpless foreboding at the thought of walking away at the end of the school year. And it damned well wasn't lust that squeezed his heart when she turned those loving green eyes on him and smiled.

He knew so much more about her now. She still said almost nothing about her father, but he understood her utter devotion to her brother, who'd been the only loving influence in her life.

"...Andre believed in me, even when I was too much of a coward to believe in myself. My father...there was a time when he tried to arrange a marriage for me, before I went to Oxford. I tried to tell him no, but he would not listen to me. I was so terribly afraid I would have no choice, but...Andre...he stopped it. I do not know how,

just that he did. Everything I have achieved I owe to him because he freed me...

"...*Winter was always my favorite time of year when I was a little girl, because Andre would descend upon the nursery and drag me out to play in the snow. He could be imperious even then, but never for himself, only for me. 'Come, dernya,'—that means 'little treasure' in my language, Andre's pet name for me. Overriding all objections—my nurse, at first, then my governess, then my tutors—he would hold out his hand to me and insist I accompany him, with a wicked smile that made me dare anything. He had a sled that flew like the wind upon a certain snowy hillside near the palace, and he would take me with him, laughing all the way...*

"...*Andre taught me to ride without fear. I think I was only three and he was eight when he first took me up in front of him atop his favorite mount. But even then he was protective of me. I knew nothing bad could happen to me with him there. It is the same feeling I have now...with you...*

"...*Suleiman the Magnificent, that is his full name, and he has lived up to it. He is the brother of Alexander the Great, out of Andre's own stables. Alexander won the Grand National three years ago, before he was put out to stud. Suleiman had the potential to be another winner for Andre, just as great as his older brother, but...instead, he was Andre's gift to me when I obtained my PhD. Never, never, will I forget the first moment I saw him. It was love at first sight, the same way I felt when I saw y—*"

Mara never completed that sentence, but Trace knew

what she had almost said. Her love shone like a bea-
con in the night. Luring him. Weaving spells around
his heart. Fairy tales he'd never been young enough to
believe in suddenly seemed possible when her green
eyes smiled at him.

Something had to give—either his sanity or his self-
control. And what he was afraid of most was losing his
iron grip on his self-control.

Damon cursed under his breath, as did Lukas, when
the SUV they were following from a safe distance
turned onto an unmarked dirt road that appeared to
lead nowhere, the SUV rocking and bouncing a little as
it traversed the snow drifts. "I dare not turn," Damon
muttered as he drove steadily by the turn off, never
slacking pace.

The SUV had already disappeared from sight, but
Lukas aimed the long-lens camera in his hands at the
dirt road as they passed it, snapping off a few shots. The
digital camera would record more than just photographs
of an empty landscape. It would also embed the GPS
location in the digital files for future evaluation. They
would return another day and reconnoiter in private,
when there was no chance their target might realize
he was being followed and put two and two together.

A few minutes later the two soldiers in civilian cloth-
ing found themselves in Keystone. Damon turned the
car around without discussion and headed back toward
Boulder. They weren't tasked to tail their target everywhere he went, to never let him out of their sight. That
would have required at least two more teams, possibly

three, and would have dramatically increased the risk of being spotted by their target. No, their job was merely to watch from a distance, record what they could, and report in detail. And be ready to kill him, of course... should the order come. Their target would return to Boulder eventually. And they would be waiting.

The cabin was cold when Trace and Mara walked in. Trace had the programmable thermostat set at fifty-five degrees so the pipes wouldn't freeze, but the air inside was decidedly chilly. He quickly turned the heat up, then got a roaring fire going in the fireplace before turning to face the princess, who stood quietly by the door, still bundled up against the Colorado cold.

"What is it?" he asked Mara when she didn't smile, didn't walk into the middle of the room, didn't remove her jacket. Just stood there watching him with a grave expression on her usually animated face.

"That is what I wanted to ask you," she said with solemn dignity. "All the way here you barely said one word to me. If you did not wish to come here, why are we here?"

Trace closed his eyes momentarily and swore under his breath. His voice was a deep rasp when he admitted, "I've wanted to bring you back here every day for the past seven weeks." A shudder rippled through his body, shaking him to the core. "And every night."

"Then why did you not bring me before this?" she whispered.

"Because..." He turned away, not wanting her to see

the desperate need he was afraid was reflected in his face. "Because I wanted it too much."

"I do not understand."

The bewilderment in her voice made him whirl around to face her, and he violently suppressed the urge to stalk across the short distance between them and drag her into his embrace. Anger shook him. Not anger at her, but at himself. "Because I'm responsible for you. For your safety. I'm supposed to be the professional here. Every time I let myself forget that, I put you at risk."

"Is that the only reason?"

He shook his head slowly and drew a deep breath before continuing. "Because no matter what happens," he said softly, holding her eyes with his, wondering if she could read him as easily as he read her, "no matter what we feel, I'll never be the right man for you—you deserve better than what I have to offer."

"Do you love me?" By the way her hand covered her mouth and the startled expression that crossed her face he knew she'd surprised herself with the question as much as she'd surprised him. When he didn't respond, she removed her hand from her mouth and said quietly, "If you love me, then nothing else matters." Her fingers twisted together, the only sign she wasn't as confident as she seemed. "If you love me, please do not talk of what I deserve." She took one step toward him. Then another. "Since I have known you all I have wanted to be was a woman. Your woman. Is that so wrong?" she implored. "Just a woman with the man she lo—"

He kissed her to stop her from making that declaration, to stop her from saying the words neither of them could retreat from. But once he touched her he was lost. When his lips took hers she made a soft, glad sound, and one arm circled his neck as she strained to get closer to him.

Heat scorched him from the inside out, and it was like the first time, only worse. Better. Trace couldn't think of anything to compare it to. Couldn't think, really. All he knew was that they both had too many clothes on. He stripped her jacket from her arms then fought to remove his own, all the while their lips clung together in a series of kisses that threatened to steal his sanity…to steal his soul. Fire raced through his veins. He wanted. Needed. But so did she. She was as wild to touch him as he was to touch her. Everywhere.

"I have to see you," Trace whispered, drawing away from Mara only far enough to gaze at her with wonder and pain. "Just once I have to see you as God made you." The air in the small room was warming up quickly, the heater and the fire in the fireplace doing their job. A faint tremor shook his hands as he reached for the buttons on her blouse. She stood there passively at first, as one button then another slid open. But then her hands were tugging at the pullover sweater he wore beneath his jacket, and when that was off she reached for his buttons, too. She whispered something in Zakharan he didn't catch, and it was a race between them.

When he unbuttoned her last button his hands tugged the ends of her blouse from her jeans, then slipped inside and slid the blouse off her shoulders. He tried to be gentle, but his heart was slamming inside his chest, and all he could think of was hurry. *Hurry.* A wisp of a silk-and-lace bra cupped her full breasts the way his hands longed to do. He reached behind her; first unsnapping her bra, then removing the clip that held her hair so that it tumbled around her shoulders in a silken curtain.

Then his hands moved beneath, sure and strong, sliding the bra straps down, down, until she was naked from the waist up, with only her honey-brown hair partially concealing her from him.

A little panicked sound escaped her and she made as if to cover herself. "No, Princess," he breathed reassuringly. "Don't hide. Not from me. Please."

His hands reached for the zipper of her jeans, but she stopped him. At first he thought she'd changed her mind, and disappointment exploded through him. But then she smiled up at him, her obvious desire to please him overcoming her shyness, and she undid the zipper herself. Holding his gaze she skimmed her jeans over her hips. But then she stopped.

His hands replaced hers. "Let me. I've dreamed of doing this." His hands slid inside the waistband and slipped the denim down, kneeling before her. She rested her hands on his shoulders, balancing herself as he gently lifted one foot, then the other, so she could step out of her jeans.

She was trembling, but so was he. He hooked his fingers in the scrap of silk that shielded her womanhood from him and tugged it down and off. Then she was completely bare to his gaze, and he sat back on his heels to take in the sight of her. "Hallelujah," he whispered finally, reverently.

She laughed, just a breath of a sound, and he realized from the delicate pink flags in her cheeks it was more from the release of the stress of standing naked before him while he was still completely clothed than from humor. He wanted to say something more, to express the complex emotions roiling through him at the sight of her. But he couldn't think of words strong enough, sweet enough, meaningful enough to describe what this moment meant to him. What her trust meant to him.

He stood up slowly, his hands moving her silky tresses aside so he could caress the pink nipples that tightened even before he touched them. Then he was bending to take one nipple into his mouth, loving it with his tongue. "God, you are beautiful, Princess," he whispered, as his lips moved to her other nipple and loved it the same way.

"That is not—" Her breath caught. "That is not true," she said. "I am pretty, yes, but not… Oh!" He'd slipped his hand between her thighs, parting them until his fingers could slide into her velvet tenderness.

"Yes," he told her, his voice husky with desire. "Beautiful. If Eve had looked like you, Adam would have gladly left Eden." *If Eve had felt like you,* he told her in his mind as his fingers moved slowly in and out of her melting softness, *Adam would have thought he was still in Eden.*

A wave of heat swept through Trace so powerful his whole body tightened, and he knew he had to hold her against his bare skin just once, or die. His hands made short work of the rest of his clothes, and then he was as naked as she was. His heart was pounding so savagely he was almost beyond caring about anything but having her when he drew her into his arms and felt her all along his body—soft and yielding everywhere he was hard and immovable. But he managed to hold on to his sanity—and his self-control—by his fingertips.

Then he was touching her again, fingers stealing into her body, stealing her breath, making her melt and run, making her clutch at his arms with desperation. His mouth trailed down to suckle the pink nipples that peeked at him through her glorious hair, tugging first one, then the other into his mouth until she moaned and her knees buckled. He held her up with one strong arm while he bent her backwards and continued his assault on her senses, until she shuddered uncontrollably and cried his name again and again, giving to him so sweetly, so completely, he knew he would remember this day forever.

His arms were iron bands around her body as he pressed her head against his shoulder, holding her close until the last tremor faded away. His body throbbed and he let her feel his desire, hot and hard against her stomach, begging for release. But he wouldn't let it go further. He couldn't. He knew there was a bed…soft… inviting…in the next room. But he didn't dare trust himself anywhere near it. He yearned to lay her down and come into her welcoming body, sealing himself to her in the most elemental way. But once wouldn't be enough, would never be enough. If he once made her his, he would kill to keep her his forever.

And he knew he couldn't keep her. She could never be his. Even if she loved him anywhere approaching how much he loved her, she could never be his. The school year would end and she would have no choice—she would return to Zakhar, abandoning him. Leaving him in hell.

But that wasn't the worst thing he could imagine. That wasn't what caused his eyes to burn as he stared sightlessly into the distance over the top of her head. That wasn't what caused the ache that shuddered desolately through him. He'd been abandoned before, and he'd survived. He was tough—he could take it. But she wasn't.

She was completely vulnerable. The trust in her eyes when he'd knelt at her feet and she'd let him see all of her was his undoing. She loved him—how much he was afraid to know. She would give herself to him and never count the cost until it was too late. But he would. He would rather die than let anything happen to her—because of him.

He'd let his control slip twice now, and that was two times too many. It would be like dying to give her up, but he needed to end it. Now. Somehow. Not just the physical side of things, although that would be hard enough. No, he needed to end everything. The sharing. The emotional bonding over which he seemed to have no control. The way her smile had twisted itself into his heart. The way she looked at him as if he were her world.

That all had to stop before it was too late. If it wasn't already too late. He had to find a way to cut himself out of her heart, even if it meant leaving his heart bleeding on the floor. He *had* to do it. For her sake, and his own.

Chapter 12

Trace deliberately took a corner much too fast, then swung the steering wheel sharply to the right and brought his car to a dead stop beside the curb. Then waited, his eyes on the rearview mirror.

There! There it was again, that dark sedan he'd spotted a few miles back. It turned the corner quickly, too, then drove right past him as if it wasn't following him. But in the few seconds as the car passed him he saw the two men in the front seat exchanging glances when they realized he'd spotted their tail. He quickly memorized the make and model of the car and the license plate number, then jotted the info in the little notebook he carried in his pocket as soon as the other car was far enough away.

He cursed under his breath. The same car had been

following them the week before as the princess drove to school in her Lexus SUV—he was sure of it now. The university had been closed for Thanksgiving week, but the princess had left two research books in her office at the university that she needed to work on the textbook she was writing, so they'd gone there last Monday to fetch them. He'd only tagged the car once, noting it in his subconscious as he was trained to do, but the vehicle had turned off several blocks away from the faculty parking lot where the princess usually parked, so he'd dismissed it as a tail. But now…

They weren't following her, they were following me.

He turned cold at the thought. If that was true, the princess was in far more danger than anyone realized, especially him. His thoughts flew to memories more than two years old, and a bloody scene in a hospital parking lot. Two men dead in the front seat of their pickup truck, his then-partner, Keira, sprawled on the ground bleeding out, a bullet that had come within inches of her heart lodged in her shoulder.

Michael Vishenko, the New World Militia, and the Russian mob all had reason to want revenge on the four of them—Ryan Callahan, Keira and Cody Walker, and…himself. They'd been extremely careful for the first year after the arrests of Vishenko and the others, but as one conviction after another had piled up with no attempts to silence them, they'd…well, not exactly grown careless, but they hadn't been quite so sharply watchful. At least he hadn't. He couldn't answer for the other three.

We'll never be safe *as long as we live.* Wasn't that

what Keira had told him her husband had said when she asked him to be Alyssa's godfather? Wasn't that one of the reasons they'd picked him as a godfather, because they knew he understood the danger they all lived under, because he'd watch over Alyssa with the same fierce protectiveness they felt toward their daughter should anything happen to them?

For a few precious months he'd let himself forget about the price on his head. He'd let himself forget he was a target, and always would be. He should have remembered they were still out there…watching…and waiting for their chance to exact revenge. Anyone close to him shared that danger.

He had no proof the New World Militia or the Russian Brotherhood was tailing him—not yet, anyway. But he had a license plate number now, and that was a start.

Trace stood in Cody Walker's office the next day. He'd compared notes with the Jones brothers the night before, making damned sure it wasn't the princess who was being followed. Both men had been emphatic there was no tail on the princess when they were guarding her—and they assured him he'd have been the first to know if they'd had even a whiff of a suspicion. That confirmed his assumption he was the one who was being followed, not her.

So he'd immediately requested the interview with Walker, knowing it shouldn't be put off. He was frustrated because he hadn't been able to trace the license plate on the car he'd spotted following him the day before to Michael Vishenko, the New World Militia, or the Russian mob, but it was the only thing that made sense.

He was still being tailed. He hadn't seen them, but he knew they were there. And now it was time to let his boss know what he knew, because he wasn't the only one involved. If he was under surveillance, then it seemed likely Callahan and the Walkers were, too.

But when he entered Walker's office he found it difficult to begin because he had no proof, just instincts, and he paced back and forth in front of the big desk, struggling for the right words. Then he realized the right words weren't necessary, not with Walker, and he said abruptly, "I'm being followed."

Walker glanced at him sharply, but Trace didn't see it. He'd come to a halt in front of one of the pictures on Walker's wall—a large, blown up reproduction of Walker's cabin in the woods of the Big Horn Mountains of Wyoming. Remembering. Fairly certain what had happened in Wyoming more than two years ago was the reason he was being followed now. It was the only working theory he could come up with.

"You're sure."

From the tone of Walker's voice Trace knew it wasn't really a question, but he answered it anyway. "I'm damn sure they're back there, if that's what you mean. It could be someone scoping out the princess, but I doubt it— Keira's brothers are adamant the princess isn't being followed when they're on duty, and the tail is there on me even when I'm not with her."

Walker cursed under his breath. "That's a complication I hadn't counted on."

"Yeah." Trace turned from the picture to stare at his boss. "Anyone following you? Keira?"

"Not that either of us have noticed, but…" Trace nodded. *But.* That was the operative word. "How long has it been going on?" Walker asked him.

Trace thought about it for a minute. "A week, maybe?" he said finally. "Two weeks? Hell, who knows?" he added, making a gesture of frustration with one hand. He hated admitting it to Walker, because it meant he hadn't really been doing his job protecting the princess. Had he let his emotions distract him, throw him off guard? How had he missed them? Those thoughts galled him, but he wasn't about to make excuses for himself, except to say, "Whoever they are, they're damn good at keeping to the shadows, better than anyone I've ever seen. Better even than Callahan."

Walker's eyes widened, and Trace laughed without humor. "Yeah. Go figure. It's not a constant thing, that much I *can* tell you. Sometimes they're there, but not always. I got the first twitch yesterday, but once that sank in I realized I'd seen the same car last week." He paused, then added honestly, "For all I know it could have started before then. Maybe even months ago. You know how it is. Nothing you can put your finger on, just a gut reaction, like when you found out you were being tailed. Like when you knew your truck had been tampered with."

Agents of Michael Vishenko within the New World Militia had rigged Walker's truck with gelignite—*turn the key, step on the gas, and boom!*—was how Walker had referred to it, trying to make light of the situation.

The bomb in his truck hadn't exploded because Walker's sixth sense had warned him something was wrong even before he knew exactly what. That's when he'd noticed the thin film of dust missing from the hood of the truck, dust that should have been there. He'd been quick to warn Ryan Callahan, too. Callahan was the sheriff of Black Rock, Wyoming, and Trace had been guarding him at the time. It was very possible Walker had saved both their lives because Callahan's official sheriff's SUV in Black Rock had also been rigged that night with the same type of explosives as Walker's truck in Denver.

Callahan and Walker had been targets of Michael Vishenko and the revived New World Militia, as had Trace and Nick D'Arcy, along with two federal prosecutors who were—unfortunately—now dead.

Six names had been on Vishenko's personal hit list to avenge his father, David Pennington. But Vishenko had only succeeded in eliminating two of them, and not even the two he most wanted dead. That would be Callahan and Walker, who together had killed David Pennington more than eight years ago while saving the woman who was now Callahan's wife.

David Pennington was long dead. Michael Vishenko was now behind bars, and unless his conviction was overturned that's where he would stay for the rest of his natural life. But he still had ties to the Russian *Bratva* through his uncle, Aleksandrov Vishenko. And although the New World Militia had been badly crippled by the prosecutions over the past two years and the loss of Vishenko's fortune, it was still in existence. So the threat to all of them was real.

Now Walker said one word. "Proof?"

"Nada. I got a license plate number yesterday, but it doesn't lead anywhere." He tore the page from his notebook and tossed it onto Walker's desk. "Maybe Keira would have more success than I did. She always could track down the damnedest things no one else could. It's worth a shot anyway."

Walker steepled his fingers and held them against his lips, nodding absently. "So what do you want to do?"

Trace had known when he walked in here what he was going to ask for. It was the perfect opportunity, the perfect out. And it happened to be the truth, so he wouldn't have to disclose anything about the princess and him in order to be taken off the case. "I know I signed up for the whole nine yards, but I think you're going to have to replace me on the team guarding the princess. If someone's gunning for me, she could very easily get caught in the crossfire. And that is *not* going to happen, not if I have anything to say about it."

At Walker's grimace Trace said, "State was wrong— it's not the first time and it won't be the last. But they don't need me to spy on her. She's not involved in the politics of Zakhar in any way. Hell, she's not even in the line of succession. Keira's brothers haven't overheard a single word worth reporting to the State Department in four months, and neither have I. So that part of the assignment is a total bust."

"It won't be easy finding someone to replace you at a moment's notice."

"Let State deal with it. You don't have to sacrifice someone from the agency, do you? They asked for me in the first place because I'm fluent in Zakharan, but the Jones brothers can understand it pretty well so that's no longer a prime concern…"

"I'll see what I can do. When do you want off?"

"Tomorrow too soon?" Trace laughed wryly at his boss's expression. "Just kidding. But if she's in danger because of me, the sooner the better. The fall term ends two and a half weeks from now, and the princess is planning to return to Zakhar for Christmas break. Could you arrange it so that someone else takes over when she returns? Earlier if you can swing it. It's hard enough guarding her as a target because of who she is. But if I have to guard her against *my* enemies as well…"

"You're right," Walker said. "Damn!" He slammed his fist on his desk. "I don't mind replacing you on that team. In fact, a case came up just the other day that's right up your alley, and I had to assign it to someone else because you weren't available. It'll be great having you back with the agency. But if what you suspect is true, if you're in danger, that means Callahan, Keira, and I are, too."

"And Alyssa," Trace said in a soft but deadly voice.

Alyssa's father's face turned hard and cold. "And Alyssa," he agreed in a voice even softer than Trace's. And even more deadly.

Two and a half weeks, Trace told himself as he walked out of Walker's office and headed for the elevator. *At the most. That's all I have left.*

It was devastating knowing that once he was off the assignment he'd never see the princess again. But he'd done the right thing. For her. *Love isn't about what I want, what I need. This is what's best for her.*

So why did it feel as if every instinct was screaming at him, "Don't do it!" He knew the princess was waiting for him to tell her he loved her. For the past four days he'd sensed her patiently waiting. She knew he loved her. *How could she not?* he asked himself. *You all but told her at the cabin last Sunday.* Every time their eyes met, every warm, confiding smile she gave him, told him more than the words she didn't say that she knew he loved her as she loved him. Unconditionally.

He'd badly miscalculated her. Them. The damnable situation they found themselves in. Almost two months ago he'd told himself he could show her how lovable she was and then let her down so gently her heart wouldn't be broken when they parted at the end of the school year. Two months…and a lifetime ago. *Cocky bastard, weren't you?* he told himself. Then in his head he heard the princess saying fiercely, "Do *not* use that word," and he amended his self-criticism from *bastard* to *SOB.*

But it really made no difference, not in his assessment of himself, or the situation. Time was no longer on his side, and he loved her enough to give her up now instead of later. *Being noble?* he jeered at himself, but… *Yeah*, he replied, understanding for the first time how Ryan Callahan could have walked away from Mandy Edwards rather than put her in jeopardy. In Callahan's world a man didn't place the woman he loved in the line of fire. Trace hadn't realized it before, but Callahan's world was also his. He wasn't going to risk seeing his princess in a pool of her own blood, the way Cody had with Keira.

The only problem was, the princess would never understand. Would never agree with him. She was just stubborn enough to refuse to let him leave quietly, not if she knew the truth. Which left him with only two options—walking away without a word, or lying to her.

How could he walk away from her without a word? Just disappear from her life? Let her think he was dead? Or worse, that she meant so little to him he couldn't be bothered to at least tell her goodbye?

He couldn't do it. He couldn't.

But lying to her? God, it went against the grain for him, almost as much as just walking away. She trusted him. Could he make her believe he didn't love her? Could he be that good an actor? Maybe. If he didn't have to look into her eyes when he lied.

The damnable thing was, he'd done exactly what he'd set out to do two months ago—he'd freed his princess to believe in love…just in time to break her heart.

"I'll be off this assignment by the end of the year," Trace told Alec and Liam later that night. He'd asked them to join him in the guest house living room after the princess was in bed for the express purpose of sharing this news with them.

The two brothers exchanged startled glances, then Liam said, "Because of the tail on you." A statement, not a question.

"Yeah. I didn't tell you last night when I asked if anyone was following the princess when you're guarding her. But I have reason to believe I might be the target, not her. There was a case—"

"The case where Keira was shot?" Alec broke in. "That one?"

Trace was glad he wasn't going to have to go into detail because he wouldn't have given them the specifics even if they'd asked. It was still a highly secret case, with *Need to know* stamped all over it. "Yeah. What do you know about it?"

Alec shrugged. "Not a hell of a lot. Keira clammed up when we asked her. Said she couldn't talk about it, and Walker said the same thing. Pissed us off royally at the time. Keira's our baby sister, and knowing she almost died, well...we understood the necessity for the secrecy surrounding that case in theory, but in practice it wasn't easy accepting it. We didn't like not knowing. Neither did our older brothers, Shane and Niall. We wanted to be sure nothing and no one was going to hurt Keira again." His eyes hardened. "Even if we had to take matters into our own hands." Alec paused, and the hard look about his eyes faded somewhat. "But that was a long time ago. Are you sure it's the same organization?"

Trace shook his head. "No. Not sure at all. But I discussed it with Walker today, and he agrees it's a strong possibility. Better safe than sorry, so he's going to talk to the State Department about replacing me on this team no later than the end of the year. Sooner, if possible."

"Does the princess know?" This from Liam.

"Not yet but she will, as soon as I have a definite date. I want to tell her myself, so please don't let on to her that you know." He thought for a moment. "Might be a good idea to tell her first thing tomorrow it's possible she's being followed. We don't know if it's true, and you should tell her that, too—we don't want to alarm her unnecessarily. We just want to put her on her guard, especially since she's driving herself. I've taught her a few defensive driving techniques I hope she'll never need to use, but if she wants to practice them, let her. Just don't say anything about me."

Liam looked as if he was going to ask something, but he glanced at his brother who shook his head slightly. And Trace figured he knew what Liam and Alec were both thinking but wouldn't ask. *How will the princess take the news?*

Trace didn't know exactly how she'd react, but he knew one thing for sure. She wasn't going to take it well. The thought of hurting her made him say more roughly than he meant to, "In the meantime, there's still a chance this doesn't have anything to do with that old case, or with me, so keep your eyes peeled. And make sure she takes a different route to and from school every day, so if she is being tailed they don't latch on to a pattern."

Liam started to protest, and Trace knew he was going to say that they always did that. "Sorry," he said, holding up a hand to cut Liam off. "I know you know what to do. You don't need me to tell you how to do your jobs, but just bear with me, okay? I don't want anything to happen to the princess just because nothing's happened up till now. I don't have a clue how long that tail's been out there. If they're following me that's one thing. It's something completely different if they're following her. I don't have to tell you to be extra careful when you're on duty."

"You're right," Alec replied for both of them, his voice as hard as steel. "You don't have to tell us that."

Damon pressed the button to turn off the encrypted laptop, waited for it to power down, then closed the lid. He tapped an impatient finger against the side for a moment, considering the new orders they'd just received. When Lukas walked into their hotel room ten minutes later carrying a bag of take-out chicken and fixings—spicy chicken for him, original recipe for Damon—Damon was ready. More than ready. Eager, in fact. Almost excited, although being the professional soldier he was he knew better than to let excitement control him. They had trained for this type of covert operation for years, and now the word had been given. The rest of the team was on its way, a rendezvous had been arranged, and a target—a new target—had been designated.

The two men dug into their rapidly cooling dinner, and as they ate Damon relayed their new orders. "Difficult," he told Lukas when he was done. He tore the meat from a chicken leg with strong teeth, then tossed the denuded bone back into the box.

Lukas leaned back in the easy chair drawn up to the hotel room's tiny table. "Difficult?" he murmured as he considered the word. "Yes." He nodded. "And dangerous." He smiled, but the smile didn't soften the hard planes of his face, it just made him look more sinister. More threatening. This was not false advertising. Lukas lived for danger. So did Damon. Why else were they here?

"The slightest mistake could be fatal."

A bark of laughter came from Lukas. "You speak of mistakes with *him* involved?" He shook his head. "You know him. When has he *ever* failed at anything he set out to do? He has meticulously planned this to the last detail, see if I am mistaken. Failure is never an option. Not for *him*."

They spent the next hour discussing various scenarios, different outcomes. They accepted with a shrug that death for one or the other was a possibility, just as they had accepted the potential for death or incarceration with their original mission. Neither had a death wish, but it wasn't something they would dwell on either.

The two men were unusually close, almost like brothers, having come up through the ranks together, and were now part of the same elite cadre. Not just *doing*, but training others. They were not without ambition, but both had eagerly volunteered for this dangerous mission out of a near-fanatical devotion to the man whose word was law to them. They had carried out their original orders with military precision and thoroughness, and treasured the few words of praise they'd received.

Now, with this new mission, they would not only have the opportunity to show what they could really do in a more dangerous and challenging campaign, they would do it under the eagle eye of the man at the helm. What more could an ambitious man ask for?

* * *

Less than a week later Trace got the call he was both hoping for and dreading. The State Department had found a replacement for him—a top notch DSS agent with fifteen years under his belt, including two years guarding the Secretary of State. He didn't speak Zakharan, which was why he hadn't been tapped for the job the first time around, but the DSS was putting him through the same language crash course the Jones brothers had gone through. Keeping the princess safe was still the top priority, and this new man had what it took to do that.

Trace was on duty that Thursday, and had planned to tell the princess as soon as he saw her that when she returned from Zakhar after Christmas break there would be someone new on the team guarding her. But he kept putting it off. Somehow the conversational opening never appeared. He couldn't tell her when she was driving, of course. Even though her driving had vastly improved over when she'd first arrived, there was no point in telling her something that would upset her when she was behind the wheel.

He figured he'd break it to her gently once he had her alone in her office—she had no classes on Thursday after her lecture hall calculus class, just office hours. But first her teaching assistant and then a string of students appeared at her door needing help, and before he knew it the day had zipped by without him breaking the news to her. He started to tell her as they were walking to the parking lot and her SUV, but then he feared she might be too upset to drive after that.

Telling her at the dinner table was impossible. Neither of the Jones brothers was in attendance, but the majority of the princess's household was, so Trace postponed the conversation. *Conversation?* he asked himself. *Confrontation is more like it.* And confrontation was what he wanted to avoid, although he was afraid that's exactly what it would be.

He almost managed to tell her right after dinner, but she disappeared into the kitchen to consult with the chef on duty before he could catch her. And from what he overheard of their conversation in French he knew she would be in there for a while, so he finally gave up.

Coward, he mentally jeered. He knew he *had* to tell her. He'd even rehearsed what he was going to say and how he was going to say it. He just couldn't bring himself to do it. Couldn't bring himself to erase that glowing expression on her face. Couldn't bring himself to hurt her. Not until he absolutely had to.

Tomorrow, he promised himself grimly as he headed to bed early. No matter what, he would tell her tomorrow.

Chapter 13

The covert team came out of the night, garbed in black, cloaked in darkness. The leader, taller than the rest, held up one hand for quiet when they approached the rear gate, although the team was stealth personified. He punched in the access code turning off the active alarm, then silently swung the gate open just far enough for the five men behind him to file through. Alert, their eyes watching in all directions for any sign they'd been spotted, they waited until their leader noiselessly shut the gate and took the point again.

He nodded to them, and they fanned out, each man already knowing his assigned target—this one heading for the stables, that one heading for the garage, and a third standing guard near the rear gate with an earphone plugged into a police scanner, protecting their escape route.

The leader and his two most trusted men made for the main house some distance away, their soft-booted feet making almost no noise in the snow. They stole around the side of the house to the front door. One of the men picked the lock and would have entered, but the leader caught his arm and shook his head. The leader slipped inside, found the alarm pad on the wall near the door with its timed red light blinking, counting down the seconds before the alarm would shrill, and keyed in the access code to turn the interior alarm off.

The house was shrouded in darkness, silent as a tomb. But the leader waited a moment, his hand up-raised to hold his men still, listening closely for any sound of movement. Then he smiled his faint smile. Although the plan had already been discussed in explicit detail, the leader warned his two men with just an exhalation of sound that reached no further than their ears. "Neutralize the household, then follow my lead," he breathed before fading noiselessly into the shadows.

Trace woke instantly when the passive alarm went off. No grogginess—just asleep one minute and sharply alert the next. The digital alarm clock on the night table by his bed glowed in the darkness, telling him it was almost 1:00 a.m. Trace had already automatically reached for his gun even as he was responding to the passive alarm lights blinking above his bed.

The passive system had been his idea. He'd approved the active alarm system already in place before the princess had moved in, but had recommended beefing it up with a supplemental active system, as well as the addition of a complex series of motion sensors. Alec and Liam knew the location of every sensor, which were tied into a sophisticated computer with its own backup power source. The computer not only pinpointed the location of which sensor or sensors had gone off, but was also smart enough to not set off the alarm unless more than one sensor was tripped, so that it wouldn't go off if a rabbit scurried across the lawn. The light panel above his bed told him that not one but five of the exterior sensors had lighted up, and two of the interior ones as well.

They were under attack.

Forty seconds later Trace was dressed and moving silently through the guest house, SIG SAUER in one hand. Even though he was fairly sure neither Alec nor Liam was there because they were both off until Saturday, he quickly checked their bedrooms just in case. He didn't waste any breath cursing when he found their bedrooms empty, just triggered the silent alarm signal to the Boulder police. But he couldn't wait—intruders were already in the main house, and his princess was in peril.

He eased out the back door of the guest house, his senses keenly attuned to every sound, every flickering shadow. *Dark of the moon,* he thought gratefully. He wouldn't have much light to see, but neither would his foes. And he'd been trained by the best. The night was his ally.

He made his way around the back of the guest house, the way he, Alec and Liam had trained in their spare time, in endless variations. Knowing that if time was of the essence, they needed to be prepared to react instantly. Moving through the shadows, he quickly worked his way to the back door off the kitchen, and unlocked it with his key.

This time Trace cursed mentally when he saw the active alarm had been turned off, but he didn't waste any seconds thinking about what that meant, just headed for the princess's bedroom at the back of the house. Even before he got there he saw the door gaping open, and two of the princess's Zakharian bodyguards bound, gagged and out cold beside it. He stealthily made his way toward the open door, flattening himself against the wall just outside.

Eyes flicking every which way, Trace listened intently for sounds from the room, but heard nothing... until the princess gasped. He gripped his gun with both hands to steady his aim, and swung into the open doorway in a two-handed firing stance, confronting the room's occupants. "Federal agent—freeze!"

Two lithe men dressed all in black, with hoods over their heads that concealed everything except for slits for their eyes, stood beside the princess's bed. But she wasn't in it. One of the men easily held her captive with a gun to her head. The second man was crossing her wrists and binding her hands.

Then a third man stepped forward from the shadows beside the bed, taller than the other two but dressed exactly like them. Drawing a knife that glittered in the faint light. Eight inches of wicked steel.

"Drop the gun," the third man hissed at Trace.

"No!" The princess struggled against the arms holding her until the barrel of the gun was pressed against her temple. Trace couldn't see her expression in the darkness, but despite her brave front he knew she had to be terrified.

He considered his options in the space of three heartbeats, and discarded them all except one. He raised his hands in a universal gesture of surrender, then flicked the safety back on his gun and slowly lowered his gun hand until he could drop his weapon on the carpeted floor.

"Kick it away," the man with the knife ordered, still in that whispered hiss, and Trace obeyed. The gun was still threatening the princess, but Trace knew this wasn't an assassination attempt. If it was the princess would be dead already. *Kidnapping*, he thought, his mind going on autopilot. But that was bad enough. When trapped, kidnappers could be just as deadly as assassins. And if they managed to escape with their victim the odds of recovering the victim alive weren't good. Especially not when the victim was an adult and able to testify.

The problem was, he didn't know how many of them there were besides these three. And the meaning of the disabled alarm was flashing a warning signal in his mind. *Inside job.* He remembered the princess saying, *"There is always a chance that this man is not loyal, or that man carries a secret agenda. Even within my own household, within my own bodyguards, who can say for sure?"*

But the Boulder police were on the way. *Time,* Trace thought. *If I can stall them long enough...*

"You're not taking her out of here," he told the man with the knife, his voice cold and determined.

"Who is to stop us?" the man hissed. "You?"

Trace didn't answer. He merely moved fractionally so the men would have to pass him to get to the door, but at the same time making sure he could see if someone else tried to enter the room.

A shadowy movement from the open doorway and a *pssst* drew the attention of the three kidnappers as well as Trace. The sound was followed by one word in Zakharan, "Police!"

The taller man, obviously the leader, slipped into place behind the princess and took control, one powerful arm encircling her waist. He still held the knife in his other hand—not directly touching the princess anywhere, but a definite threat. He made a motion with his head and the other two men slid obediently from the room. Trace let them go, his attention riveted on the princess and the man holding her prisoner.

When the others were safely out of reach, their faint footsteps no longer audible, the third man moved blindingly fast. He pushed the princess toward the bed and darted for the door, but Trace was already waiting for him. The knife slashed once and Trace danced back out of range, then closed on the man, grasping the man's knife hand above the wrist in an iron grip. The two men were equally matched in strength and determination. And while the black garbed man had the knife, Trace had seen a gun held to the head of the woman he loved and had seen her threatened with the knife held by this man—his repressed fury over those images coalesced into a steely resolve not to let this man escape, too.

They struggled for endless seconds, strength against

strength. Then out of the corner of his eye Trace saw a shadow move from the doorway. He tried to shift, to turn so the man he was fighting had his back to the door, but it was too late. Something crashed down on Trace's left shoulder, and his grip on the knife hand slackened momentarily. It was just enough for the man in black to twist free.

He feinted at Trace, but then someone else was there between them. "No!" Small bound hands pushed the knife away from Trace's chest, and when the blade was jerked back the princess cried out in pain.

The soft curse issuing from the other man's mouth barely registered in Trace's consciousness, and he was gone before Trace could close with him again. Then the only sounds were footsteps running lightly down the hallway…and a tiny moan close by. Part of him wanted to give chase, but he needed to see how badly the princess was injured before he did anything else.

He clicked on the light switch and saw her crouched on the floor cradling her bound hands against her body. Blood seeped from between the tightly clenched fingers of her left hand and stained her nightgown, but she didn't seem to care about that. "You are okay?" she asked Trace anxiously, her gaze running over him from head to toe. "He did not hurt you?"

Her question sliced through him, and he didn't trust himself to answer. He knelt beside her and quickly unbound her wrists, noting automatically and filing away the fact that they weren't tightly, cruelly tied. It was something to think about. Later. Not now.

He tried to take her left hand in his, and she resisted

at first. "Let me see it, Princess," he said softly, prying her fingers open with gentle hands. Then he cursed fluently under his breath. The knife blade had left a gash across the entire palm. It wasn't deep, but it was long and still bleeding. Trace knew that at the very least it would leave a hell of a scar, and might possibly involve some nerve damage.

He curled her fingers closed to contain the bleeding and stood up. A minute later he was back with a clean washcloth and a towel. He used the washcloth as a pressure bandage, then wrapped the towel carefully around her fist before knotting it securely. "That'll hold until we get you to the hospital, but it's going to need stitches, maybe even surgery."

He drew the princess to her feet and sat her in the armchair in the corner of the room—away from the windows—then picked up the phone and dialed 911. When he was done he told her, "The ambulance is on its way. How do you feel? Light-headed? Dizzy?"

She shook her head. "I am fine."

She wasn't fine, and the bloodstains on her nightgown bore mute testimony to that fact. "Stay here," he said in a voice that came out more harshly than he knew. "Keep that hand elevated and don't try to stand up—I don't want to come back and find you out cold on the floor. I won't be long, I'm just going to see if anyone else was injured, and open the gate for the police."

Trace sat in the emergency waiting room, staring futilely at his hands as he waited to hear about the princess. His left shoulder ached abominably, but he hadn't bothered to have anyone at the hospital look at it. He'd received his share of injuries over the years, and knew his body well enough to know there'd be a bad bruise, but nothing worse than that. Nothing compared to the injury the princess had suffered.

He'd been in touch with the Boulder police, who had been and gone, then reported back to him that they had found next to nothing. No DNA evidence. No fingerprints. Just a few footprints in the snow, two overpowered Zakharian bodyguards, and two disabled active alarm systems. He'd already contacted the DSS and called the Jones brothers to bring them up to speed. Then he'd called Walker, waking him from a sound sleep, and gotten the agency involved. Even if the Boulder police couldn't find anything, it was still possible the agency might uncover something, but he wasn't holding his breath.

The more he thought about it, the more convinced he was it couldn't be anything except an inside job. If it was the last thing he did, he was going to find out who it was. Someone was going to pay. Someone was going to pay dearly for every drop of blood the princess had shed…protecting him.

Trace stood in Cody Walker's office early Saturday morning, the second time he'd been there in less than two weeks. He'd asked his boss to meet him at the agency instead of going to the house because he had to raise a question—not an easy question, but one he couldn't ignore—and he didn't want Keira around when he asked it. He knew that if Walker couldn't help him find the answer no one could. Next to his former boss, Nick D'Arcy, there was no one he respected more than Cody Walker.

"This can't go beyond this office," he told his boss flat out. He drew a breath, then added, "Keira can't know I'm even thinking along these lines, so you can't tell her. You can't even let her *suspect* I'm thinking it."

Walker's expression had been serious before because he'd known something was up, but now his face hardened and his blue eyes turned cold. "So you're going down that road," he said softly.

Trace made an impatient gesture. "I've got no choice. The State Department and the DSS are investigating. The Boulder police are investigating. Even the agency gave the estate a thorough once over. But you already know that except for the disabled alarm systems everyone has come up with squat. It's an inside job—nothing else makes sense. There are only two people I *know* aren't involved—the princess is one. I'm the other." One corner of his mouth quirked up into an ironic smile. "And the State Department and the DSS aren't so sure about me. But I am."

"I am, too."

"Thanks for the vote of confidence," Trace said sincerely. "But where does that leave me? Only a few people knew the alarm codes, and Keira's brothers are on the list. They were both off duty, which looks suspicious…if you've got a suspicious mind. And I do."

Walker nodded. "I do, too."

Trace grimaced. "I can't rule out either of them as suspects, and God knows I want to. Everything in me says they're innocent, but without some kind of proof they're not involved… Hell. What am I supposed to do? I changed the alarm codes immediately, of course. But I had to give the new codes to Alec and Liam—Alec's on duty today and tomorrow, then Liam Monday and Tuesday. If one or the other is involved—or both—I don't think they'll let anything happen when one of them is guarding her, especially now—that would be too suspicious. And I just don't see either of the Jones brothers letting suspicion fall on the other one. They're pretty close. Besides, it's too soon after the first attempt. So I think the princess is safe until I go back on duty on Wednesday. *If* they're involved. If they're not, who knows if she's safe for a single minute?"

"You want me to ask the State Department to beef up her security?"

"They're already working on that. The DSS has a plan. And the Boulder police department is adding an extra ride-by patrol at night. I can't fault their response time the other night—they got there damn quick—but that extra patrol won't hurt."

"Then what? You want me to have Keira's brothers pulled off the assignment? Replace them?"

Trace made a sound of frustration and sank into one of the chairs in front of Walker's desk. "Hell, I don't know. What would you tell State and the DSS?" he said, playing devil's advocate. "That one or both of them *might* be involved? Ruin their careers when I haven't got even a shred of proof? When it's more likely one or more of the Zakharians who work for her? They had the codes, too." He recounted what the princess had told him about why her brother had sent her to the

US, and about not really trusting anyone—not among her household or her bodyguards. "God, I can't imagine what that's like," he said, shaking his head, "wondering if the people who're supposed to protect you are going to betray you."

He sat lost in thought for a moment, then continued. "And if the Jones brothers are innocent, then I've just put the princess in more danger because she knows them and trusts them a hell of a lot more than she trusts her Zakharian bodyguards. And they've done a damn good job until now. I'll be gone by the time she returns from Christmas break, and I don't want to leave her with total strangers. Not if I don't have to."

"Okay," Walker said in that reasonable way he had. "Let's go over it from the top then. Together. Walk me through everything that happened. Let's see if we can spot something. If we can rule Keira's brothers out, we'll both feel a lot better." He added drily, "I'll be damned if I want to break news like this to Keira."

Twenty minutes later Walker picked up a pen from his desk and leaned back in his chair. A hint of a smile tugged at the corners of his mouth and he whistled tunelessly.

"What?" Trace demanded. "What did I miss?"

"I think you were just too close to it." His eyes met Trace's. "And your personal involvement isn't helping your objectivity."

Trace froze. "I don't know what the hell you're talking about."

"If that's the way you want to play it, fine," Walker

said. "But I'll tell you exactly what Callahan told me two and a half years ago when I was falling for Keira. 'Just don't let it get in the way of the job. You can't fight what you feel. But you *can* lock it away. I know.' And the hell of it was, he was right." He laughed softly. "The hell of it is, Callahan's *always* right, damn him."

When Trace didn't respond, Walker said, "Okay, forget I ever brought it up and focus on what you just told me."

Trace replayed everything in his mind and was just about to shake his head, indicating he wasn't seeing what Walker was seeing, when the light popped on. "If the Jones brothers are involved, why weren't all three security systems disarmed?" he asked softly. "Why was the passive system left on? That doesn't make sense. It's as if someone wanted the alarm tripped. As if someone wanted me to respond to the intrusion."

"Exactly. If either of them gave the access codes to the intruders, why not give all of them? If the passive alarm hadn't gone off, those men would have succeeded in kidnapping the princess and getting clean away. You wouldn't have known a thing until it was too late."

"Also, why weren't the princess's hands bound tightly?" Trace added. "It didn't even take me a minute to untie her. And why wasn't her mouth taped? Real kidnappers wouldn't give a damn about hurting her, and they would have wanted to make sure she didn't cry out, call for help."

"Right again."

A thought occurred to Trace and he voiced it. "You

don't think the State Department… No, that doesn't make sense. Does it?"

"Some kind of convoluted plot to make the king of Zakhar think someone's trying to kidnap his sister? What would that accomplish?" Walker chuckled wryly. "Except make him *not* trust us to protect her?"

"Not that exactly," Trace said slowly. "But what if the State Department wanted him worried about his sister's safety? And at the same time, wanted to make him grateful to us for saving her? That tracks, doesn't it? You said when you asked me to take this assignment that Zakhar is critically important to the US's strategic plan for NATO and Europe. And if the king is grateful to us…" He deliberately left the sentence unfinished. "I know those men spoke a few words in Zakharan," he added, "but that could have been a ploy to make the princess think they were Zakharian nationals—something she'd be sure to mention to her brother—so he wouldn't suspect a setup."

Walker cursed fluently, then said, "I hate to say it, but there's sort of a crazy logic to the idea. It makes as much sense as anything else makes sense, I guess." He tossed the pen he was playing with back onto the desk. "Damn it. That means Keira's brothers could still be involved."

"Yeah." The two men exchanged serious looks. "But if so," Trace said, "at least they were acting under orders from our government, and not selling out the princess."

"You really think…"

After a minute Trace shook his head, quashing the possibility he'd just raised. "No, not really. Some smart idiot in the State Department might have cooked up the plan, but if so, why not bring me into the loop? Too dangerous not to, don't you think? I could have killed one or more of those men. Easily. They couldn't possibly predict what I'd do, how I'd react in that situation. If bullets started flying, the princess could have been killed or gravely injured. And that would have serious negative consequences for our government. Besides, I don't think Alec and Liam would have gone for it, even if they were ordered to. They're too smart. They would have seen the same holes in the logic that I just did, and they would nix it immediately."

"That brings us right back to the question of why. Why was the passive alarm system left on?"

Trace let his breath out in a whoosh. "No idea. But at least I can cross Keira's brothers off my suspect list. That's a load off my mind."

Walker hesitated, then said, "I think I'll run a little background check on them anyway. It won't hurt, and Keira doesn't have to know. And I'll bet you anything they're telling the DSS the same thing—to run a background check on you, just in case."

Trace laughed under his breath. "Yeah. No bet." Then his expression turned serious. "The next question is, what has the State Department told the king? They had to tell him something—he and the princess are really close. They talk fairly often on the phone, and I'm sure she wouldn't keep something like this from him."

"I can find out for you."

"Thanks. I'd appreciate it."

Trace had jumped up and was heading for the door

when Walker stopped him with a question. "You still want off the assignment, right?"

Trace turned, his hand on the doorknob. "That hasn't changed. Besides, the State Department has already lined up my replacement. Didn't you know?"

"Yeah, but this is still your assignment until he comes on board in January. I wasn't sure if this incident had changed your mind or not."

Trace shook his head. The self-recriminations he'd submerged during his conversation with his boss came roaring back as he remembered how he'd failed to protect the princess. As he remembered the blood staining her nightgown. As he remembered the seventeen stitches that had been required to close the wound she'd received trying to protect him.

"It's possible the tail on you isn't related to Vishenko or the New World Militia after all," Walker said. "I spoke with Callahan yesterday, and he's sure no one's following him or his family. And if he says he's sure, I believe him. So maybe it's related to the kidnapping attempt. Have you considered that?"

"I thought about it," Trace said grimly. "I've done nothing *but* think about it. I even wondered if someone was trying to maneuver me into thinking I was putting the princess in danger so I'd withdraw from the team. They might be gambling it would be easier to get to her if I'm not around. Anything's possible. But no matter what, I still need off."

"Because of that personal involvement you're *not* having with the princess?" Walker shot at him. A question for which Trace had no answer.

Chapter 14

Finals week was almost over, and since Mara had no finals to give on Friday, she gathered up all the books and personal items she wanted to take with her to Zakhar and packed them in her briefcase on Thursday afternoon. The next week was Christmas, but she had delayed her scheduled departure until the morning of Christmas Eve, wanting as much time with Trace as she could possibly manage before she left. Andre had been understanding—he had assured her one of Zakhar's royal air force planes would be available to her whenever she was ready.

She hadn't asked Trace to reconsider his decision not to go with her to Zakhar. She'd thought about it after the last time at his cabin, but ever since the kidnapping attempt last week he'd been...unapproachable. Distant.

And for much of the time he simply hadn't been around to ask. He'd gone with her to the hospital after the attack, then had accompanied her home and watched over her in silence, pulling a chair up beside her bed and sitting in it until she fell asleep.

He'd still been there when she'd awakened two hours later. He hadn't argued with her when she'd insisted on going to school—it was the last day of classes before finals, she'd told him, and she couldn't possibly be absent. He'd just looked at her with shadowed eyes, red-rimmed from lack of sleep, and said three words in a tone of voice that brooked no defiance, "You're not driving."

Her chauffeur had driven Trace and her to and from the university that Friday. Mara refused to admit it to Trace, but she was completely exhausted by dinnertime, and fell asleep right afterward. When she woke Saturday morning Alec was there and Trace had disappeared. He hadn't returned until late Tuesday night, long after she'd gone to bed. He'd shown up for duty right on time yesterday morning and did his job with his usual thoroughness and efficiency, but the man she'd come to know, the man hidden inside the one the rest of the world saw, was gone.

He wouldn't even talk to her. She'd tried to initiate a conversation with him yesterday, but after several monosyllabic answers she'd given up. And today was no better. He hadn't uttered a single word other than what was absolutely necessary. Now he sat in a chair by the door, ostensibly reading one of the three newspapers he always carried with him, but he hadn't turned a page for the past hour.

Mara sighed and double-checked the grades she'd already posted via computer. No mistakes there. She felt a little thrill of pride that every one of her students had done no worse than pass. She had her share of weak students in her calculus class, not to mention her share of malingerers, but somehow she'd pulled it off. Her tests weren't easy, and she had a reputation as a tough but fair grader. Mathematics wasn't a "fuzzy" subject, after all—the answers were what the answers were, and that was that. But she'd patiently tutored the weak students, and somehow had managed to either inspire the malingerers or put the fear of God into them—not a single student had failed. And she had a handful of incredibly gifted students in her graduate classes who were her pride and joy as a professor.

Her professional life was in splendid shape, and she could hardly wait for Christmas break to be over so she could get back to teaching next semester. It was only her personal life that was in a shambles—because of the man sitting like an immovable block of granite right beside her office door.

She checked her email one last time, posted her congratulations to her students on her blog along with a "see you next year" farewell message using only the fingers of her right hand, then shut her laptop off and packed it away in her computer bag. She fetched her parka from the stand, shrugged it on and zipped it up. She pulled the woolen mitten she wore over the bandage on her left hand from her pocket. She briefly considered asking Trace to help her because the bandage made it awkward to get the mitten on, but decided against it and struggled on her own until she was successful. Then she pulled her right glove out of her other pocket and donned it, too. With nothing left to do, she finally had no choice but to speak to Trace. "I am ready to go."

He stood immediately, folded the newspapers she knew he hadn't really been reading, and shoved them into the backpack he carried to help him blend into the crowd of college students on campus. He drew his ski jacket on but didn't zip it up—unless the weather was too severe he always left his jacket open for quick access to his SIG SAUER. When the weather was bad the pistol was moved to his jacket pocket and his hand stayed on it the entire time, but it wasn't too cold today. He slung the backpack over his left shoulder. "Ready," he told her. But his eyes refused to meet hers.

When Mara had first started teaching at the university she had naturally expected her bodyguards to assist her with lugging all her paraphernalia between the SUV and her office, but she had quickly learned that was something they never did. Alec had explained it to her the very first day he accompanied her to school. It wasn't that they were being rude or inconsiderate— their job was to keep her safe. That meant keeping their gun hands free and their eyes alert for danger signs. Being weighted down with her computer bag or briefcase would make them less effective as bodyguards, and was simply out of the question.

It was second nature now for her to carry her own things, so even though her left hand was still mostly unusable she slung the strap of her computer bag over her shoulder, grabbed her briefcase and purse with her right hand, and followed Trace from her office. She set everything down and pulled the door shut behind her, testing it to make sure it was locked, before picking her things up again.

When she turned around she saw that Trace was watching the nearly deserted hallway with hooded eyes. Not even in the early weeks of the semester had he looked as hard and cold as this, and Mara sighed. *There is nothing I can do about it now,* she told herself. *But when we get home...I have to talk to him. I have to find out what is wrong. If I do not, he will probably disappear as he did last week, and I will not see him again until he comes back on duty next week. Then I will only have one day with him before I leave.*

Maybe his pride was bruised because she'd been injured in the attempted kidnapping, just as Keira had been a few years ago when she'd taken a bullet meant for another man. Was that why he refused to talk to her? Was he feeling responsible because he'd failed to protect her? Didn't Trace understand he *had* kept her safe? That he had foiled the kidnapping attempt—one man against three—and that she owed him her life?

She remembered the nightmare terror that had gripped her when she'd been dragged from her bed and known she was being kidnapped, terror that had changed into something even more terrifying when she thought Trace might be killed. If that had happened she wouldn't have cared what happened to her. A cut hand was a small price to pay when compared to his life. She had only done the same thing Keira would have done, after all. Somehow she had to make him understand.

They walked in silence to the faculty parking lot. On Monday Liam had suggested that with the injury to her left hand it might be best for her chauffeur to continue driving, but Mara had stubbornly refused. "I will just drive slower," she had insisted. "I will be careful." It wasn't as if she couldn't use her left hand at all, she just had to be careful not to pull the stitches loose.

Liam wasn't to know, nor Alec either, and especially not Trace, but she was trying very hard to wean herself away from reliance on the household staff that had been such a part and parcel of her life up until now. She'd had no choice the Friday before, not in the face of Trace's adamant stance on not letting her drive. But she wasn't completely incapacitated, and she didn't need her chauffeur to drive her. She was trying her best to become as self-sufficient as most American women, and one woman in particular.

When she started out she had it in her mind to pattern herself on Keira Walker. The two women had become friends of sorts in the past few months, and since Mara knew Trace thought the world of Keira, what better role model could she pick? Trace didn't know it, but weeks ago she'd started taking cooking lessons from her French chefs on the days Trace wasn't on duty. Alec and Liam had been amused, but had willingly eaten her modest efforts. It wasn't until she'd let it slip to them that she was trying to become more like Keira that Alec laughingly told her, "Keira can't cook. Our mom gave up trying to teach her because she refused to learn."

Mara had been taken aback by that, but not daunted. So maybe cooking wasn't a skill Keira had ever acquired, but it would still make Mara more able to function on her own if she had to. And she wanted to prove to Trace she didn't need a large household staff to survive. Otherwise, how would he ever come to believe she could be anything other than the princess she was? How would he ever realize the only one she truly needed in her life was him?

The drive home was as silent as the drive to work had been, and Mara had plenty of time to think. Trace's refusal to talk to her hurt, but it gave her the opportunity to consider long and hard about what was really important to her, and what she would willingly give up to keep him in her life.

Money was something she had always taken for granted. When she turned twenty-one she'd inherited a sizeable fortune from her mother, much of which resided in a trust. She didn't need the salary she earned as a professor at the university, and in fact had arranged to donate her salary anonymously to the general scholarship fund. Andre paid for her bodyguards since they were all in the Zakharian military, but she easily paid for the rest of her staff and all the household expenses out of the income she earned on the trust's invested principal. But she knew from things she'd read that some American men could be touchy about money, particularly when the woman had it and they didn't.

Trace was a proud man. A self-made man. Everything he had he'd earned himself, and Mara admired him tremendously for it. Most of her principal was in an unbreakable trust that benefited her and any heirs she might have, and if she died without issue the trust would revert to Andre and his heirs. But there was enough money under her personal control to give a proud man pause. "Fortune hunter" was an ugly title, but one she knew the tabloids wouldn't hesitate to use. She'd lived her whole life as a target of the tabloids, but Trace hadn't, and she had to shield him if she could.

To do that she had to convince him she could survive on a lot less. All she really needed was enough money to maintain her stable. Trace *couldn't* ask her to give up Suleiman—he loved riding as much as she did, and she had it in her mind to provide him with a mount worthy of him, a mount to equal Suleiman so they could race together like the wind. But other than that her needs were few. A chance to teach, to share her love of mathematics with her students. A chance to write, to leave something of herself to posterity. And Trace. She needed him. Needed his love. More than anything else she needed his love.

Then a thought occurred to her, startling in its simplicity, but something that should have occurred to her a long time ago. *Maybe the reason he never told you he loves you all this time is because of the money. Maybe he is afraid people will think the worst. Maybe he is afraid you will think the worst, too. Maybe he is waiting for you to say something first because of that.*

By the time they got home Mara had convinced herself her supposition was the truth. She turned to Trace the minute they walked in the front door and forced him to meet her eyes. "We must talk."

He stared at her, impassive. Then he said, "You're right. I've been putting it off, but…"

Mara glanced around the front hallway and saw two of her staff passing through. "Privately," she said in an undertone. He nodded, and she added, "Give me five minutes to take off my things. I will meet you in my sitting room." She didn't wait for acknowledgment, just headed for her bedroom. She dumped briefcase, purse and computer bag unceremoniously on the chair beside her bed, and in frantic haste removed her jacket, mitten, glove and glasses, leaving them lying on the bed.

She hurried to the bathroom and wasted a minute rubbing away the little indentations her glasses left, and tucking in the stray tendrils of hair that had escaped her careful chignon. Then she stared at her reflection for another half a minute, wishing she was as beautiful as Trace was handsome. A wasted wish. She pressed her lips firmly together and gathered up her courage. "He loves me as I am," she reminded herself solemnly. "I am beautiful in his eyes."

If Eve had looked like you, Adam would have gladly left Eden. Trace had said those words to her less than three weeks ago. And he had meant them, she knew it. He'd bared his soul to her that day. Now it was time for her to do the same. She headed straight for the sitting room before her courage failed her.

Trace had steeled himself for the upcoming confrontation, but he was afraid of what the princess might say if he let her start the conversation. So the minute she entered the room he whirled to face her. But as his gaze focused on the white gauze bandage wrapped around her palm, the words that came out of his mouth weren't the ones he'd planned to say. "Why the hell did you do it?" he asked her abruptly. "Don't you know any better than to get in the middle of a knife fight?"

He couldn't drag his eyes away from that bandage, beneath which were those seventeen stitches. The cut had been straight and not too deep, and thankfully hadn't required surgery, but each stitch was an indictment of him, and what he had failed to do. His anger at himself made him lash out at her. "Don't you know any better than to grab at a blade that way with your bare hand?"

She stared at him for long seconds as if taken aback by his accusation. As if she had no idea this was what he'd wanted to talk to her about. "I thought he was going to hurt you," she said finally, in a low voice. "I thought you might be killed."

Trace swore, and she flinched. "It's my job to keep *you* safe," he said. "Not the other way around."

"Do you think I care about that?" she asked intensely. "Do not talk to me about whose job it is to protect whom when I know I am more to you than a job."

He swallowed hard and turned his back on her so he didn't have to see her pain. It had to be now—he would never have a better opportunity. But he couldn't look into her eyes and lie to her. "No," he said. "You're a job. One I should have taken more seriously. That's why I'm angry you risked your life. If anything had happened to you it would be a black mark against me, and I could kiss my career goodbye."

She hesitated. "And love? Where does that fit in?"

Still with his back to her, he pretended he was staring

out at the landscape through the window even though it was nearly too dark to see anything except his own reflection. The face of the man in the glass was the face of a stranger. As if he were standing outside of himself Trace answered, "It doesn't."

She moved quickly, coming to stand in front of him, forcing him to look at her. The expression in her eyes was one he'd seen once before, the night she'd struggled to save Suleiman. And he knew she wasn't giving up without a fight, not when she loved him with every fiber of her being. Exactly what he'd feared. "I love you," she said in a rush. "You must know. And you love me."

"That's what I was afraid you were thinking. That's why I've asked to be reassigned."

"Reassigned?" She stared at him in shock. "You... you are leaving?"

He nodded. "I'll finish out this month, but come January someone else will replace me on the team guarding you." When she didn't say anything he tried to break it off gently. "What you feel isn't love, Princess. You would have felt the same toward any man who—"

She cut him off, her voice low and fierce. "No!"

He continued as if she hadn't spoken. "Toward any man who showed you what your body was capable of. It just happened to be me. But don't fool yourself it's love you're feeling—you would react the same way with any other man."

"You cannot believe that," she whispered, obviously appalled. "I could never...no other man..."

Her expression tore at him, weakening his resolve, and he had to remind himself of all the reasons why they could never be together. "Okay, maybe what we had wasn't just…sex." He caught himself before he could reach out and caress her cheek at the stricken look in her eyes. "Maybe it was…special…in its own way. But it was going to end sooner or later. We both knew that. A year from now you'll look back on this as a pleasant interlude, but not something to build a life on. You'll meet someone you really love, and forget all about—"

"That is not true!"

He overrode her vehement interruption. "You'll forget all about the special agent assigned to guard you. Just as I'll forget about you."

"No," she said, shaking her head with determination. "You love me." She placed her hand over her heart and tapped lightly. "I know it here. You will not forget me any more than I will forget you."

He schooled his expression into one as hard as his voice. "I don't love you."

"You are lying to me." Her voice broke as she pleaded, "Why are you lying to me?"

"Why can't you just accept the truth?" he said harshly. "I had a job to do. That's all. I shouldn't have taken advantage of your inexperience, but I did, and I'm sorrier than I can ever tell you. I broke a cardinal rule in my line of work—never let yourself get personally involved. Never let yourself fall—" he corrected himself quickly "—get attached to the person you're guarding. I regret it more than you'll ever know, and it has to end. I'm moving on. End of story."

She took a step toward him. "You are not like that," she whispered on the edge of tears. "I *know* you are

not. You are lying and I want to know why." She stared
at him for endless seconds. Then a light came into her
eyes, her face. "You are trying to be noble. Yes! That
is like you. You think I have not thought it through,
loving you, and you are trying to be noble. But you are
wrong. I—"

Desperate to convince her, Trace said brutally, "You
just don't get it, do you? Do I have to draw you a picture? The State Department didn't just *happen* to pick
me to be your bodyguard. I'm not a DSS agent like the
Jones brothers—they couldn't just assign me. They had
to borrow me from the agency I really work for. If you
don't believe me, you can ask Walker."

She stared at him. "Why?" She barely breathed the
question. "Why did they…"

"Because women find me attractive, damn it!" He
threw the words at her like stones, and he suddenly realized he could tell her the truth…the truth that was
also a lie, but which just might do the trick. "Because
they wanted me to seduce you!"

She stood there pale and still, as if carved in marble. Then she blinked. "Seduce…" She shook her head
slowly. "I…I must be very stupid because I do not…
Why? Why me?"

"Leverage," he said, with a cynical twist to his lips.
"Zakhar is politically important, and…" He let her fill
in the blanks for herself.

"Leverage." There was no emotion in her voice. No
tears in her eyes. Just a face deathly white. "Then…
those times at your cabin…?"

"You made my job easy." Trace bitterly regretted that

statement as soon as he'd uttered it, and he wanted to take it back. But it was already too late.

She blinked again, but that was the only sign she'd heard him. "I...see," she said eventually, her eyes very dark in her pale, expressionless face. She opened her mouth to speak, and for just a second her bottom lip quivered, but she caught it with her teeth and bit it into submission. There was blood on her lip when her teeth finally let it go, and she asked in a voice barely above a whisper, "Photographs?"

Raw pain savaged him, talons ripping into his heart. He couldn't have lied to her about that to save his soul. But his silence was enough.

"I see," she said again. She stood immobile for a moment, her lips parted as if she wanted to say something else, but she didn't. The thin line of blood on her bottom lip bore mute testimony to the control she had exerted on herself. Then she licked her lips, tasting the blood there, and Trace tasted despair when he saw it.

Mara touched a finger to her lip as if she'd just realized what she'd done, then stared at the blood on her fingertip for endless seconds. She whispered something in Zakharan that sliced through Trace like a razor, but she'd already turned away and didn't see his reaction.

He fought the overwhelming desire to call her back, to tell her it was all lies, every word, that he loved her more than life itself. That he would *never* betray her love in that degrading fashion. But he'd chosen his course deliberately. He *had* to be cruel in order to drive her away. Now, before it was too late. Before she ended up dead or injured again because of him. Before he took what she ached to give him and he ached to have.

His eyes burned, but at first he didn't recognize what it meant—it was so long since he'd cried. But he knew he would never forget her last words to him. Would never forget the desolate emptiness in her voice when she said, "I should have known I could not be loved."

Chapter 15

Mara stood at her bedroom window, staring out at nothing in the gathering darkness. Wondering why everything seemed so distant. Wondering why the woman reflected in the pane of glass didn't weep. She touched her right hand to the image on the glass, and wondered why she didn't feel the cold seeping through the window to her skin. Wondered why she felt absolutely nothing.

She glanced at her bandaged left hand, but it was as if it belonged to someone else—another woman, not her. Some other woman had grabbed at the knife to push it away from the heart of the man she loved. Some other woman had felt the blade slice into her flesh. Some other woman had felt the blood gush, warm and sticky, between the fingers she clenched tightly against the blood and pain. And some other woman had anxiously asked Trace, *You are okay? He did not hurt you?*

Some other woman. Not her.

She leaned her forehead against the cold window, and her warm breath misted the glass, hiding her reflection from view. Somewhere beneath her frozen emotions something moved, and memories crowded in. Memories that made her shiver as the cold could not. Memories that threatened her fragile control.

Trace touching her with loving, lying hands, stroking her, making her cry out his name as pleasure burst through her body for the first time. *Click.* And a photograph was taken. Herself bending over Trace, touching him with her hands, her lips, taking him into her mouth and loving him the only way she could think of, the only way he would let her. *Click.* And a photograph was taken. Trace caressing her bare nipples through the veil of her hair, making her tremble with a rolling tide of love and desire. *Click.* And a photograph was taken.

Each click in her head was like a lash against her heart, and she flinched again and again, fighting the memories and what they meant. Fighting to keep the pain at bay. Fighting to keep the ice shield in place. Because what lay on the other side of that shield was too terrible to contemplate.

Click. Click. Click.

Suddenly she knew she couldn't stay here. Not another day. She would rather smash the window and slash her wrists against the shards of glass than see Trace again, knowing the truth about him…and about herself. The truth her father had tried to teach her. The truth

Andre had repeatedly denied. The truth she'd fought against accepting when she'd fallen in love with Trace and resolved to earn his love if she could. Until now.

Worthless. Nothing as herself, just a tool, a means to an end, a way of controlling her brother. A way of insuring his "loyalty." Just a pawn in someone's macabre, twisted game of political espionage.

Click. Click. Click.

She darted to the purse she'd dumped with her briefcase on the chair by her bed when she'd come home from work, and fumbled in it until she found her cell phone. She thought for a moment, trying but failing to remember what time it was in Zakhar. Then she realized it didn't matter, and pressed the one number she had on speed dial.

After a minute a deep voice sounded in her ear in the musical cadence of Zakharan…the sound of home. "Mara?" Andre asked, and though he didn't say it she knew she had woken him. When she didn't answer, he asked, "What is it, *dernya*? Is something wrong?"

The loving concern, the use of the endearing nickname only he used, shattered the ice encasing her. "Andre," she began, but then tears clogged her throat and she sobbed.

"Mara!" She could hear the anguish in the way he spoke her name, and knew she had to tell him…something.

She sank to her knees beside the chair, her legs no longer able to support her, and fought the sobs wracking her body until she could speak coherently. "I need to come home," she managed in a voice that shook with grief. "Please, Andre. Please send a plane for me. Now. Tonight. I cannot stay here. I need to come home. *Please.*"

How long she knelt by the chair after she'd hung up the phone she never knew. But her body was stiff and aching when she finally stood up. There were no more tears. Tears were a luxury she couldn't afford. She needed to start preparing to leave, needed to mobilize her household, needed to think of everything that had to be done. And to do that she needed to be strong. Strong…like Keira. *No, not like Keira.* Keira made her think of Trace. And she couldn't think of Trace. Not now. Not ever again.

Click. Click. Click.

Trace keyed in the electronic code to open the estate's driveway gate, and thrummed his fingers impatiently on the steering wheel until the gate was open and he could drive through. Then he electronically closed the gate securely behind him. He drove up the winding driveway and parked his truck in front of the guest house, noting absently that the four-wheel drive Alec drove was already parked there, but Liam's wasn't. His brows drew together in a frown. *Liam's supposed to be on duty today,* he thought. *Did he and Alec switch and they forgot to tell me?*

He rubbed his hand tiredly over his face—he hadn't slept much the past few nights away. His conscience had been brutal, denying him sleep. He'd finally reached a decision this afternoon, and had hightailed it back here determined to make things right with the princess. To take back the lies he'd let her believe. Even though they still had no future, he'd hurt her more than he'd ever believed he could hurt a woman, and he would have no peace until he begged her forgiveness.

He jumped out, headed straight for the main house and rang the bell, but no one answered the door. He rang again, but still no answer. Wondering, but not really worried, not yet, he pulled out his key ring to unlock the door. But just as he was reaching for the doorknob he heard footsteps crunching in the snow behind him, and he swung around.

Alec stood there bareheaded, his jacket hanging open as if he'd just shrugged it on and hurried outside when he heard Trace's truck. "She's gone."

"Gone?" Trace asked blankly, staring at the other man. "What do you mean? Why didn't you call me? She wasn't supposed to leave until Christmas Eve."

"They left Saturday. Not just the princess, her entire household. And I don't think she's coming back. She had her horses shipped by rail to the coast and then by sea to Zakhar—her groom accompanied them."

An icy, empty feeling settled over Trace, but Alec wasn't finished. "She left you something," he said, his voice as cold as Trace felt. "Liam and I drew straws to see which of us got to be the one to tell you—and I won."

"Tell me what?"

"That whatever you did to her, we hope you're satisfied." Contempt mingled with repressed anger in Alec's face and voice, and was reflected in the rigid tenseness of his muscles. "Because Liam and I—we just wanted to cry."

Trace's right hand slowly clenched into a fist. "Just spit it out, damn it," he grated.

Alec shook his head. In a soft but deadly voice he said, "See for yourself. She left it in your room."

Trace held Alec's gaze for a minute, then stalked toward the guest house, his footsteps in the crisp snow the only sound in the stillness. Foreboding clutched at him, and a fear such as he'd never known filled his chest. When he reached his room he pushed the door open. And froze.

Alec's words reverberated in his mind. *Liam and I— we just wanted to cry.* Now he understood what Alec had meant. Because he wanted to cry, too. Strewn across his bed was the gift she'd left him. Her hair. Her glorious honey-brown hair. *If Eve had looked like you,* he'd told her when he'd seen her naked except for those cascading waves, *Adam would have gladly left Eden.*

He took two steps toward the bed, and then stopped short as her message hit him like a physical blow. She'd left it all behind. For him. Because he'd made her feel ashamed. Ashamed of every intimate moment they'd spent together. She'd hacked it off and discarded it, as if she couldn't bear the reminder of the times he'd caressed her body through the silk of her hair, as if she couldn't bear the reminder of how he'd wrapped her hair around his throat and breathed in the scent of her. As if she couldn't bear any reminder of *him.*

A slight sound alerted him to Alec's presence behind him before the other man spoke from the doorway. "What the *hell* did you do to her, McKinnon?" he asked, the rage in his voice even more a challenge than his words. And a threat.

Trace didn't answer. Couldn't. He didn't even turn around. He just pushed the door shut in Alec's face and locked it. Locked himself in with his anguish. "I'm sorry, Princess," he whispered in a ravaged voice, his eyes squeezing shut as the enormity of what he'd done washed over him. "Oh God, I'm sorry. Please forgive me." There was no answer except the harsh sound of his tormented breathing.

Trace spent Christmas Day holed up in his cabin in Keystone. He hadn't wanted to go back there—memories of the princess at the cabin would haunt him until the day he died—but he had nowhere else to go. His condo was sublet until June; he couldn't possibly stay at the estate now that he was no longer guarding the princess; and although he'd long since been invited to spend Christmas with the Walkers, he couldn't envision himself making convivial small talk with the Walkers' other guests. Especially since two of them—Keira's brothers, Alec and Liam—would be staring at him with the contempt decent men reserved for rapists and child molesters.

He'd brought a bottle of Johnny Walker Black along with the intention of getting wasted, but he couldn't even bring himself to break the seal. The bottle sat unopened on the counter in the cabin's tiny kitchen. Nor could he bring himself to start a fire in the fireplace, so he stoically sat on the sofa in the main room, staring at the cold, empty grate, huddled in his ski jacket and woolen scarf until the heater warmed up the room.

He was exhausted. His body craved the respite of dreamless sleep, but for the past five nights he'd only slept in snatches. Every time he dozed off he dreamed of the princess as he'd last seen her, her eyes huge in a face from which all color had fled. All except for that thin line of blood on her lip, crimson as she whispered her worst nightmare come true. *Photographs?*

How could he have let her believe him capable of such a vile act, such a desecration of her love? She'd cried atop Mount Evans and told him, *I would turn around, and there they would be—the paparazzi.* Click. Click. Click. *I used to have nightmares when I was young...I honestly believe if I were being raped or murdered and the paparazzi were there, instead of trying to help me they would just photograph it.* He'd been desperate to break it off with her, but...he should have found another way. With the crystal clarity of hindsight he realized it would have been better to have just walked away without a word than to let her think...

And as if that memory wasn't enough to rob him of sleep, there were her last words to him—*I should have known I could not be loved.* How did a man live with that on his conscience? How could he live with that memory and still call himself a man?

Despair ate at him. Not just the despair of knowing he'd destroyed her fragile confidence in herself as a woman. The despair of knowing he'd lost her trust, something precious, something so rare in his life there weren't words to describe it.

It was easy to say he'd done it to protect her from his enemies. But if he was honest—*by all means, let's be honest at last,* he told himself ruthlessly—that wasn't the only reason. Long before he'd noticed he was being followed, he'd unilaterally decided there was no future for them.

Who gave you the right to make that decision for her...without discussion? He would never have dreamed of doing that with his former partner. Why had he done it with Mara?

The answer, when it came, was brutal in its self-assessment—he'd judged himself as unworthy of her. Because of that, he'd callously ignored her feelings in the matter, and had determined he wouldn't let her throw away her life...and her love...on a no-name bastard no one had wanted. Not his father. Not his mother. Not his grandparents.

No one had wanted him—the man he was inside—except her.

Pain returned in waves. *There is no such thing as a bastard child,* she'd told him with fierce determination that first time at his cabin. Was that when he'd realized it was already too late? That the battle against loving her was lost? And when she'd touched him with loving hands, giving to him so selflessly, healing him when he hadn't even known he was wounded—was that when he'd surrendered his heart?

But not his trust. He'd never surrendered that.

Trust. His princess had freely given him her trust, but he hadn't given her his in return. He hadn't trusted her love, hadn't trusted she knew what she was doing.

She'd seen something in him that had torn down the barriers in her heart that had stood for most of her life. But he hadn't believed she could see the man he really was and love him. No one else ever had, not in thirty-six years. Why should she be any different?

Harsh reality deluged him like an icy rain. *You weren't protecting her, you were protecting yourself. That's the real truth here. You were desperate to protect yourself from being hurt, so you hurt her instead. You drove her away so you could fool yourself you were being noble. But that was as much a lie as telling her you seduced her on command.*

Like an old, old man, Trace removed his ski jacket and let it drop unheeded on the floor. He reached for the SIG SAUER nestled in his shoulder holster, drew it out, and laid it on the coffee table in front of him. Then stared at it for several long minutes. He'd known men who had taken that way out, when the pain of living had made it seem the only escape. No one he was close to, thank God, but men he'd worked side by side with in Afghanistan, men he *knew.*

He'd always told himself it was the coward's way out. Had always felt that a *real* man could tough it out, could take the worst that life dished out. He hadn't understood. Now he realized that if he'd been a better friend, maybe those men could have confided in him. Maybe he could have made a difference. Even if only one man had changed his mind... But he had shielded himself from feeling too much all his life. Had shielded himself from getting too close to just about everyone... including his ex-wife.

Was that why Janet didn't trust me? he wondered, seeing the failure of his marriage clearly for the first time. *Because I didn't trust her enough to let her see the man I really am?*

With a sense of shock he realized that only twice in his adult life had he ever let anyone inside his defenses. Only two people had been allowed to get close to him emotionally—Keira and the princess. And only once had he trusted. The woman he'd trusted *hadn't* been the woman he loved more than life itself.

He buried his face in his hands.

Two hours later his cell phone rang, startling Trace from a restless, dream-disturbed sleep. He fumbled for the phone, wondering who the hell could be calling him on Christmas Day. "McKinnon," he growled once he finally managed to get the cell phone answered.

"It's me," Keira said in his ear, "so don't think you can scare me off with your big, bad, bear imitation."

Trace sat up and rubbed a hand over his face. He tried to see what time it was, but his eyes wouldn't focus. "What time is it?"

"Never mind that," his former partner told him sternly. "I have someone here who wants to say something to you." There was a brief silence, followed by a faraway, "It's Trace, Alyssa. Tell him what you want to say."

Alyssa's little girl voice gurgled in his ear. "Dank-oo, Dace."

"You're welcome, sweetie," he managed. "I hope you liked it."

Keira came back on the phone. "She loved it. You knew she would. But you've got to stop spoiling her."

"Is she having a good Christmas?"

"All four of my brothers are here. My mom's here. And Cody, of course. All dancing attendance on her. And Santa Claus left her a boatload of presents under the tree and a stocking filled with a dentist's worst nightmares. But her 'Dace' isn't here, so she's miserable."

Trace laughed. "Yeah, right."

Keira laughed, too. "Okay, maybe I'm exaggerating a little. Hang on a sec. Cody, can you take Alyssa for a few minutes?" A deep rumble answered her, followed by a moment of silence, and then Keira came back on the line. "Okay, I'm back. Cody's got Alyssa and I'm barricaded in the laundry room, so I might have ten minutes, tops."

"Don't interrupt your Christmas for me."

"Please," Keira said drily. "Don't give me that crap. This is me, remember? Your former partner? The one you didn't hesitate to ask if I was in love with Cody two and half years ago? The one you didn't hesitate to ask if I was sleeping with him? Does that ring any bells?"

Trace winced. "Yeah. I seem to recall having the gall to ask you those questions."

Keira's voice turned serious. "Alec just told me Mara went back to Zakhar. Lock, stock and barrel."

For a moment he'd let himself forget, but now it came roaring back, a freight train thundering down the track, smashing right into his heart. "Yeah."

"He didn't say, but he didn't have to—I saw the look

he and Liam exchanged when I told them you weren't coming for Christmas dinner. You had something to do with it. Right?"

"Right."

"Are you out of your ever-loving, freaking mind?"

Trace was startled into laughing again, a rusty sound that held echoes of pain. "Don't pull any punches, Keira. Tell me what you *really* think."

"I'll tell you, but I'm not sure you want to hear what I have to say."

He didn't respond at first, just rubbed his hand over his face again, then he said slowly, seriously, his tone an indictment of himself and his actions, "Whatever you're thinking, it can't be any worse than I've already said to myself."

"I wasn't planning on calling you names. I was just going to tell you the real reason I wanted you to be Alyssa's godfather, and let you take it from there."

Trace hesitated. "Because you knew that if anything happened to you and Cody, I'd protect her with my life?"

"No. That might have been Cody's reason, but it wasn't mine."

Puzzled, he asked, "Then why?"

He could hear her draw a deep breath in his ear and expel it slowly. "It's two things, really. Because there's a capacity for love in you far beyond most men. I don't even know if you're aware of it yourself, but I see it in you. And because you respect women. I mean really *respect* them, and not just as women, as people. If anything happened to Cody and me, I wanted my daughter raised by a man who could give her roots and wings.

The roots that can only come from unconditional love, and the wings that can only grow strong when you're allowed to fly free as far as they will take you."

Trace squeezed his eyes shut and swallowed the lump in his throat that threatened to overwhelm him. But Keira wasn't finished.

"I love my brothers, you know that. But I grew up with them. I know them inside and out. They would give Alyssa the roots she needs, but I don't know if they would give her wings. And *that's* why I wanted you to be her godfather and not one of them."

"Keira..." He couldn't go beyond that one word.

"Alyssa deserves the best. And that's you." She cleared her throat. "There's just one more thing I have to tell you, and then I'll let you go. Liam told me—he thought it was funny, and it is, in a way, but it's a little pathetic, too—Mara was taking cooking lessons from her chefs, did you know that?"

"No."

"Apparently she was trying to make herself more self-sufficient, like me."

"That doesn't make sense—you can't cook."

"No, but she didn't know that until Alec told her. What she *does* know is that you hold me in high esteem. And do you know what she told Alec when he asked her how she'd been injured? She said, 'I only did what Keira would have done in that situation.'"

Trace uttered a pithy, four-letter word.

"That's all I wanted to tell you. Okay, that's *not* all I wanted to tell you, but I don't think I need to tell you anything more. You're a smart man—you've never given yourself the credit you deserve, but you were a great teacher and I owe you a lot. The only thing I regret about marrying Cody is losing you as a partner—and if you *ever* tell him I said I regret anything about marrying him I'll call you a liar to your face," she ended with a laugh that had him laughing, too. "He feels guilty enough about it as it is. Oh, and that reminds me," she said swiftly before he could hang up. "Cody asked me to check on a license plate number for you, along with the make and model of the car it belongs to. He said you thought the New World Militia or the Russian mob might be tailing you."

"Yeah."

"You had him so worried he would barely let Alyssa and me out of his sight, and he opened an agency investigation immediately. He even called Callahan to warn him. And that was *not* a comfortable conversation, let me tell you."

"Forewarned is forearmed."

"Yes, but…you were way off base."

Despite his lack of sleep Trace was suddenly alert. "How do you know?"

"Because that car belongs to—hold on to your hat—the king of Zakhar."

Chapter 16

"*What?*" Trace couldn't believe what he'd just heard.

"That's what Cody said when I told him. I had to trace it through a couple of shell corporations, but I nailed it down yesterday. So if you were being followed—and I'm not saying you weren't—it was probably just the king being an overprotective brother."

"You're positive?" *The princess wasn't in danger because of me,* he thought with an overwhelming sense of relief. *I didn't put her at risk.*

"I'm not positive he was just being an overprotective brother, but I *am* positive the tail didn't involve the New World Militia or the *Bratva,* the Brotherhood. Unless the king of Zakhar is a member of the Russian mob," she added drily.

"You're the best, Keira. I've said it before, and I'll

probably still be saying it when we're both old and gray. Thank you *very* much!" After he hung up Trace put the cell phone down and stared at the SIG SAUER still sitting on the coffee table. Thinking about what Keira had just told him.

They weren't gunning for me, he thought thankfully. *Whatever the explanation is, they weren't gunning for me. Which means I can put that fear for the princess to bed.*

Then he thought about the other things Keira had told him earlier—and everything she hadn't said. He thought about Alyssa, about the sweet, darling girl she was, and the woman she would someday become. His princess would have been just as sweet and darling as a child, and she had grown into a woman who had flown far beyond anything anyone could ever have imagined, knowing her crippling childhood with the father who never loved her. Who besides her brother had given *her* roots and wings? How had she found the courage to fly? Yet somehow she had.

...I cannot ask you to be less than the man you are. But I can *ask you to let me be a woman for you... If you love me, then nothing else matters. If you love me, please do not talk of what I deserve... Since I have known you all I have wanted to be was a woman. Your woman...*

His woman. No, that wasn't true. She didn't just want to be his woman, his lover. That's what she'd said, but he knew her better than that. His princess might try to be a modern American woman, but she was old-fashioned in some endearing ways. Cooking lessons? That wasn't her trying to be self-sufficient. That was her wanting to be his wife in the traditional Zakharian sense.

He didn't give a damn about her cooking skills—they could eat frozen dinners or fast food every night for all he cared. But he suddenly saw a vision of the two of them messing around in the kitchen together after a long, hectic day—teaching for her, an agency investigation for him. He wouldn't be able to share much about his job with her, but then she had never pushed him to tell her things; she respected the boundaries he couldn't cross. And she wouldn't be able to share much about her job with him, either. Not because of security restrictions, but because her specialty was beyond his comprehension—if he'd learned nothing else attending her classes while guarding her, he'd learned that.

But those things didn't matter. She just wanted to belong to him...and have him belong to her. Simple... yet profound. Wasn't that what he wanted, too?

He pulled out his wallet and picked up his cell phone. He had to call information to get the number, and the last-minute purchase put a dent in his credit card balance, but fifteen minutes later he had a flight to Zakhar booked for New Year's Eve, the earliest flight available.

Exhaustion tugged at Trace and he made his way slowly into the bedroom, afraid he still wouldn't be able to sleep. But whether it was because he'd never brought the princess to the bedroom in his cabin, or because he was literally weaving on his feet or because his conscience was finally at peace now that he'd made his flight reservation, he slept the clock around and then some.

When he woke the next evening he had a vague memory of waking once or twice and stumbling to the bathroom, then falling back into bed almost immediately, but he couldn't have said exactly how many times it had happened. Now when he woke he was aware of two things: the sun was already setting and he was ravenous. He tried to remember if he had any food in the kitchen. He didn't feel up to driving in to town to one of the restaurants there, but he would if he had to.

I should keep this place stocked better, he told himself a few minutes later as he dumped a can of Beefaroni into a pot with a can of green beans, both cans near their expiration dates. He stirred it all together and watched impatiently until it was warm enough to be edible— he was too hungry to wait for it to be truly hot. Then he stood over the sink and wolfed the mixture down. It was surprisingly good. *Or maybe I was so hungry old shoes would have tasted good,* he thought humorously. He had just run water in the pot to let it soak before washing, when he heard a faint sound at the front door.

He automatically reached for the SIG SAUER in his shoulder holster and cursed when his hand came up empty, then remembered he'd left his gun on the coffee table the day before. He made a diving leap for the gun just as both the front and back doors burst open. And that was the last thing he remembered clearly for a long, long time…

Drugged. They'd kept him drugged. He'd been trussed up like a chicken, blindfolded, drugged and transported. Where? For what purpose? And who was it? The New World Militia? The Russian mob? Someone else? And why? Why bother transporting him? More dangerous that way, more likely that something would go wrong and they'd be discovered. Why not just kill him and get it over with?

He didn't realize he was floating in and out of consciousness. Didn't realize that after the first time he was no longer bound, gagged or blindfolded. Just drugged. He didn't realize he'd been fed three separate times, and that the drugs had been administered in his food. He also didn't realize a physician had carefully monitored his vital signs the entire time he was a captive.

But some part of him *had* recognized he was on a plane—that droning sound was unmistakable, and in his drugged state he sometimes thought he was back in the Marine Corps, flying in a military transport into and out of Afghanistan. Other times he thought he was dead, waiting in limbo for God to decide his fate—heaven or hell. He examined his conscience and figured it was a toss-up, unless God gave him the benefit of the doubt for good intentions.

He woke for the last time as he was being strapped down on a stretcher, then carried gently out of a plane. His first confused thought was that he'd woken up in Brigadoon, the fairy-tale city of stage-and-screen fame that only appeared once every hundred years. Snow-capped peaks ringed the city around him; the air was fresh and pure; and quaint, winding streets led upward from the airport toward a palace on a hill. Then he knew where he was. And unless he was much mistaken, he wasn't about to die anytime soon.

* * *

Trace was ushered into a long, spacious room, and the door was closed behind him. His kidnappers had given him time to recover, time for the drugs to be completely washed from his system, but they hadn't told him a damned thing. His clothes had been taken, cleaned and returned to him, although he felt partially naked without his shoulder holster and gun—he'd gone strapped for so long he didn't feel dressed without it. Then they'd brought him here…and left him.

He took a look around. Mirrors interspersed with life-size portraits lined one side, tall windows the other. It made the room look twice as big as it really was, although it was big enough to play flag football in. Not that anyone would, because the furnishings were priceless antiques.

He wandered down one side, casually glancing at the portraits of long-dead rulers of Zakhar until his attention was riveted by a relatively recent family portrait of a man, a woman and a baby. The man he recognized as the previous king of Zakhar—Mara's father. And the woman, the woman could have been Mara, but he knew it must have been her mother.

I didn't realize the princess resembles her mother so closely, he thought. But the more he studied the portrait the more he realized there were noticeable differences. The woman in the portrait had hair that was more golden than Mara's honey-brown color, and there was an expression on her face he'd never seen on Mara's— a haughty superiority that matched the expression on her husband's face. On occasion the princess had been haughty, even peremptory at times, but never superior.

And the beauty of the woman in the painting owed a lot to artifice. Her face was meticulously made up to enhance her beauty, but it was a cold, impersonal look, like a fashion model in a glossy magazine. There was none of the soft, natural warmth Mara exuded.

The vast, marble-tiled room was empty of people save for himself, but not for long. A side door opened and a man walked through, closing the door firmly behind him. He was tall and well built, and he carried himself like a soldier, but there was something else about him that Trace couldn't put a finger on. Then it came to him. This man had that same regal air Mara did.

He stopped a few feet away from Trace. His eyes flickered to the family portrait that had held Trace's interest. "Yes," he said without preamble. "Mara resembles our mother. That only complicated things for her where my father was concerned, especially as she grew older."

He turned his attention back to Trace. "I apologize for the necessity of kidnapping you," he said in the same precise English his sister used, the precision a dead giveaway it wasn't his first language. "I needed to talk to you and it was impossible for me to leave Zakhar at this time."

Trace shifted his stance belligerently. Being kidnapped still rankled. "You couldn't just do it over the phone?"

"No." Nothing more, just that no.

The silence stretched out as each man assessed the

other. Trace saw a man a shade taller than his own nearly six feet two, just as fit, a few years younger. He could see the family resemblance in their coloring and their eyes, but whereas the princess was feminine down to her fingertips, the king was very much a man's man. There was also a sense of physical power held in check, and Trace remembered how Mara had once described her brother—*he is a man who will always be stronger than anyone who goes against him.*

Now Trace knew she hadn't been exaggerating. Zakhar's king was a man first, and a king second. He waited for the king to say something, but the silence between them remained unbroken until Trace finally said, "So what did you want to talk to me about?"

Without warning the king asked, "Is my sister pregnant?"

It took a second for the question to sink in. Then Trace swore and hit him. The king had an iron jaw, and though he was staggered by the blow, it didn't knock him down. Trace expected a return punch and readied himself for it, but the king just stood there rubbing his jaw with one powerful hand, a faint smile on his face.

When it was clear he had no intention of starting— or finishing—a brawl, Trace relaxed slightly and flexed his fingers, pain that had been blocked out in the heat of the moment suddenly making itself known. It hurt like hell, but he didn't regret it.

He raised his gaze from his throbbing knuckles to the man in front of him. "I never touched your sister," he told the king in a harsh tone. His innate honesty made him add, "Not that way. You slander her by insinuating—"

Only then did he realize the original question hadn't been asked in English, and his vehement response had been the same. Only then did he realize the king had used a crude Zakharan term for pregnancy, one that only a native Zakharian would know. He'd been baited deliberately for exactly the response he'd given.

"That is why I could not ask you over the phone," the king said, in English this time, still with that faint smile. "Your reaction tells me three things." He ticked them off. "One, you understand and speak Zakharan. Unless I am mistaken—and I rarely am—you probably speak it like a native." He didn't wait for Trace to either confirm or deny this statement before continuing.

"Two, you do not give a damn who I am. That is good," he said approvingly. "Better than I had hoped." His smile faded. "And three, you would defend my sister's honor as if it were your own." He considered Trace for a moment. "So I have to ask—why is she here and not in America?"

Taken aback, Trace could only say, "I... It's Christmas break. The university is closed until school starts up again in mid-January." It was a lie, because he knew she had no intention of returning. But it was the only thing he could think of.

"Yes, but she is here and you are there. At least, that is where she thinks you are. So why is she here... alone?"

A dozen responses went through Trace's head, but none he could say to the king of Zakhar. So he just pressed his lips sternly together and refused to speak.

"What do you know of my father?"

The question came out of the blue, and took him by surprise. "Enough," Trace said, glancing at the portrait on the wall. His tone was grim, bitter. "Enough to know I'm very sorry he's dead…because I would have liked to meet him in a dark alley."

The king nodded his agreement. "If that is how you feel then you know Mara has been wounded in a way no child should ever be wounded." For a moment his eyes were hard and cold, and Trace could relate. "I tried to make it up to her, but I am just her brother, and it was not enough. For years I thought she would never recover, that she would live apart in her own little world forever, no matter what I did."

The king's jaw tightened. "Seven years ago my father tried to force Mara into an arranged marriage. Some women could have survived that kind of marriage, but not Mara—it would have destroyed her. I could not let that happen, so I put a stop to it."

"How did you—" Trace began, then remembered little things Mara had told him about her brother, and understood. "Leverage."

"If you like," the king said. "Some would call it blackmail. The end result is the same."

Curious, he asked, "What did you do?"

A stillness settled over the king in a way that reminded Trace of Mara when her father was mentioned. "Even before my mother's death the monarchy was nearly everything to my father—Marianescus have ruled Zakhar in an unbroken line for more than five hundred years. After her death it became his all-consuming passion. I told my father if he forced Mara into marriage he would have no heir—the unbroken line would be broken." He smiled coldly. "There is one thing about leverage—or blackmail—you *must* be willing to follow through on your threat. My father knew me. And so he let Mara go."

Trace let out the breath he was holding. Though his expression didn't change, his opinion of Mara's brother—already high—ratcheted up several notches.

"I sent Mara to university in England. I hoped that once she was away from my father's debilitating influence she would... But no." The king sighed. "She came back to Zakhar after she obtained her doctorate and taught at university here in Drago. Two years, and the man did not appear, the one who could break the chains my father placed on Mara's heart."

The king glanced away, as if seeing something in the past only he could see, something that pained him to remember. Then his eyes moved to the family portrait for a few seconds before his gaze met Trace's again, and Trace sensed the steely determination in the other man. "I could not let things continue that way. And so I magnified a small crisis here in Zakhar into a major one, and used that excuse to send Mara to your country."

"You sent her there on purpose?" Trace asked. The king nodded. "Why?"

After a minute's reflection the king said, "I hoped something might happen there that could not happen here, and it did." His eyes softened. "Two months ago Mara called me. She told me she had met a man...a man like no other. A man who understood. A man who made her believe she could be loved the way she had never believed before."

The unexpected, gut-wrenching words stabbed through Trace like a knife thrust, a near mortal wound that left him mentally gasping for air.

"At first I was…concerned. Concerned enough to send men to America to check on this man, to make sure I had not made a terrible mistake sending Mara there. I had to be *sure* she would not be hurt." His gaze was direct. "I will be honest. The men I sent had orders to quietly eliminate this man to protect Mara…if necessary."

"So that's who they were," Trace said softly. "I thought they were related to another case, one from years ago. But *you* sent them. Keira was right when she said—"

"Yes." The king cut him off. "They reported back to me that the man was exactly what he seemed to be. And despite how Mara feels about photographs I had no choice—my agents sent me pictures of Mara with him. In all of them it is obvious Mara is in love, the kind of love I have prayed she would someday come to know. But the man…the pictures showed a man who did not betray his emotions. A man who shielded them from the eyes of the world. A man after my own heart." The faint smile had returned. "Except for one picture. One picture, and then I knew almost all there was to know of this man and how he felt about Mara."

Trace's voice was husky when he said, "I'm surprised you didn't eliminate him then and there."

The king's brows drew together in a frown. "Is that

what you truly think? Can you honestly believe *any-thing* is more important to me than Mara's happiness?"

Trace's jaw tightened, and he took a step forward, his stance a challenge. "You don't give a damn about your blue-blooded sister taking up with an American bastard who doesn't even know his father's name?" he threw at Mara's brother.

"I knew that about you even before Mara told me she loved you. I knew that about you as soon as you were assigned to guard her."

"And it didn't *matter*?"

The king shook his head. "Once upon a time that may have been important. But there is one thing that trumps where you came from and who your father is or is not." His eyes bored into Trace with intensity. "You would give the blood from your veins to keep Mara safe. *Not* because it is your job, but because she is your world. Yes?"

Trace swallowed hard. He didn't want to answer, but he couldn't help it. "Yes."

"That is the *only* way to judge a man's worth where a woman is concerned." The king was breathing harder now with the force of his emotions held sternly in check. He didn't say anything more until he had regained his iron control. His next words shocked Trace.

"But I had to be sure, for Mara's sake. I could not trust in just that picture, not with Mara's whole future at stake. I had to test you."

Comprehension dawned swiftly. "You son of a bitch," Trace said, anger flaring. "*You* were behind the kidnapping attempt." The king inclined his head. "You sent men… What if something had gone wrong? What if—"

The king interrupted him. "I could not take the chance that something would go wrong. So I did not send men. I led them."

Trace stared in disbelief, but then the meaning of the soft curse the assailant had uttered when the princess was injured sank in. *It is Andre's favorite curse,* the princess had said long ago. Now it made sense. "*You* led them? You did that to your own sister? You terrorized her? You risked her life by having someone hold a gun to her head?"

"There were no bullets in the gun—she was never in danger." A muscle twitched in the king's jaw. "That is, she would not have been if she had not tried to save *you.*" He shook his head. "I did not expect that—not from Mara. She took me by surprise when she jumped for the knife—*that* is how she was injured. I had no intention of killing you, but she did not know that. I had not expected that kind of bravery from my little sister." His face softened again, and a smile of admiration played over his lips. "When that happened I knew she loved you more than I had ever imagined."

Trace had known, too. Wasn't that when he'd realized he *had* to break it off with her, before it was too late? And *not* just because he'd thought he was a target, but because she was willing to risk her life for him?

"But just as she did not know the truth, you were not to know she was never in danger," the king continued, "That would have defeated the purpose. I deliberately planned the attack for a night when the other two bodyguards were away, so only you were there to rescue her. But did you not question why the two active alarm systems were so effectively disabled, yet the passive alarm system was left activated?"

"Not at the time," Trace admitted. "Not until afterward, when I had time to think it over and assess everything. You wanted me to know she was in danger."

The king nodded. "I tested you the only way I could, and then I knew for sure you were the man for Mara." His smile faded. "So I will ask you again. Why is Mara here alone? Why is she grieving as if you are dead?"

Trace was still trying to come to terms with everything the king had just told him, trying to put all the pieces into their new places in his mind. Trying to comprehend the single-mindedness, the ruthlessness that could put Mara through that ordeal. *Love that is cruel to be kind,* he thought. *No matter the cost. Because the end result is worth any price.* He steeled himself to answer the king's question. "If she's grieving," he said, "it's because I sent her away. Because I told her…" His throat ached. "I told her I didn't love her."

"I see. You lied to her."

"Yes."

"And she believed you." It wasn't a question, but Trace nodded anyway. "I should kill you for that," the king said softly, his chest heaving suddenly, and Trace knew he wasn't talking about having him killed; he *literally* wanted to kill Trace with his own hands.

But Mara's brother couldn't hate him any more than he already hated himself. He would never forget the expression on Mara's face when he told her… "There's more," he said, holding himself straight, meeting the sharp accusation in the king's eyes. "She knew me too well. She wouldn't believe I didn't love her. She thought I was trying to be noble. So I had to tell her…" He couldn't say the words.

"Ahhh. I see it now. Seducing her? Was that also part of your assignment?"

"I never seduced her!" The harsh words echoed through the vast room.

"There is seduction…and then there is seduction," the king said softly. "Perhaps you did not seduce her into your bed, but you seduced her into loving you, did you not?"

"That was *never* part of my assignment," Trace rasped. "That was…" Mara's face rose before him, her lovely green eyes smiling shyly at him as she offered him the gift of her body…and her heart. As she offered him her trust. The fierceness in her eyes and her voice as she said, *there is no such thing as a bastard child.* "That was…" *Inevitable,* a little voice whispered in his skull. *To know her…really know her sweet and loving heart…is to love her unconditionally.*

"If you love her, can you not see you have wounded her far worse than my father ever did?"

The words scourged Trace and the blood drained away from his face, leaving him cold and light-headed. "No," he said, shaking his head slowly, even though he knew it was the truth. Wasn't that why he'd gone back to the estate before Christmas, only to find her gone? Wasn't that why he'd booked his flight here even before he'd been kidnapped? To try to undo the damage he'd caused? "No."

"I tell you yes. You have killed her as surely as if you had stabbed her, but not quickly, not cleanly. She will go on living, dying by inches, her heart already dead inside her. If you could have seen her as I saw her when she stepped off the plane…" A muscle twitched in the king's jaw. "I could have killed you for that alone."

Chapter 17

Trace tried to defend himself. "I *had* to push her away. I thought I was putting her in danger." The king's brows drew together in a questioning frown. "Those men following me—*your* men—I thought they were stalking me from a case I worked on a while back. I can't give you the details, but they were stone-cold killers. I knew damned well if they tried to take me out she might get caught in the crossfire. I wasn't about to risk that. No way in *hell* was I going to let anything happen to her because of me."

The king cursed long and fluently in Zakharan, but the words and the expression on his face told Trace the curse was internally directed. "I did not think of that," the king whispered finally, more to himself than to Trace. Then his lips tightened as he went back on the offensive. "But you did not tell her that was the reason, did you?" he said shrewdly, his words clipped and precise. "If you had, it would not have broken her heart. Wounded her, yes. But not crushed her soul as you have done."

Trace shook his head, facing the bitter truth. "I thought I had to find a way to kill her love," he insisted. "I wanted to free her. Free her to find a better man than me."

"*Free* her?" The king stared at him in disbelief. Then one hand made a sharp gesture of denial. "You are not Zakharian, no matter how fluent you are in our language, so perhaps you do not know. Marianescus mate for life. It started with the founder of our house, and that character trait has flowed through our blood for more than five centuries." Pain slashed across his face for a moment before he controlled it. "We love once," he said softly, his eyes looking beyond Trace at a long ago memory, and Trace sensed he wasn't just talking about Mara. "Then never again."

The king's eyes sought the portrait on the wall beside them. "Even my father could not escape that fate. I have often wondered if he could have married again after my mother died, perhaps he would not have blamed Mara for her death. Perhaps he would not have hated her so completely."

The king's mouth hardened and his eyes turned to stone as he faced Trace again. "My father could never admit it was *he* who caused my mother's death by insisting on another child, another son to secure the Marianescu legacy." His eyes looked nothing like Mara's at this moment, and Trace saw the same implacable hatred for the old king that he himself felt. "But it is too late for that. What my father started, you have nearly finished."

Trace shook his head, unable to speak, but Mara's brother wasn't done. "I cannot reach her. I cannot heal her. I can only take a desperate chance and kidnap the man she loves, praying you can somehow undo the damage you have done to someone who never deserved such cruelty. Not from my father. Not from you."

"That wasn't what I intend—"

The king cut him off. "Perhaps not. But do they not say the road to hell is paved with good intentions?" He looked at Trace, his face hard and implacable. "You have put her in hell. What are you going to do about it?"

The two men stared at each other for endless seconds. "Where is she?" Trace asked finally, the words rasping in his dry throat.

"Stay here. I will send her to you." The king turned on his heel and strode toward the side door. He glanced back with his hand on the knob. "Do not tell her I brought you here by force. Let her think you came to her of your own free will. I will not contradict you." Then he was gone.

Trace moved to one of the long windows on the east side of the room, staring unseeingly out into the garden. He had no idea what he was going to say to the princess; he only knew her brother was right. If he loved her— and he did, so much so that life had not seemed worth living once he had driven her away—he somehow had to find the words to undo the damage he'd done. What had he intended to say to her when he'd booked his flight to Drago for New Year's Eve? He hadn't known then, just that he *had* to see her. Had to explain. He'd thought he would have time to think of what to say. But now he had mere seconds to find the words.

The hell with protecting myself, he told himself. *The hell with that. I don't know what I'll say to her, but every word will be the truth, even if it damns me.*

Andre dismissed his bodyguard and walked into the little library on the second floor, where he'd been told he would find his sister. She was sitting at the large table in the middle of the room where she and her best friend in high school, Juliana Richardson, had studied long ago. Textbooks were strewn haphazardly across the polished surface, some faceup, some facedown, others with strips of paper marking pages. Mara was busy scribbling in a notebook, and Andre heaved a sigh of profound relief. For the first time since she'd returned home she was showing an interest in her work, the work that had once been the cornerstone of her life. And that meant she was no longer completely devastated by what had happened to her at Trace McKinnon's hands.

Mara looked up as the door closed behind Andre, and smiled. A real smile, the first one she'd given him since her return. The smile didn't banish the shadows from her eyes, nor did it return the roses to her cheeks. But it gave Andre hope that his sister was moving beyond the pain, to a place where—even if McKinnon weren't waiting downstairs—Mara would be able to return to something akin to a normal life.

"What are you working on, *dernya*?" he asked her curiously.

"I was going to surprise you," she told him. "I was going to wait until I was finished, but I can tell you now."

"Tell me what?" He came to stand by her side, looking at the incomprehensible notations on the page in front of her and laid a gentle hand on her shoulder.

"I have been working on a textbook. Differential equations. I started on it when I began teaching at the University of Colorado." Her smile faded for a moment before she pasted it back in place. "The dean was most encouraging. And I let the head of the mathematics department critique the first few chapters. He was impressed."

"Why am I not surprised?" he teased her, tucking a wisp of hair behind her ear. "My little sister is a genius. Anyone would be impressed. Anyone who understands differential equations, that is. It is merely Greek to me."

She laughed, as he had intended. "It *is* Greek," she averred. "The symbols, at least. The text is in English. I told Liam it would be easier if I could write it in Zakharan, because it is not always easy to find the right English words for what I want to say." This time when her smile faded it didn't return.

"But you will not give up, will you, *dernya*? How many times have I heard you say you do not like half measures?"

Andre watched as Mara's eyes went blank for a moment. Then her lips tightened. "No, I do not like half measures," she whispered, almost as if to herself. She raised her face to Andre's, a new light in her eyes. "You are right, of course," she told him. "I cannot run away like this. I must go back." She drew a deep, trembling breath. "I must finish out the school year. My students are depending on me." She glanced at her notebook. "I will not let him make me a coward again," she vowed, and she didn't have to say his name for Andre to know to whom she was referring. "If nothing else, I will at least finish what I started."

Andre smiled his faint smile. "That is the sister I know and love," he said, letting his pride in her reflect in his tone. "The sister who could throw her heart over any fence and land safely." He tilted her chin up so she was forced to look at him. "You are not a coward, *dernya*. You never were."

She shook her head in denial. "I was," she insisted. "You know I was. I could never stand up to our father. You always had to fight my battles for me with him—I could never fight my own. Not even for something I have always loved." She swallowed hard.

"Love makes cowards of us all," Andre said, paraphrasing Shakespeare. "The longing to be loved for ourselves makes us afraid. And that fear makes us weak. Ahhh," he said when she gave him a wondering look. "Did you think I was immune?"

Mara hesitated. "Juliana?" she asked after a pregnant pause.

Andre closed his eyes for a second and breathed deeply. He let a self-derogatory smile play over his lips, then nodded. "Juliana," he acknowledged. The word was soft as a sigh.

"Still? After all these years?"

"I am a Marianescu," he said simply. "As are you."

"Yes," she agreed after a moment. "We are Marianescus, first and last. That is our fate." Andre watched her face, watched her expression morph into determination, as if she were drawing strength from the knowledge he understood there could never be another man for her, the same way there could never be another woman for him. But that didn't mean her life was over. She could build a life of purpose for herself just as he had done. Alone. "We never get everything we want in life," she said softly. "But we cannot give up, can we?"

"Never." They shared a smile of commiseration, then Andre said, "Would you do something for me, *dernya*?"

"Anything."

"There is an envoy waiting in the Hall of Mirrors. I have spoken with him but he also insists on seeing you about an important matter."

Mara touched fingertips to her cheeks, emphasizing the shadows under her eyes, and said, "I...I do not think... I am not quite ready to see anyone other than you."

"As a favor to me, yes?"

"What does he want? Why does he need to see me?"

"He will tell you that, *dernya*. But I promise you will not regret seeing him."

A door opened behind Trace, reluctant footsteps tapped across the marble tiles, and a voice as familiar to him as his own heartbeat said in Zakharan, "My brother, the king, says you insist on seeing me. I do not understand, but I—"

Trace turned around. "Hello, Princess."

"Trace!"

She caught her breath and her eyes widened until they were huge in her pale face, and for just an instant the intense light of joy shone there. But then she flinched, agony wiping away the joy, and her hand came up to cover her eyes. Her breath came in little pants and her mouth moved soundlessly. Then she crumpled.

Trace caught her as she fell, lifting her into his arms and carrying her swiftly to one of the antique sofas that lined the room. He laid her on the sofa and knelt beside it, his hand checking her pulse. It was far too rapid, and her breath fluttered in her throat.

He'd known she'd cut off her hair, but it was still a shock seeing her without it. After the first shock, though, it barely registered. Feathery wisps of golden brown hair framed her face, giving it a gamin look even more appealing than the sophisticated chignon she'd usually worn before. But the knowledge that he'd caused her such devastating pain she'd felt she had no choice but to do what she'd done made him bleed inside as he'd bled the night he'd seen her discarded tresses strewn across his bed.

"Princess," he said, caressing her cheek with a hand that trembled. "Open those green eyes for me. Come on, Princess. Curse me, slap me, yell at me. Do anything you want to me, but please open your eyes."

Mara came back to consciousness slowly, fighting it every step of the way. Someone was calling her, but not by name. *Trace,* she thought, smiling. Only Trace called her *Princess* in just that way, like a loving caress. Only Trace…

Then she remembered…and whimpered. "No…" Trace didn't love her. He didn't need her. He didn't even want her. He had just been doing his job. When he had touched her body, made her feel those incredible, indescribable things, he had just been doing his job. When he had made her believe in him, when he had made her believe herself loved, he had just been doing his job.

Mara opened her eyes. Trace was there, bending over her, his bluer-than-blue eyes dark with concern. One hand was holding her wrist, feeling for the pulse there. The other hand was caressing her cheek with the exquisite gentleness that had once convinced her she was loved…but not anymore.

"Do not touch me—I do not need your help," she told him coldly, struggling to sit up, to escape those lying hands. Although she'd just decided she had to return to the US to finish out the school year, she would never have sought Trace out, and would have done everything she could to avoid seeing him again. Courage was one thing. Masochism was another. Humiliation coiled inside her now as she remembered how she'd trusted herself to this man. How he'd seduced her into wanting him, loving him, all the while he was just doing his job.

And somewhere there were explicit photographs of the two of them.

Mara went hot and cold now just thinking about it. She had not been ashamed to let Trace touch her intimately when she thought he loved her. She had not been ashamed to touch him in ways she had never imagined she would want to touch any man, because she had loved him. Loving him, being loved by him, had made her feel blessed. Until he had told her there were photographs...

She closed her eyes as if she could blot out the memories by refusing to look at him, but she knew that couldn't happen. She couldn't escape her memories any more than she could escape this moment. When she had viciously hacked off her hair she had sworn no man would ever make her weep again. No man would ever make her ashamed again. And yet that was exactly what she was feeling now—scorching shame that made her want to weep and weep, until the shame was washed away. "Do *not*," she said again, pulling away sharply from his hands.

Trace let her go and sat back on his heels. This close to her he could see the visible signs of her suffering, the ones her brother had also seen. Her green eyes could never be anything but lovely to him, but there was a bruised look around the skin there that told its own tale. And her face was somehow thinner than he remembered, little hollows beneath her delicate cheekbones. But it was her mouth that hurt him the most. Those lips that had once smiled lovingly at him were tightly compressed, as if guarding her from further pain. Guarding her from him.

My God, he thought, dismayed. *What have I done?* "Princess—"

"My name is *Mara*," she said in a voice like ice, cutting him off. *"Mara Theodora."*

Her words clanged in his heart like a death knell. *Bitter divine gift,* she'd told him once, believing that assessment of her worth. Then he'd made her believe differently, only to cast her back into that bottomless well of despair, thinking herself unloved and unlovable. The way he'd once thought of himself.

"No," he said, his voice deep with emotion. "Not to me. You will always be my princess. The sweetest gift God ever gave a man."

She closed her eyes and swallowed convulsively. "Do not," she whispered, shaking. "*Please* do not."

Her tortured plea to be left with the tattered shreds of her dignity intact ripped through him. "I know I hurt you, Princess," he said softly, keeping his hands from her with an effort. "I didn't mean to. I told myself I was protecting you…from me. I thought, 'She'll forget me in time. She'll forget…and thank me for letting her go before it was too late.'" She made a small sound of pain, but he went on.

"I wanted to keep you. I wanted to lock you away and keep you forever—you have no idea how much I wanted that. But I couldn't believe a woman like you even existed for me. Couldn't believe there was a chance in hell of overcoming who you are, who I am." He took a deep breath, but he knew it had to be faced. "And then there was the job I was sworn to do."

She buried her face in her hands but she didn't cry. It would have been easier for him if she had. "My job is as much a part of me as you are," he said. "Guarding you…even spying on you…those were things my country asked me to do, and I did them. I'm not proud of spying on you, but I won't apologize." He hesitated, but he had to be honest. "I would do it again if I had to."

Her body shook, and he gently touched her arm. "But, Princess, everything else I told you was a lie. Holding you, loving you, letting you love me—those were never part of my assignment."

She shuddered. "But you let them take...photographs," she whispered in a voice that trembled and broke on the last word, a voice that betrayed the depth of her humiliation.

"No," he said, wishing with all his heart he had never let her believe that. "There were no pictures. That was a lie, too. Do you really think I could do that to you?"

She didn't speak, and he wondered what else he could say to convince her. Trust, once lost, might never be regained. He cast about frantically in his mind. Then it came to him. "Do you remember the day we went to Mount Evans, when that tourist took your picture at Summit Lake?" A faint murmur of assent answered him, but she still refused to raise her face. "Do you remember how I made him give me the camera—how I erased the picture from the memory card and told him he was a dead man if he ever took your picture again?"

"Yes," she answered in a tiny, muffled voice. "I remember."

His voice was low and deep when he said, "If I wouldn't let him have even an innocent picture, do you think I could let *anyone* take intimate pictures of you?" Slowly her hands fell away and she raised her face to his. Her expression told him she wanted to believe... but the uncertainty refused to be banished.

"That first day in my cabin…from the moment you told me there is no such thing as a bastard child, I knew I loved you. I fought it, but it was a losing battle. Then you gave yourself to me so sweetly, so completely. I knew I was the first man to touch you that way, and I wanted to make it so perfect for you. I wanted to give you that gift, so you would always remember your first time as a wondrous thing. So you would always remember *me* that way—as the man who gave it to you."

Her eyes, her lovely green eyes told him she *did* remember it the way he'd intended, despite everything, so he went on. "Then you let me give myself to you. Oh God, you touched me as if I were a priceless gift, and I…" His voice was husky with emotion, and for a moment he couldn't continue. "You gave me your trust. Do you have any idea what that meant to me? You were like a dream of perfection. My dream. My princess." His eyes held hers steadily. "There are no pictures except in my memory."

She closed her eyes for a moment and a sigh shuddered out of her, and when she looked at him again, her eyes swimming in tears of thankfulness, he knew she finally believed him. "After you left…after I drove you away…I had nothing," he went on. "I didn't even have the certainty that I had done the right thing…for you. Because I realized then it was all me—the whole time I thought I was protecting you from me, I was protecting myself from you. I can't explain it, but it's the truth. I just didn't realize until afterward. But cutting you out of my life didn't protect me—you were always there in my heart. And in my dreams. I couldn't escape from loving you, and I realized deep down I didn't want to. I was just afraid."

He thought for a moment, considering, and then discarding her brother's warning not to tell her the truth of how he'd arrived here. He wouldn't lie to her ever again. "Then your brother had me kidnapped and brought here."

"Andre?" He saw the returning doubt in her eyes, the sudden suspicion. "Oh, why did he do it?" she cried softly. "Now it is even worse…"

Trace rose slowly to his feet, staring down at her. "No," he told her. "He did the right thing." Later he would tell her about the plane ticket he'd already purchased. Later he would tell her other things, too, the thoughts that had run through his head as he stared at his gun in the desolate emptiness of his cabin—the place he'd first realized he loved her, the place that had become like a tomb to him without her there. For now, something inside tore loose and set him free to let her see him as he truly was. No defenses. No secrets. In fluent Zakharan he said, *"For such is the will of God that by doing right you may silence the ignorance of foolish men."*

She gasped.

Still in Zakharan, he told her, "I was that foolish man," letting her see his pain. "Too ignorant, too blind to see what your brother was wise enough to know— that the only truth that mattered is I would gladly die to keep you safe. Now and always."

He reached down and pulled her gently up into his arms. She came willingly. He pressed her head against his shoulder, letting her hear the thud of his heartbeat, letting her know his own uncertainty where she was concerned. He switched back to English. "If you can still love a man so blind, Princess, if you can still trust him…"

Her voice was muffled against his shoulder, but he heard her clearly. "I do," she whispered on the edge of tears. "I always will."

Later he would marvel at how easy she had made it for him. Later he would wonder why she still loved him after he'd caused her so much pain and humiliation. Later he would be awed and humbled that she still trusted him so completely. For now all he could do was be grateful.

"Then come back to Colorado with me. Marry me. Build a life with me. Teach me—" He swallowed hard. "Teach me how not to be so afraid of losing the most precious thing in my life I make it happen." His voice dropped a notch. "And then…when you're ready…let me give you children we will both love and cherish the way children *should* be loved and cherished. The way I love and cherish you. Always. In all ways. I swear I will never again give you cause to regret loving me."

"Yes," she said, raising her face to gaze into his eyes. Her green eyes were alight with the blazing fervency of her love. "Oh, yes."

King Andre Alexei IV stood on his private balcony overlooking the formal gardens that encircled the palace, watching as his beloved sister walked in the moonlight arm in arm with the man she loved along one of the winding, snow-dusted pathways. The twinkling lights of the sleeping city of his birthplace, Drago, shone in the distance, lights that didn't dim the silvery starlight from above.

She is free, he told himself thankfully. *Mara is finally free after all these years. I did it. I brought her out of the darkness into the light just as the first Andre Alexei did with his beloved Eleonora. But not alone— I could not have done it without* his *help. I could not have done it without the help of a man who by his own words is an American bastard who does not even know his father's name.*

He had told McKinnon no more than the truth that afternoon—he had deliberately engineered this by sending Mara to America, praying he was doing the right thing. And for once God had answered his prayers. Mara was finally free of the past, finally free of the malignant shadow cast by their father.

A touch of bitterness crept in as the king wondered what it would take to free himself in the same way. Wondered if his one-time threat to his father would be realized after all—that the unbroken line of Marianescus ruling Zakhar for over five hundred years would be broken. Wondered if he would ever have a son to follow in his footsteps as son had followed father since the first Andre Alexei had ruled Zakhar in the sixteenth century. *Must I pay forever for one mistake?*

His expression settled into determined lines. *No,* he resolved. *Now that Mara is free, I am free to seek my own salvation—or my own hell. Everything is ready. Everything is in place. The waiting is over. Now I will act.*

He breathed deeply, letting the strain bleed out of his

muscles, and cast one last lingering glance at the lovers below him before walking back through the French doors of his balcony and closing them firmly behind him. He wasn't there to see as Mara and Trace stopped abruptly, turned toward each other, and their two shadows blended into one.

Epilogue

Mara thundered across the open Colorado landscape on Suleiman's back, then took the fence flying, not slackening her pace for an instant. The sound of another horse just behind her made her bend over Suleiman's neck and urge him to even greater speed. "Come on, boy!" she whispered in Zakharan, though she knew he couldn't hear her, not at this speed. The cool October wind slashed across her cheekbones—if she wasn't wearing her riding helmet her hair would be flying wildly, blinding her.

Another fence loomed, and she threw her heart over it mere seconds before Suleiman took it in his powerful stride. Then she was pounding along the home stretch. Now the other horse—her wedding gift to Trace—was drawing closer, until the two horses were neck and neck, first one then the other in the lead. *Half a furlong,* she thought with a fraction of her brain as she lay herself almost flat against Suleiman's neck and pressed her heels into his sides. *Faster. Faster!*

One last fence, which Suleiman and the other horse sailed over side by side, and then both riders were pulling up sharply as the stables came into view. Trace's arm snagged her body as soon as they stopped, pulling her close for his fierce kiss. Mara's heart had already been pounding from exertion, but now it kicked into overdrive as she gave him back kiss for kiss.

"You witch," he whispered breathlessly in Zakharan between kisses. "God, you scare the hell out of me every time you ride Suleiman that way. But somehow you always come off unharmed."

"Me?" she responded in kind. "What of you on Alexander? You take risks I would never dare, and you do not even wear a helmet. If you were thrown…"

He laughed and switched easily back to English. "Cowboys don't wear riding helmets even if princesses do. You should know that by now."

Mara laughed, too. She pulled away reluctantly and quickly dismounted, then removed her riding helmet with a tug at the strap, letting her hair tumble around her face. She led Suleiman into the stables, praising him as she went, and Trace did the same for Alexander. Twenty minutes later, their mounts groomed, fed and watered, Mara and Trace paused together to look back as they were walking out.

"You would think two stallions would never co-exist peacefully the way Alexander the Great and Suleiman the Magnificent do," she said with a soft smile.

"Maybe it's because they're brothers. Or maybe it's because they were raised together. Either way it doesn't matter. I'm just thankful they do. Which reminds me, you never did tell me how you convinced your brother to sell Alexander to you."

"He knew how much I wanted a horse for you equal to Suleiman in every way. What horse could match Suleiman except his own brother?" she said simply. "Perhaps I took advantage of Andre," she added, a guilty expression creeping into her face. "He never could say no to me."

Trace's eyes softened. "Now why am I not surprised? I have the same problem." Mara and Trace walked arm in arm to the main house, her riding helmet dangling by its strap from her husband's arm.

Everything had fallen into place with amazing ease. They had been married for nearly ten months now, and the things Mara had so worried about—the money, the paparazzi, the tabloids—had somehow lost their significance. Trace took everything in his stride. He'd struggled with his pride, but had finally accepted there were some things Mara would always need because of who she was—the security of the estate in Boulder the king of Zakhar had bought for her was one of them. A household staff—a greatly reduced household staff—was another, as were bodyguards. Not federal agents. That really wasn't necessary. And not Zakharian bodyguards, either. Just agents from a reliable Denver firm, licensed for concealed carry—there were still crazies out there, not to mention the threat still hanging over his head. Trace wasn't taking any chances with Mara's safety, so bodyguards were still a necessity. And her stables. Their stables, now. But other than that their life together was composed of simple, homey things.

Mara was still teaching at the University of Colorado; Trace was back working for the agency. They had agreed their jobs were off limits as topics of conversation, but they had so much else to talk about they didn't miss it. They were friends as well as husband and wife. Friends as well as lovers. The nearly ten months since their quiet wedding on New Year's Day had flown by.

She smiled to herself as she ran a hand through her tousled hair, which had finally grown long enough to curl wildly around her face, trying to bring some order out of the chaos. "Don't bother," he told her. "I like it that way. Makes you look as if you've just tumbled out of bed. My bed."

"Hah!" she teased him in English. "You would like that, yes?"

"Hell yes!" He pulled her roughly into an enveloping embrace as his lips descended on hers, and everything was forgotten for the moment.

Later that night Mara lay nestled in Trace's arms beneath the covers, her frantic heartbeat slowing as she breathed deeply and nuzzled against his warmth. Would he always have this effect on her? she wondered. Would he always make her crazy with longing, then drive her wild until nothing else mattered but the release only he could give her? *Let me always feel this way,* she prayed. *And let me never fail to thank God every day of my life for Trace's love.*

He had already brought her to completion once with his magic hands, just as he had their very first time. Now his muscled arm tightened around her shoulders and tugged until she lay on top of him. "Tell me again," he said, his hands cradling her face.

"I love you," she whispered, then repeated it in Zakharan. English was good enough for most things, but Zakharan was the language of love. Her love. The language of her heart.

He shook his head. "Not that. I *know* that. Tell me the other." He spread her legs and fitted himself at the portal of her womanhood. And waited.

She smiled slowly at him in the darkness. "I am ready," she breathed in Zakharan, knowing he knew exactly what she was talking about. "I am ready if you are. I will even give up riding as we did today if you will give me your chil—" She caught her breath sharply as he arched his hips and thrust smoothly inside her. Then she was riding a wild wave until it crashed thunderously upon the shore, taking her with it.

As she fell asleep in her husband's arms, Mara knew with unalloyed certainty that nine months to that very day she would give Trace the first of what she hoped would be many children, the children they both craved to seal their love for all eternity. The children they would both love and cherish the way children *should* be loved and cherished.

Always. And in all ways.

* * * * *

Watch Andre meet his match in
KING'S RANSOM

And if you missed them, check out
REILLY'S RETURN &
CODY WALKER'S WOMAN

#1847 HEIR TO MURDER
The Adair Affairs
by Elle James
When his father is murdered, a newly found heir to a fortune and his far-too-attractive best friend hatch a plan to catch a killer...but will the painful secrets she's keeping destroy the growing bond between them?

#1848 CAPTURING THE HUNTSMAN
by C.J. Miller
FBI special agent Nathan Bradshaw pairs with campground owner Autumn Reed to capture the serial killer who murdered his sister. But when Autumn becomes the next target, it's a race against time to capture the Huntsman before he wins again.

#1849 KILLER EXPOSURE
by Lara Lacombe
Scarred, quiet chemist Dr. Hannah Baker wants nothing to do with the case Detective Owen Randall brings to her doorstep, nor the desire between them that reminds her of what she can't have. But as the killer carries out an attack, both of them must let go of the past to survive.

#1850 PROTECTING HIS BROTHER'S BRIDE
by Jan Schliesman
After a devastating tragedy, Kira Kincaid's job becomes her life. When she's framed for medical fraud, the only man who can help her clear her name is the last man on the planet who would ever trust her...*especially* once he finds out who she really is.

REQUEST YOUR FREE BOOKS!
2 FREE NOVELS PLUS 2 FREE GIFTS!

Ⓗ HARLEQUIN

ROMANTIC suspense

Sparked by danger, fueled by passion

YES! Please send me 2 FREE Harlequin® Romantic Suspense novels and my 2 FREE gifts (gifts are worth about $10). After receiving them, if I don't wish to receive any more books, I can return the shipping statement marked "cancel." If I don't cancel, I will receive 4 brand-new novels every month and be billed just $4.74 per book in the U.S. or $5.24 per book in Canada. That's a savings of at least 14% off the cover price! It's quite a bargain! Shipping and handling is just 50¢ per book in the U.S. and 75¢ per book in Canada.* I understand that accepting the 2 free books and gifts places me under no obligation to buy anything. I can always return a shipment and cancel at any time. Even if I never buy another book, the two free books and gifts are mine to keep forever.

240/340 HDN F45N

Name   (PLEASE PRINT)

Address   Apt. #

City   State/Prov.   Zip/Postal Code

Signature (if under 18, a parent or guardian must sign)

Mail to the **Harlequin® Reader Service:**
IN U.S.A.: P.O. Box 1867, Buffalo, NY 14240-1867
IN CANADA: P.O. Box 609, Fort Erie, Ontario L2A 5X3

Want to try two free books from another line?
Call 1-800-873-8635 or visit www.ReaderService.com.

* Terms and prices subject to change without notice. Prices do not include applicable taxes. Sales tax applicable in N.Y. Canadian residents will be charged applicable taxes. Offer not valid in Quebec. This offer is limited to one order per household. Not valid for current subscribers to Harlequin Romantic Suspense books. All orders subject to credit approval. Credit or debit balances in a customer's account(s) may be offset by any other outstanding balance owed by or to the customer. Please allow 4 to 6 weeks for delivery. Offer available while quantities last.

Your Privacy—The Harlequin® Reader Service is committed to protecting your privacy. Our Privacy Policy is available online at www.ReaderService.com or upon request from the Harlequin Reader Service.

We make a portion of our mailing list available to reputable third parties that offer products we believe may interest you. If you prefer that we not exchange your name with third parties, or if you wish to clarify or modify your communication preferences, please visit us at www.ReaderService.com/consumerschoice or write to us at Harlequin Reader Service Preference Service, P.O. Box 9062, Buffalo, NY 14269. Include your complete name and address.

HRS13R

SPECIAL EXCERPT FROM

H HARLEQUIN®

™ ROMANTIC suspense

*Noah Scott inherited a fortune from his biological
father, who was murdered. With his best friend
Rachel's help, Noah must find the killer, but will her
secrets destroy their growing attraction?*

*Read on for a sneak peek at HEIR TO MURDER
the latest in* New York Times *bestselling
author* **Elle James**'s **THE ADAIR AFFAIRS** *series.*

Tonight, Rachel would tell him the truth. If he couldn't
forgive her or trust her after that, well then, that was the
end of the time she'd spend with him. She swallowed hard
on the lump forming in her throat. She hoped and prayed
it wouldn't come to that. In the meantime, she would look
her best to deliver her confession.

In her bathroom, she touched up the curls in her hair
with a curling iron, applied a light dusting of blush to her
cheeks to mask their paleness and added a little gloss to
her lips.

Dressing for her confession was more difficult. What
did one wear to a declaration of wrongdoing? She pulled
a pretty yellow sundress out of the closet, held it up to her
body and tossed it aside. Too cheerful.

A red dress was too flamboyant and jeans were too
casual. She finally settled on a short black dress with thin
straps. Though it could be construed as what she'd wear
to her own funeral, it hugged her figure to perfection and
made her feel a little more confident.

As she held the dress up to her body, a knock sounded
on the door.

"Just a minute!" she called out. Grabbing the dress, she unzipped the back and stepped into the garment. "I'm coming," she said, hurrying toward the door as she zipped the dress up.

She opened the door and her breath caught.

Noah's broad shoulders filled the doorway. Wearing crisp blue jeans and a soft blue polo shirt that matched his eyes and complemented his sandy-blond hair, he made her heart slam hard against her chest and then beat so fast she thought she might pass out. "I'm sorry. I was just getting dressed and I haven't started the grill…"

He stepped through the door and closed it behind him. "My fault. I finished my errands earlier than I expected. I could have waited at a park or stopped for coffee, but…I wanted to see you."

"Hey, yourself. I'm glad you came early." And she was. The right clothes, food and shoes didn't mean anything when he was standing in front of her, looking so handsome.

He leaned forward, his head dropping low, his lips hovering over hers. For a moment, she thought he was going to kiss her…

If you loved this excerpt, read more novels from *THE ADAIR AFFAIRS* series:

CARRYING HIS SECRET by Marie Ferrarella
THE MARINE'S TEMPTATION by Jennifer Morey
SECRET AGENT BOYFRIEND by Addison Fox

Available now from Harlequin® Romantic Suspense!

And don't miss a brand-new **THE COLTONS OF OKLAHOMA** book by New York Times bestselling author Elle James, available September 2015 wherever Harlequin® Romantic Suspense books and ebooks are sold.